**REMO GRINNED**

"Hey, Chiun. When is a bee not a bee?"

"When it is not," Chiun said flatly.

"Care to elaborate?"

"My wisdom would be wasted upon small minds."

"I saw a bee. A very tiny bee."

"And you do not question what your eyes see?"

"Hardly ever."

"Then you saw a bee."

"What did *you* see?"

"A not-bee."

"Is that anything like a not-hole?"

"I will not answer your riddle because it has no answer," Chiun said elliptically.

"Suit yourself. I'm going to catnap. It's a long way to L.A."

"With you snoring at my side, an̲ ̲ ̲ ̲ ̲ ̲ ̲ ̲ ̲ ̲" Chiun sniffed.

Created by
# WARREN MURPHY
## and RICHARD SAPIR

THE Destr☉yer™

## FEAST OR FAMINE

A GOLD EAGLE BOOK FROM
# WORLDWIDE.®

TORONTO • NEW YORK • LONDON
AMSTERDAM • PARIS • SYDNEY • HAMBURG
STOCKHOLM • ATHENS • TOKYO • MILAN
MADRID • WARSAW • BUDAPEST • AUCKLAND

First edition April 1997
ISBN 0-373-63222-3

Special thanks and acknowledgment to
Will Murray for his contribution to this work.

FEAST OR FAMINE

1

At first, no one connected the hideous death of Doyal T. Rand with the greatest plague to threaten America's breadbasket since the Dust Bowl.

Doyal T. Rand wasn't a farmer. He was a geneticist. His chief accomplishment in life was the discovery of the sex gland in roaches. Learning to shut off the pheromone-producing gland was the same as shutting off a roach's genetic ability to replicate itself. No more replication, no more roaches. While human birth control remained a subject of controversy, many on both sides of the argument practiced roach birth control without giving the moral implications a second thought. Nobody cared about roaches. Not even Doyal T. Rand, who had become a millionaire many times over defusing and frustrating their furtive little sex lives.

Doyal T. Rand was on his lunch hour on a sunny April morning when he forgot a simple truism. There is no such thing as a free lunch.

Technically, it wasn't a free lunch that killed him, but a candy sample.

Doyal T. Rand stood on the corner of Broadway and Seventh Avenue in New York City making faces at the rows of restaurants while trying to decide whether he was in the mood for Chinese or Thai. Actually, he hungered for Korean barbecue, but the nearest Korean restaurant was in Herald Square, which was too long to walk, and Doyal T. Rand was too cheap to take a cab.

While he was mentally tasting Bi Bam Bap on his hungry tongue, Doyal T. Rand heard what was to him music.

"Free sample!"

Rand turned. On the corner behind him, a man was standing in the cool of April, with a tray slung from his shoulders like those that cigarette girls carried in old B movies. He wore some kind of team jacket and cap. Doyal T. Rand didn't follow sports, so his eyes flicked from the team logo to the man's hands.

He was handing out free samples of something to anyone who would accept them.

"Free. It's free. Free to all," the hawker kept saying. His face was an animated shadow under the bill of his cap. He wore mirrored sunglasses tinted an iridescent emerald.

Doyal T. Rand stepped closer. At first, it was curiosity. Then greed. And when he noticed people unwrapping the samples and popping them into their mouths, he had to have one. It didn't matter what it was. It was free. Doyal T. Rand liked free stuff. If someone were to can puppy poo and offer them two for the price of one, Doyal T. Rand would buy four cans and walk away grinning.

"I'll take one," he told the vendor.

"It's *guarana* candy," the vendor said.

"I don't care. Just give me one."

"It's made from a Brazilian berry supposed to have aphrodisiac properties. Not that we're guaranteeing anything."

"I don't care what it is. I just want mine," Doyal T. Rand said impatiently because he took a strict forty-five minutes for lunch. Enough to wolf his food down and slide out the door before the waitress realized she'd been stiffed on her tip.

The tray was filled with what looked like amber marbles wrapped in cellophane. When Doyal got a good look, his undersized heart sank. The stuff looked like hard candy. He didn't like hard candy. He preferred caramel or nougat. Bull's-eyes were his favorite. He loved chewing through sweet caramel to the dry, powdery confection center.

Still, this candy was free.

"Gimme," Doyal T. Rand said.

The vendor ignored the dull amber candies rattling around his waist-high tray and palmed one from his pocket. That one was slightly larger than the others and slightly redder. Doyal, his eyes on all those free samples, failed to notice his came from the hawker's pocket.

"Is it hot?" he asked, thinking of a peppery candy called Red Hots, which he detested.

"No. Sweet."

"I don't like hard candy," Doyal T. Rand muttered, ever the ingrate.

"You'll like this."

"We'll see," said Doyal T. Rand. Just as he turned to go, he caught himself and asked, "Can I have another?"

"One to a customer."

"It's for my secretary. She has a sweet tooth."

"One to a customer."

Shrugging, Doyal T. Rand walked off, absently unwrapping the ball of hard amber sugar. He still had to figure out where to eat. Lunchtime was ticking away.

Rand finally decided on Thai food. He stepped off the curb as the light changed and, without thinking about it, popped the hard amber candy into his mouth.

It was pleasantly sweet. There was a kind of tang to it that took the edge off the sweetness. Doyal T. Rand rolled it around on his tongue, paying more attention to the taste. It began tasting familiar. Then he remembered a soft drink that had come on the market last fall. It tasted just like this. It was good. The candy was good, too. Best of all, it was free.

Rand was halfway across Seventh Avenue when he decided the candy was worth going after seconds.

He turned, biting down on the hard, sweet ball, and instantly his head filled with a weird buzzing.

Not his ears. His head. It started low, then swelled with incredible speed. He had a wild thought. He wondered if this was the aphrodisiac effect the vendor had mentioned kicking in.

Then the buzzing filled his entire head, and the world winked out as if he had been struck blind by the very sweetness of the taste in his mouth.

Doyal T. Rand took a halting step, then another. His head swayed, then jerked, and then he pitched forward on his face in the middle of the crosswalk.

The light changed, and a phalanx of capsulelike yellow cabs surged toward him, honking and blaring for him to pick his lazy ass off the intersection so that Manhattan traffic could flow with its normal multi-directional pandemonium.

When Rand refused to move, they went around him. At first, with care, but once traffic flow resumed, several vehicles left short stretches of smoking tread as testimony to their brake-pad strength.

All that honking brought NYPD traffic cop Andy Funkhauser surging into the blaring congestion, blowing his whistle like a fury.

Officer Funkhauser all but tripped over the body, dropped the whistle from his mouth and used his hands to direct the traffic flow while he tried talking into his shoulder radio.

The ambulance pulled up while the light was red, and a pair of EMTs jumped out.

"I didn't touch him," Officer Funkhauser said, one eye on a fresh barrier of yellow cabs that eyed him with hungry headlights as they waited for green.

"Drunk?"

"Could be diabetic."

One of the EMTs got down on his knees. "Hey buddy, can you hear me?"

The body of Doyal T. Rand declined to answer. So they rolled him over.

Officer Funkhauser had one eye on the impatient

traffic. The light had finally turned green, and engines were growling. He was keeping them at bay with only the upraised palm of his hand.

He heard one of the EMTs say "Ugh."

He had never heard an EMT go "Ugh" before. The poor bastards saw everything. Officer Funkhauser thought he had seen everything, too.

So he took his eyes off the line of cars and cabs and glanced down.

What he saw hit him like a mule's kick.

The victim's face was turned up to the sky. The sun was shining down with a clarity New York City only enjoyed on cloudless days.

The victim's eye sockets were scarlet caverns. There was no blood. No eyeballs. Just the red bone that was designed by nature to hold the human eye in place.

"Jesus, where are this guy's eyes?" blurted the EMT who hadn't said "Ugh."

At that point, the dead guy's mouth—there was no question he was dead—dropped open. The sun shone directly into it. It showed the interior of his mouth. And showed without a doubt that the dead man had no tongue. No uvula, either.

"I think we have a homicide here," the first EMT muttered.

"Fuck," said Officer Funkhauser, who knew he had to call for Homicide and a morgue wagon and didn't think his upraised hand and his badge could hold off the growling cabs much longer.

"I think it was a mob hit," Officer Funkhauser

volunteered when two homicide detectives made their appearance.

"What makes you say that?" the black one asked while the white one knelt over the body.

"Guy had his eyes gouged out, and his tongue is missing. That says mob hit to me."

The homicide detective grunted and said, "We deal in facts."

"And it's a fact that poor guy's lacking eyes and a tongue. They didn't melt in the heat. It won't break sixty-five today."

"We deal in facts," the detective repeated. "Harry, what have you got?"

"I think we'd better get this guy photographed and off the street before we all get run down."

That took all of thirty minutes, and when the body had been photographed from every angle and the outline traced in metallic silver to withstand tire prints, the coroner's people laid him on a gurney and started to cart him off.

The body wobbled on the gurney, and as they raised it to the level of the wagon, the eyeless head rolled to the left. Out of the left ear poured a pinkish gray gruel, and the seasoned veterans on the scene recognized it as brain matter.

"Jesus."

They gathered around the gurney as it was set back on the ground.

"Brains don't liquefy like that, do they?" Funkhauser muttered.

"How long has this guy been dead?" an EMT wondered aloud.

They poked and prodded and noticed the flesh hadn't even cooled, and decided less than an hour.

"Brains don't liquefy," the homicide detective repeated.

No one disputed him. But they were looking at human brain matter lying like so much custard beside the man's left ear.

The medical examiner got down on one knee and shone a light into the corpse's right ear.

"What do you see?" asked Officer Funkhauser, who was by this time fascinated. He had always wanted to go into Homicide. This was very educational.

"Step aside," the M.E. barked.

When he did, the M.E. gasped.

"What is it?"

"I see daylight. I can see clear through this man's skull."

"Is that possible?"

"If the man's head was empty, it is," he said, climbing to his feet. His knees were shaking. He said, "Load him up and get him out of here."

Officer Funkhauser watched the body slide into the back of the meat wagon and spoke the obvious.

"The mob doesn't normally mess with a guy's brains. Do they?"

AT THE MANHATTAN MORGUE, the body was identified as that of Doyal T. Rand by the contents of his wallet.

Chief Medical Examiner Lemuel Quirk X-rayed his skull and determined it was empty of all soft tissue. No tissue, brains or soft palate. Other organs were missing, too. The pineal gland. The thyroid. The sinuses. And the entire auditory canal.

When they cut him open, they discovered an undigested mass in his stomach that caused Quirk to go as pale as sailcloth.

"If I didn't know better, I'd say I was looking at human brain matter," he muttered.

His assistant took a quick look, gulped hard and grabbed at his mouth. As he ran from the autopsy room, he could be heard retching all the way down the hall.

Dr. Quirk scooped out the contents of the stomach, weighed them and, with a stainless-steel scalpel, probed them.

Brain matter all right. Liquefied, like scrambled eggs that had set. But mixed in were red bits of pulp and flecks of matter he realized with a heart-pounding start were the clear lenses of a human eye.

"How...?"

Going to the head, Quirk pried open the mouth and shone a penlight down the man's gullet.

"No soft palate...yes, it was possible."

Somehow the man's brain, eyes and other soft tissues had been churned to a liquid and simply slid down his unobstructed esophagus into his waiting stomach via natural apertures in the basal skull like

the foramen magnum, the clivus and possibly the cri-
biform plate. Since there had been no digestion, the
liquefaction had occurred at or just before the time of
death. It was all very logical, the biology of it.

Except it was impossible. People's brains did not
turn to liquid and go sliding down their gullets.

Not unless there was a terrible new agency of death
out there.

**2**

His name was Remo, and he didn't look like a walk-ing sanction.

In fact, he was the United States of America's ul-timate sanction. He stepped off the plane at Sarajevo looking like a typical American tourist. Except for the fact that tourists don't come to the former Yugoslavia. No one comes to the former Yugoslavia. They only try to get out. Ethnic fighting had reduced the nation to the status of a Third World hellhole with former neighbors accusing one another of genocide, ethno-cide, patricide, matricide, infanticide and even worse horrors.

At the bottom of the air-stairs stood a uniformed agent who directed Remo to customs.

"Where can I get a cab?" Remo asked him.

"After undergoing customs and baggage reclaim, you will find signs."

"I'm not carrying baggage."

"What? No baggage?"

"I travel light," said Remo, who was attired for shooting pool. He wore gray slacks, a crisp white T-shirt and Italian loafers that fit his sockless feet per-fectly.

"You must come with me if you have no baggage."

"No," Remo corrected. "I must catch a cab."

"Why?"

"Because the quicker I catch the cab out of here, the quicker I can get the cab back to my return flight."

The uniformed man looked at Remo with unhappy eyes.

"When are you leaving Bosnia-Herzegovina, sir?"

"Four-thirty."

"You are in Sarajevo for only four hours? What is your business here?"

"My business," said Remo.

"You are reporter?"

"No."

"UN observer?"

"I heard the UN got chased out."

"They are forever trying to sneak back in," the customs official said pointedly.

"I'm not UN. If I had a safe area to protect, it wouldn't be overrun by a bunch of big-mouthed goons with guns."

The uniformed agent flinched. "You must come with me."

"If with you means to the cabstand, sure. If not, go screw."

"Go screw what?" asked the agent, who was obviously unfamiliar with current U.S. slang. Actually, Remo's slang wasn't that current, but it usually got the point across.

"Go screw yourself onto a cactus and go for a spin," returned Remo.

The Yugoslav—Remo couldn't tell if he were a Serb, a Croat or a Bosnian—probably didn't know what a cactus was, but he knew an insult when he heard one. And he was convinced he had heard one. Even if he didn't exactly understand it.

"I am insisting," he said, his voice and spine turning to ice.

"Okay, but only this once," said Remo, changing attitude because he had been ordered to Sarajevo not to clean up Dodge, but to take out one Black Hat.

"Come with me," the man said, turning around like a man used to being obeyed.

In an interrogation room, they sat Remo down and surrounded him.

"Empty pockets, please."

Remo laid his billfold with its Remo Novak ID and approximately three thousand in U.S. bills and the folded article from the *Boston Globe*. He figured the money would distract them from the clipping. He was wrong. The Serb who detained him slowly unfolded the article. It was headlined A "Wanted" Poster That Leaves Pursuers Wanting.

"What is this?"

Remo decided what the hell. They didn't sound as if they were planning to let him go any time soon, and he had that plane to catch.

"It's the reason I'm here," he said nonchalantly.

"You are reporter?"

"Assassin."

"Again, please?"

"I'm here to nail one of the war criminals on the list."

"This is a reproduction of a Wanted poster for UN war criminals."

"That's right," Remo agreed.

"It is useless."

"Next to useless," Remo corrected.

"These are posted all over former Yugoslavia. There are almost no photos. Just silhouettes. The descriptions are a joke. Look at this one. It said, 'Bosko Boder. Six feet tall. Known to drive a taxi in Sarajevo. Wore gold.'"

"Know him?" asked Remo.

"I could be he. It could be any Serb who drives a taxi and stands so tall."

"I'm not allowed to nail just any Serb. I have to nail the correct Serb."

"What means this 'nail'?" asked a brooding-faced man who looked like the local torturer. He had a scar running across his forehead like an exposed red vein. Remo grabbed the clipping from the lead interrogator's grasp. The third blacked-out face down in the second column mentioned a Serb concentration-camp guard with a jagged scar running from temple to temple.

"Your name wouldn't be Jaromir Jurkovic, would it?" asked Remo.

"I deny being Jurkovic!"

"And what if he is?" pressed the lead interrogator.

"If he is, I get to nail his sorry butt."

"It is illegal to nail Serbs in Sarajevo. Whatever that is." And the man snapped his fingers.

At that, Jagged Scar Jurkovic stepped behind Remo and laid two meaty paws on Remo's shoulders. Remo sensed the nearing pressure waves and allowed this to happen, although his reflexes screamed at his brain to strike back with all the power at his command. Which was considerable.

Instead, Remo reached up and casually slapped the crushing fingers to loose sausages.

Jaromir let out the screech of screeches and turned it into a high howling yowl. Coming out of his seat like casual lightning, Remo turned and quieted the man with an equally casual slap. His jawbone flew off its hinges and tried to jump out of his mouth. The envelope of skin that was his stubble-blue chin kept it from hitting the opposite wall. Finally, it stopped wobbling and just stayed slack. Jaromir's tongue hung out like a panting dog's.

He tried to speak, but without working mandibles, all he could manage was a hollow groan and a slow drool.

"That," said Remo, "is one definition of the verb *to nail.*"

The interrogation room was quiet long enough for the alleged Jaromir Jurkovic to finish his groan. Then tensed hands slapped for side arms. That gave Remo permission to defend himself, and he did.

In place, he spun around. Arms floated high. One foot came up and out. Centrifugal force made the rest automatic.

The stiff fingers of Remo's left hand reamed out a man's eye sockets while the right jabbed another's Adam's apple. The foot, still rising, impacted a groin. The groin became suddenly and forever concave. The owner didn't care. The pain traveled up his spinal column and literally short-circuited his brain.

Remo left four groaning Serbs on the floor in various degrees of distress, thinking that it had been a detour worth taking.

Like most Americans, when the fractious ethnic cleansing in the former Yugoslavia had broken out, he hadn't known for five months who was who. If the Russians had declared war on the Canadians, he would have known whom to root for—after some thought. If Germany had reinvaded France, he would have had a clue. If Korea had bombed Japan, he would have had a rooting interest.

But he didn't know what a Bosnian was. A Croat might as well have sat on a grocery shelf labeled Croats. Remo early on figured out that a Serb was a kind of low-rent Russian. But it was months before the TV news anchors had added the qualifier *Muslim* to the noun *Bosnian* and Remo was all set to cheer on the Croats because these days the only Muslims fighting anyone were car-bombing civilians. Until the first pictures of the emaciated Bosnians in Serb concentration camps started coming out, and it began to look as if the Serbs were the real bad guys.

To this day, he had no clue what a Croat was or did or looked like. But he knew that the Serbs were being bastards and Bosnians were being victimized.

He gave up on the United Nations before the UN rolled in. The UN was fine if there was no shooting. But they had simply stood around with their hands in their pockets while helpless families were being massacred in so-called safe haven after safe haven.

That lasted until NATO came in, but NATO wasn't much better. They actually surrendered confiscated weapons so Serbs could start up all over again. And when the call came to arrest war criminals and detain them, they ignored it. War criminals were celebrities in the former Yugoslavia. No one dared touch them because it threatened the fragile peace hammered out in Dayton, Ohio—of all places.

The way Remo saw it, a fragile peace in which war criminals were issued free passes was no peace at all.

Finally, Upstairs saw it this way, too.

"Go to Sarajevo," said the lemony voice of Remo's superior, Dr. Harold W. Smith. "And get General Tanko."

"Done," said Remo, who by trade was an assassin. In this case, he was an unofficial U.S. government sanction.

The idea was to nail the biggest war criminal of them all. Maybe that would scare the others into hiding or surrender.

Remo walked through the terminal at Sarajevo past bullet-pocked windows and other evidence of the long war that had shattered a once semicivilized nation and found his way to the cabstand.

The cabs were green. They looked as if they had been salvaged from a junk heap. Consulting his clipping, Remo went from driver to driver asking, "Are you Bosko?"

The fourth cabbie in line said, "I am Bosko."

"I need a ride to General Tanko's house."

"You have business with Tanko?"

"He said to ask for you," Remo lied.

"Come in. Come in. I will take you to Tanko."

The drive was depressing. Bombed-out buildings. Open sewers. All the amenities of warfare. The international community kept talking about rebuilding, but with all three sides still at one another's throat, no one wanted to pour money into the rat hole its inhabitants had made of Yugoslavia. So the people lived in squalor.

"You bring drugs, eh?" Bosko asked.

"I bring the most potent narcotic of all."

"Heroin, yes?"

"Heroin, no. It's called Death."

"Death. Is designer drug, yes?"

"Is ultimate drug," said Remo. "One hit, and you never want to wake up."

"You tip me with Death, of course."

"You read my mind," said Remo, smiling with thin lips that bordered on cruel.

Remo didn't look strong. He looked wiry. His build was average for a six-footer, but his wrists stood out. They were freakishly thick, as if they belonged to someone else. But there they were, holding his long-fingered hands to his wiry forearms. The tendons in them stood out like white cord.

He didn't look old enough to have been a Marine

in Vietnam, but he was. He didn't look like a former cop, except maybe around the eyes. Remo was that, too. And he certainly didn't look like the most dangerous killing machine wearing white skin. But he was. Remo was a Master of Sinanju, the first and ultimate martial art. The discipline that gave rise to every Asian fighting skill from kung fu to *yubiwaza*, Sinanju had been practiced exclusively by the head of a Korean house of assassins that originated in the village of Sinanju high in rocky, forbidding North Korea.

For five millennia, the House of Sinanju had been a Korean power. Now the secrets that transformed an ordinary man into the perfect fighting machine had fallen into non-Korean hands and were dedicated to furthering American aims. And Remo was the disciple who was focusing now on one aim in particular.

The house of General Tanko was in a suburb and very well maintained. No bullet holes. Intact glass. The paint looked fresh. It had once belonged to a Muslim doctor whose blood had seeped into the front door after they stood him before it and shot him to bone splinters. The fresh paint was to mask the blood.

The cab rolled up the graveled path, and at the entrance, the driver turned and smiled with big yellow teeth.

"You tip me with Death?"

Bosko's eyes were on Remo's eyes. They were dark and set deep into his skull. They were the eyes of a death's-head. In his last moment, Bosko thought exactly that.

Remo didn't know or care. He simply brought the heel of his hand up from his knee and applied it to Bosko's aquiline nose. It was a good nose for shattering purposes. The cartilage bent to the left, snapped and, when the heel of Remo's hand impacted on the bone, it shattered like shrapnel.

Splat!

Bone splinters riddled Bosko's unsuspecting brain.

Remo reached up and pulled him by the hair over the seat and down onto the back-seat floorboards.

Getting out, Remo walked confidently to the front door. He liked front-door hits. No one ever expected his assassin to come knocking in broad daylight.

While he waited for a response, Remo put on his polite-encyclopedia-salesman face.

The door opened. It was General Tanko himself, eyes black as a crow's and his pugnacious features unconcerned. He wore the gold braid and tinsel that was his Serbian army uniform. General Tanko liked to wear his dress uniform. He was proud of the innocents he had butchered.

"General Tanko?"

"I am he. Who are you?"

"I'm from the U.S. Board of Unofficial Sanctions."

"Sanctions?"

"We sanction people like you. I'm pleased to announce that you are this month's sanctioned Serb."

"You cannot sanction a person. It is preposterous. Nations are sanctioned. Not persons. It is unhumane."

"You mean inhumane."

"Yes. Inhumane. Not to mention ethicless. How dare you come to me with this announcement of sanctions."

"We tried sanctioning your country," explained Remo. "But it's so poor, it can't get any poorer. So in its infinite wisdom, Uncle Sam has decided to sanction you personally. Think of it like having the Publisher's Weekly Prize Van roll up and take instead of give."

"I have rights."

"Everyone has rights," agreed Remo, still polite.

"Yes, everyone."

"Except the innocents you butchered."

"I am not butcher, but a Serb."

"In your case, it's the same thing. Now if you'll step out of your nice, ill-gotten house, we can get this sanction over with."

General Tanko blinked. "What does this entail?"

"A lecture on niceness."

Tanko blinked again. Then a slow smile spread over his coarse features. "I am to be lectured?"

"On being nice."

"By you?"

"Yep," said Remo.

"By an undernourished joke of an American such as you? You dare to sanction the great Tanko, the Scourge of Srebrenica?"

And General Tanko threw back his black head and roared his amusement.

Splat.

Remo couldn't wait. It was the description *under-*

*nourished.* Nobody called him that. He was not undernourished. It was that his body contained almost no body fat. He looked thin. He didn't look muscular. But he could erase General Tanko from existence with a sweep of his hand, which he did.

Remo's sweeping hand came up and impacted the cutting edges of General Tanko's upper teeth. The force was enough to shatter the general's teeth, but the angle was perfect. Instead, the teeth were forced into the jawbone, and the entire top of General Tanko's large head snapped back and, like a pineapple breaking off its stalk, it fell to the ground behind his back.

General Tanko's lower jaw remained attached to his stump of a neck. It sagged. The tongue remained attached to the lower jaw. It gave a meaty little toss as the nerves controlling it waited for signals from the disconnected brain and, receiving none, plopped dead onto the sagging jaw.

Remo pushed the tottering body back into the foyer and drew the door shut. Body and door impacts blended in one sound.

Reclaiming the cab, Remo drove back to the Sarajevo airport whistling.

He had made the world a safer place. And he would make his flight.

**3**

Word of the ultimate sanction befalling General Tanko of the Bosnian Serb Army raced from Sarajevo to the capitals of Europe and to Washington, D.C., within thirty minutes of the discovery of his body.

It reached the lonely desk of Dr. Harold W. Smith in Rye, New York, at the same time it hit Washington.

The Associated Press report was sketchy.

Sarajevo (AP)
General Tanko, otherwise Tanko Draskovic, indicted Serbian war criminal, was discovered in his home, the victim of a savage attack perpetrated by persons unknown. General Tanko was found with his head ripped from his body as if by a tremendous force. Initial reports are he was not beheaded. What was meant by this statement in the context of his fatal injuries is not known at this time. Draskovic was fifty-six.

Dr. Smith read this without his gray eyes registering any reaction that it meant something to him. His gray, patrician face likewise registered no emotion. But the news told him that his enforcement arm had succeeded in his assignment.

If all went well, Remo would be en route to Kaszar Air Base in Hungary and safe passage home. If not, well, the Serbian authorities would suffer unacceptable casualties trying to prevent him from leaving the former Yugoslavia. Smith had no concerns for Remo's personal safety.

A long time ago, he had selected Remo to be his enforcement arm, framing him for a murder he didn't commit. Remo had been a Newark beat cop in those days. Smith had railroaded Remo through a kangaroo court trial to the Death House. He had been one of the last men electrocuted by the state of New Jersey.

Remo Williams, believed dead and buried by the world, had been given over to the last Master of Sinanju for the training that transformed him into a virtually unstoppable killing machine. For over two decades, in missions great and small, Remo had never failed.

A phone rang. There were two on Smith's black glassy desk. One blue, the other gray. It was neither of these. The ringing came from the right-hand middle drawer of his desk. It was muffled but insistent.

Sliding open the drawer, Smith dug out a fire-engine red desk telephone and set it on the desktop. He picked up the receiver and said, "Yes, Mr. President."

"I was just handed an intelligence report that General Tanko is dead," the familiar presidential voice said.

"I have read that report," Smith said noncommittally.

"Between you and I, was that your man?"

"Do you need to know the answer?" returned Smith in his natural lemony voice. It wasn't disrespectful. Neither was it inviting. It could be read either way.

"I was just curious," said the President. His voice was not exactly offended. Neither was it hurt.

"Intelligence came to me that General Tanko was considering a terroristic attack on the NATO Implementation Forces in Bosnia. Orders emanating from his political masters in the rump Yugoslavia. An expression of U.S. displeasure had to be undertaken."

"That's good enough for me," the President said. "This conversation never happened, by the way. You won't read about it in my memoirs."

"I intend to write no memoirs," said Harold Smith, who meant it.

The President hung up, and Smith returned the red telephone to the desk drawer and shut it. Before he left for the evening, he would lock it with a small steel key. It was a dedicated line directly to the White House, and was linked with its identical twin in the Lincoln Bedroom of the White House.

For the thirty years since Harold Smith had been plucked out of the CIA's data-analysis department to head CURE, the supersecret government agency that didn't exist, he had lived with the only private hot line to the Commander in Chief at his side. A President of the United States had created CURE in the lonely womb of the Oval Office. He had told no one of his idea until he had found the man to head the organization—Harold Smith.

"The nation is sinking into chaos," the President had told Smith, then many years younger but just as gray as today. Smith thought he was being interviewed for a security position with the NSA. That impression was dispelled once he found himself alone with the young, vigorous President who was soon to die a martyr's death. The month was June, 1963. Smith had forgotten the exact date, but the conversation remained etched in his memory like glass scored by a diamond.

"I see," said Smith, letting the President talk.

"Crime is out of hand. Our judges and unions are corrupt. The police—the good apples—are not equal to the demanding task at hand. I don't control the FBI. And the CIA is forbidden from operating on U.S. soil—not that they don't try."

Smith said nothing to that. He was strictly an analyst. His days of action were far behind him, as were the President's. Both had seen action in the Big One, the President in the Pacific, Smith in the European theater of operations.

"I see chaos, perhaps civil war by the end of the decade," the President continued.

Smith did not contradict that view.

"I can suspend the Constitution," the Chief Executive went on, "or I can declare martial law."

He paused, fixing Smith with his crinkling blue eyes.

"But there is a third option."

"Yes?"

"Have you ever heard of CURE?"

"No. What do the letters represent?"

"Nothing. I'm not even sure what I have in mind should even have a name, but let's call it a cure for a sick world. I need an organization that will watch the watchers, get at the cancer infecting this great nation of ours and excise it like a surgeon. Quickly, cleanly and, above all, quietly. And I want you, Harold Winston Smith, to head it."

"I will require a large staff," Smith said stiffly, neither accepting nor rejecting the offer because he loved his country and if the President asked him, he would head up this CURE entity without reservation.

"You do it with next to no staff. If this gets out, it's my backside and your neck. Or maybe the other way around. You are one of the top computer men over at Central Intelligence. You'll sift though data, isolate the malefactors and arrange for them to be dealt with."

"This is extralegal," Smith warned.

"No. It is extra-Constitutional. Which is far worse," the President said soberly. "But it's this or admit the American experiment is an abject failure." The President fixed Harold Smith with his warm, humorous eyes. They turned steely. "Not," he added, pronouncing each word like a drumbeat, "on my damn watch."

"Understood, sir."

With a handshake, the secret pact was made.

Smith resigned from the CIA, ostensibly for the private sector. He took over Folcroft Sanitarium in Rye, New York, as its new director. From Folcroft, he quietly ran CURE. Funded by black budget money, using computers and confidential informants, it reached out to the cancers of American democracy and seared them dead.

In the early months of CURE, the President was cut down. Smith was on his own. The successor President, rattled by his abrupt and bloody ascension to power, signed on for the agency to continue operations.

"Indefinitely," he said. The new Commander in Chief was afraid he was next.

Over successive administrations, Harold Smith had worked to salvage a foundering nation. But the forces of social instability were greater than one man could bear.

Smith was forced to recruit an enforcement arm. A former cop named Remo Williams. Vietnam vet. Marine. Expert rifleman. Skills he would have to unlearn if he were to do the work of a wounded world.

A beeping brought Smith's reflective eyes to his computer screen buried in the black glass of his desktop. The hidden monitor connected to the mainframes and optical WORM-drive servers in the Folcroft basement, the information octopus that reached its tentacles out to cyberspace.

It was another AP report. The system was kicking it out as mission related. CURE's mission, not necessarily Remo's.

Sarajevo—Airport Altercation (AP)
Serbian authorities report a massacre at the airport at Sarajevo. As many as twenty-nine security forces were reported dead or wounded. A Serb jet has taken off. Destination unknown. It is believed the hijacker or hijackers are aboard.

Smith read this with a visible sign of relief washing over his lemony face. Remo. He had made it out of Yugoslavia. No doubt there would be a NATO security team waiting to take him into custody once he reached Kaszar.

Smith picked up the blue contact phone and placed a call to a U.S. Army major attached to NATO.

"This is Colonel Smith. Pentagon," Smith said. "The hijacked aircraft due in from Sarajevo has been commandeered by a U.S. security agent returning from a sensitive mission. He is to be granted safe passage on a Military Airlift Command flight home."

"Yes, Colonel. Where is he going? Specifically."

"Wherever he wants to," said Harold Smith.

"Understood, Colonel."

Hanging up, Smith turned his cracked leather executive's chair. Long Island Sound danced under the noonday sun. The first sails of spring were ghosting across its blue expanse. For more springs than he ever imagined back in 1963, Smith had looked out through the picture window of two-way glass.

How many more would Harold W. Smith, who had devoted his life to his nation's security, enjoy before he finally laid his aging bones in the rocky soil of his native New England?

Heaven alone knew.

**4**

As opening days went, this one was going to be a bitch.

"It's going to be a bitch," Perry Noto muttered.

"I still think it's a risky idea."

"We had to reconcept. We were going down the tubes," he said as he walked through the deserted restaurant with its French-provincial decor.

"We did better than that last reconcepting of yours."

"The novelty wore off. You can get people to try braised alligator or buffalo steak, but they get tired of it. Our clientele was getting bored. They want excitement. They want adventure."

"They want a decent meal for under forty bucks. Why can't we go nouvelle cuisine?"

"That's too eighties."

"Japanese is still popular. And with the small portions, we could make a bundle."

"Insurance would kill us. Those damn knife jugglers flipping and flinging those heavy blades in the customers' faces—before long, someone'd lose a nose and we'd lose our restaurant. No, this latest reconcept will work."

"People are finicky about what they put in their stomachs."

"Hey, they eat blue cheese. And blue corn is big now. Whoever heard of blue food? Show me something edible that's naturally blue. People eat Indian cuisine. That stuff tastes like rat in goat sauce. And Indian desserts might as well be sweetened rabbit pellets. Yet people flock to Indian restaurants."

"People also understand the four basic food groups."

"I thought it was five."

"Four. They learn in school that you need so many grams of cereal grain, fruits, vegetables and meat."

"Dairy products. That's the fifth basic food group. Not that anyone drinks dairy anymore."

"Five. Five basic food groups. I stand corrected. It's five. Not four. Not six. But five." She held up five fingers.

"Well, we just discovered the sixth."

"People will not pay to eat bugs, Perry."

"Not bugs. Arthropods. Or maybe insects. Don't say bugs. You say bugs, you might as well say snots. Or boogers."

"Might as well say boogers. That's what we're serving up."

"No, we are serving fried grasshopper on a bed of romaine lettuce. Chocolate-covered fire ants. Sweet-and-sour crickets. Yellow jacket au jus. Perfect grazing food. We are not serving anything people don't eat in other countries. This is L.A. We knock down cultural and culinary barriers every month. We'll

sweep east with this revolutionary restaurant reconcept, and by the turn of the century, we'll be over-
seeing an empire of—''

''McRoaches.''

Perry winced. ''Don't say roach. Add it to the ta-
boo list. We don't serve roach in our restaurant.
That's going too far.''

''Maybe we should put that at the bottom of the
menu in Florentine script. 'Positively no roaches
served.' ''

''Not funny, Heather.''

''Not appetizing, Perry.''

Perry Noto looked at his wife, Heather. She was
not hard to look at. Not after the tummy tuck, the
boob job and butt lift. Her face had been spared the
multiple plastic surgeries. It was a clean, sun-
scrubbed face and would be presentable for another
three or four years even under the California sun. After all, Heather Noto was only twenty-six.

''You could be blonder,'' he said, trying to change
the subject.

''What?''

''Your hair. It could be blonder.''

''The next-lighter shade is platinum. Platinum
blond went out with Jean Harlow.''

''Blonder.''

''Look. I've been ash blond, champagne blond,
honey blond—all the way down to summer blond.
I'm stopping here. My follicles can't take all this dying and rinsing.''

''Image is everything. Especially in our business.''

"If we don't imagine up a name for this latest wild hair of yours, our image will be guacamole."

"I got just the thing."

And from a shelf of New Age books—a relic of their failed macrobiotic plunge—Perry pulled down a red paperback, and opened it.

"What's that?"

"Thesaurus."

"My question stands."

"It's like a dictionary, except it shows you every possible variant on a word. Right now I'm looking up 'food.'"

"You're on the wrong page. Try 'bugs.'"

"Shh."

Suddenly, Perry Noto's eyes flew wide. They became two white grapes under pressure with their seeds squeezed out.

"I got it! I got it!"

"What?"

"Grubs!"

*"Grubs!"*

"It's perfect. 'Grub' is a synonym for 'food.' And a lot of perfectly scrumptious insects start off as grubs. We're serving them up before they get out of the larval stage."

"Why not just call it McMaggots?" Heather asked bitingly.

"Will you cut the shit?"

"Who in their right mind would pay forty dollars an entrée to eat in an eatery that calls itself Grubs?"

"It's cute."

"It's death." And with that, Heather Noto went to her own office bookshelf and took down a yellow book with a plastic cover.

"What's that?" Perry asked suspiciously.

"French dictionary."

"We're not opening a French fucking restaurant."

"And we are not opening a goddamn Grubs. Maybe a French name will take the sting out of the concept."

"Sting. Good choice of words. What's French for 'grubs'?"

"Give me a sec, will you, please?"

Heather flipped though the pocket dictionary with peach-nailed fingers. "Damn. I mean *maudit*."

"What?"

"A grub in French is *larve*. Too close to 'larva.'" Perry brightened. "I like it."

"You would." She turned her back on his curious face.

"Try 'bugs,'" Perry prompted.

"I am."

"Well?"

"'Bug' in French is *insecte*. Wait, there are synonyms galore."

"I didn't known the French had synonyms."

"Shh. *Bacille*. No, sounds too much like 'bacilli.' Oh, here's something interesting."

Perry got in front of her and tried to read the page upside down. He got an immediate headache.

"There's a French phrase for 'big bug.' *La grosse légume*."

"I like the 'gross' part."

"*La grosse légume.* It sounds like that stuff the French are forever putting in their consommé, legumes."

"Are those bugs?"

"No, beans."

"Let me see that." He scanned the page. "Hey, here's a perfectly good word. *Punaise.* What do you think?"

"Well, it rhymes with 'mayonnaise.'"

Perry Noto shifted his gaze to an imaginary spot on the ceiling. "I can see it now. La Maison Punaise..."

"House of Bugs! Are you crazy?"

"Hey, who's going to know?"

"Everyone, once the menu falls open and they see poached dung beetle," Heather said archly.

"La Maison Punaise. That's what we'll call it."

"I like La Grosse Légume much better."

"If La Maison Punaise bites the big one, that will be our fallback name when we relocate."

"If this thing fails, we're not relocating. We're reconcepting. Retro concepting."

"If La Maison Punaise doesn't go over, we're maggot meat."

"That better not be on the menu."

Perry Noto smiled. "I'm crazy, but I'm not *that* crazy."


LA MAISON PUNAISE OPENED to an A-list crowd of invitees only. The press was there. The stars were there. Most important of all, the food was going down their throats without coming back up again.

"How are the chocolate-covered ants, Arnold?" Heather asked.

A Germanic voice rumbled, "Scrumptious. I can hardly taste the ants."

"What are these?" a famous actress asked Perry, holding up a toothpick on which was speared a blackened morsel.

"That? Let me see, I think it's Japanese beetle, Cajun style."

"I love Japanese food."

"How does it taste?"

"Crunchy."

A ditzy blonde sauntered up and, with a serious face, asked, "I'm a strict vegan except for seafood. What can I eat?"

"Seafood. Seafood," Perry repeated, his success-dazzled gaze wandering the room.

"Silverfish cakes are coming up in a minute," Heather called over.

"Oh, thanks so much."

*"Bon appétit,"* said Heather, steering Perry aside. "I take back every bad thing I said," she whispered.

"How's the kitchen?"

"Busy as a beehive."

"We're golden."

"Don't count your honey until it's in the jar," Heather said archly.

The insects and champagne flowed freely, washing down swarms of cinnamon chiggers and grubs in duck sauce. There was only one problem, and that was when the *L.A. Times* restaurant critic complimented Perry on the popcorn shrimp and Perry had, not thinking, corrected him.

"Those are locust larvae."

"Larvae..."

"Grubs. You know, you're eating grubs. Your grub is grubs. Hee-hee," he added, giggling at his own joke.

The critic turned avocado and cured his suddenly active stomach by chugalugging a bottle of Château Sauterelle '61.

"Let him go," Heather urged.

"It's three hundred bucks a bottle."

"It's a million dollars in free publicity if he's spiflicated when he writes his stupid review."

In the end, the grand opening was a smashing success. The petty problems, liquor-license troubles and health-examiner payoffs were forgotten by the time the last guest left just after midnight.

Perry turned to Heather, beaming. "We pulled it off. Admit it."

"Okay, we pulled it off. Let's see if it lasts."

"Are you kidding me? Insects are forever. They'll outlive us all."

At that point, a weird humming came from the kitchen.

"What's that?"

Perry smiled broadly. "Tomorrow's profits exercising."

They went to the vault door and through the traditional swinging doors into the kitchen. The building had formerly been a major bank. Instantly, their noses were assaulted by a plethora of odors. They had learned not to retch. Bugs tasted okay if they were sauced or simmered correctly. But they sure stank during preparation. Hence the vault door to protect the clientele's delicate sensibilities.

The house chef was stooping over a wooden crate. It was buzzing.

"What's this?" Perry demanded.

"Did you order bees?" he asked, frowning.

"I don't remember ordering bees."

"This box is filled with bees—if I know the sound of bees."

"Bees aren't on the menu," Perry insisted. Heather concurred. Bee bodies contained venom that was impossible to clear out. They were worse than Japanese blowfish, which could kill if the wrong portions were ingested.

"Perhaps someone is making a suggestion."

"No," said the chef of La Maison Punaise, who was, of course, French. Just in case they had to re-concept overnight.

"Well, let's open it."

Remy the chef took a short pry bar off a shelf and attacked the crate. It was held together with black metal strapping. It wouldn't budge.

Perry found a pair of wire cutters and went snip-snip. The strapping spanged apart and coiled back, snapping at him. A piece of strapping caught him on the cheek, producing blood.

"Be careful."

Remy attacked the crate with the pry bar. The lid came off with a sharp screech of nails and the groaning of stressed wood.

When they got the box open, they all saw that it was empty.

But it was still buzzing.

"What the hell is making it buzz like that?" Perry wondered aloud.

"It sounds like *abeilles*," said Remy. "Bees."

"I know it sounds like bees. But it's empty."

At that point, the drone of the bees that weren't there changed in character. It swelled. It seemed to fill the kitchen with an all-pervasive sound. It was all around them.

Perry smacked his right ear. It was a natural reflex. The sound seemed to have attacked his ear. Only it was short and sharp, like a mosquito.

Then Heather slapped her left bosom. It jiggled. And kept on jiggling. Silicone was like that.

Remy ripped his white starched hat off his head and began swatting the empty air around them and cursing in prickly French.

The buzzing swelled and swelled, and as it ascended the scale in an increasingly angry drone, adrenaline overcame the Château Sauterelle buzz and they all looked at one another.

"Let's get the hell out of here," Perry said.

"I'm with you," said Remy.

They ran for the swinging doors. No problem. The insistent sound seemed to follow them.

They got to the vault door. It had fallen shut. No problem. Remy tackled the dog wheel.

That was when the buzzing began to attack them. In earnest.

They felt it as a pricking sensation on their skin at first. Then as heat. Hot heat. Painful heat. A million tiny red-hot needles might produce such a sensation.

But when they looked at the backs of their burning hands, they could see nothing except a creeping redness. Like a rash.

Perry looked up from his red palms to his wife's shocked face. It was turning red, too. An angry, embarrassed blush. Before his eyes, her pouty red lips seemed to twitch. And from one corner dribbled something white and vaguely waxy.

"I think my paraffin injection is leaking," she said.

Then she grabbed herself with both hands. "My boobs. They're wet."

"Oh, God! A silicone leak."

Remy had his own problems. He was scratching himself like a man with a million fleas.

"*Sacré Dieu!* I am undone," he screeched.

Then they couldn't breathe. They gasped and they began to choke. One by one, clutching their swelling throats, they fell to the stainless-steel floor.

As his sight darkened, Perry Noto looked to his wife, and his last coherent thought was, She's breaking out in hives...why is she breaking out in hives?

THE BODIES later identified as Perry and Heather Noto of Beverly Hills and chef Remy Asticot were found the next night when would-be patrons of La Maison Punaise flocked to the trendy restaurant to sample the delicious popcorn shrimp glowingly described in the *L.A. Times*.

The L.A. County coroner performed an autopsy and discovered high levels of bee venom in the bodies of the three victims.

What he didn't find was evidence of bee stings or the tiny barbs usually left in the skins of bee-sting victims. He searched every square millimeter of epidermis for a full working day to discover any hypodermic mark such as a needle might make. There were no track marks.

Finally, in exasperation, he gave a news conference.

"The victims would appear to have ingested toxic levels of bee venom during their last meal," he announced. "They died of anaphylactic shock, a condition normally the result of allergic reaction to bee toxin, or from massive bee stings."

"Then why didn't the patrons also succumb?" a reporter asked.

"Perhaps they didn't eat the same foods."

"Dr. Nozoki, were traces of bees found in the victims' stomachs?"

"I am no entomologist," said Dr. Togo Nozoki, "but the stomachs of the three victims were packed with insect materials—including antennae, carapaces, legs and other such matter. Digestion had begun. And bees lack the horny outer bodies of other insects on the menu."

"Bees usually die after they sting. Why were no bees found in the premises?" another reporter demanded.

"I can only conclude that the victims ingested every morsel of the bee delicacy that unfortunately felled them."

This seemed to satisfy the media. And if the media was satisfied, the public was satisfied.

No one thought very much of the fact that L.A. Coroner Togo Nozoki himself succumbed to a bee sting several hours later. Lots of people were hypersensitive to bee stings.

5

The Military Airlift Command C-130 Hercules tur-
boprop transport lumbered to a jolting stop at the end
of the main runway at the South Weymouth Naval
Air Station. When Remo had first moved to Massachusetts a few years before, the location had been
chosen because of its convenient access to South
Weymouth and its many military aircraft standing
ready to take Remo to any spot in the world his missions required. The base had been targeted for closure
several times. Each time, Harold W. Smith had pulled
his invisible strings to get it taken off the closure list.

Finally, the pressure to close the base had gotten
so strong that the only way to save it was to risk
showing Harold Smith's far-reaching hand.

Harold Smith didn't like showing his hand. So he
had allowed it to close. It was still technically open
with a skeleton staff during the final environmental
cleanup, so when the hydraulic ramp lowered to dis-
gorge Remo, he stepped off the plane thinking that
this would probably be the last time he was privileged
to fly out of South Weymouth courtesy of Uncle Sam.

A taxi was waiting for him courtesy of "Uncle
Harold," who preferred that Remo be whisked from

sight as soon as possible. The taxi took him to a shopping mall, where another taxi took over. Another Smith precaution. If Remo were to leave a trail of bread crumbs, Smith would personally eat them off the ground in the name of security.

As he pulled up before his home, Remo reflected that he wasn't looking forward to being back.

The reason why greeted him at the door while he was inserting the key.

The door jumped open. In the foyer stood a tiny Asian woman with iron gray hair and the same faded lavender quilted garment she had worn ever since taking up residence in Castle Sinanju, a former church converted into a condominium.

"Hi," said Remo, who still hadn't learned her name.

"Good riddance," the housekeeper cackled.

"I'm coming back, not going out."

"Bad riddance, then."

Remo scowled. "Chiun in?"

"In meditation room, gay-face."

"Will you cut that out!"

"You not die yet? What take you so long? Every night out on the town, and you still come back alive. Too skinny, but alive."

"Get stuffed."

"Stuff me. Change do you good."

Remo just gritted his teeth. It had been like this since the day Remo had returned home boasting that stewardesses didn't like him anymore.

"Faggot," the housekeeper had said, padding off in disgust.

Remo had tried to correct the mistaken impression. "I happen to like women."

"You supposed to love them. Coochie-coo."

"The trouble is stewardesses love me too much," Remo tried to explain.

"Too much love? No such thing."

The next time Remo saw her, she had handed him a pamphlet on AIDS prevention and a box of rainbow-striped condoms.

"Look," Remo had tried to explain, "women are drawn to me like flies to hamburger. I finally figured out a way to keep them at bay. Shark meat. I eat it by the ton. Something about it cancels out my pheromones and chases women off."

"Pillow biter."

"I didn't mean it like that!"

"Hah!"

It was the only fly in the ointment of Remo's current life. He had finally solved the stewardess problem only to find himself with a housekeeper problem.

Remo still couldn't figure out why Chiun had hired a housekeeper in the first place. This one was old, cranky and she sometimes smoked Robusto cigars—always outdoors.

Taking the steps to the bell-tower meditation room, Remo discovered it was empty except for the round tatami mat Chiun often meditated on. He stepped out of one shoe and touched the mat with a bare toe. Cool. Chiun hadn't been here in at least a half hour.

Descending, Remo scoured the third floor. No dice. There was no sign of the old Korean in any of his usual rooms. Not the room where he kept all his steamer trunks. Not the rice room, which was stacked with enough varieties of exotic and domestic rice for all of them to survive to the year 2099.

The room given over to Chiun's infatuation of the decade was padlocked, but Remo's highly attuned senses told him the Master of Sinanju's heartbeat and rice-paper personal scent were not coming from behind the door. Remo wondered why the door was padlocked. Chiun hadn't had an infatuation since he had grown sick of the news anchor named Cheeta Ching. Before that, he had been smitten by Barbra Streisand. He hoped Chiun hadn't fallen for the First Lady or someone equally inconvenient.

Finally, Remo found the Master of Sinanju in the fish cellar. It had only recently become the fish cellar, since Chiun had grown concerned over the dwindling fish resources of the planet Earth. Sinanju diet was restricted primarily to fish and duck and rice in vast quantities. Without all three of the allowed Sinanju food groups, their lives would be unlivable.

As Chiun once explained it to Remo, "We derive our powers of mind from the goodness of fish. Copious mounds of rice sustain our souls."

"What is duck good for?" Remo asked.

"Duck teaches us that no matter how monotonous fish and rice become, it could be worse. We could be limited to duck alone. Heh-heh-heh."

Remo wasn't sure how much of Chiun's remark

was intentional humor, but he personally only looked forward to duck when he got tired of fish.

The fish cellar had been turned into a private aquarium. The walls were set with row upon row of fresh- and salt-water tanks. It looked like one of those multimedia banks of TV monitors all turned to a remote from the New England Aquarium. Except these fish were real. They were brought in from the seven seas, and delivered every month so that Remo and Chiun had their own private food stock. Chiun had won this concession at the last contract negotiation with Harold Smith.

At the far end of the cellar were the ice boxes and smoke rooms where iced and smoked fish waited for their glorious destiny, as Chiun once put it.

Chiun stood in profile before the stainless-steel door.

He seemed oblivious to Remo. In this view, Chiun's face was something made of papier-mâché and peeled off an ancient wizard's desiccated skull.

Chiun stood not much taller than five feet. His bony, frail-seeming body was cloaked in a traditional kimono of raw, neutral-hued silk. Its sleeves hung down over the Master of Sinanju's cupped hands, which rested on his tight little belly.

His head was down. He might have been praying. Shifting light from one of the fish tanks played on his wrinkled, impassive features.

At Remo's approach, the Master of Sinanju didn't react.

Instead, he said, "You wear a face I do not care for."

"It's about that freaking housekeeper of yours."

"Who?"

"What's her name?"

"I do not know to whom you refer," said Chiun, gaze not lifting from the fish in the tank.

"I don't know her name. She won't tell me."

"Perhaps it is Grandmother Mulberry."

"Is that who she is?"

"It is possible she is Grandmother Mulberry," said Chiun, nodding. The simple nod made his wispy beard curl in the still air like paper being consumed by an unseen flame. Over his tiny ears, clouds of white hair gathered like storm clouds guarding a mountain.

"Well, if you don't freaking know, who does?"

Chiun said nothing. Remo joined him, and found himself looking at a trio of silver-blue fish zipping back and forth. They looked too small to eat, and Remo said so.

"Perhaps you would prefer suck-fish," returned Chiun.

"Not from the sound of them."

From his sleeve, a bony talon of a hand emerged to tap the screen with a long fingernail that was fully an inch longer than the others, which were very long.

"Isn't it about time you clipped that one?" asked Remo.

"I am enjoying the resurgence of this nail, which

was formerly concealed from sight." And he tapped the glass with a metallic click. "There."

The fish was black, as long as a man's palm, and it was attached to the side of the tank with its open suckerlike mouth.

"That's a suck-fish?"

"It is edible."

"If you say so," said Remo.

"But tonight we will enjoy Arctic char."

"Sounds better."

Chiun's eyes were hooded as they remained on the tank.

"You are troubled, my son."

"I am an assassin."

"Yes?"

"You trained me to kill."

"Yes."

"You showed me how to insert my fingers into the intercostal spaces in a target's ribs and nudge his heart into going to sleep."

Chiun nodded. "You learned that technique well."

"You taught me how to pulverize the human pelvis with the heel of my foot."

"A remonstrance, not a killing."

"You taught me the techniques for short-circuiting the spinal cord, bruising the brain and lacerating the liver without breaking the target's skin."

"These subtle arts you also embraced in time."

"But there's one thing you forgot to teach me."

For the first time, the Master of Sinanju's eyes

looked up at Remo, meeting them. They held an unspoken question in their clear hazel depths.

"You forgot to teach me how to strangle annoying housekeepers."

"You would not!"

"She's worse than a fishwife, Chiun!" Remo exploded. "What the hell is she doing here?"

"She performs certain services."

"I'll cook every meal forever if you get rid of her."

"She does laundry."

"All the laundry. I'll do it. Gladly."

"She mops floors. You do not mop floors. It is beneath you. I have heard you say this."

"Buy me a mop. You'll have the cleanest floors in town."

"You do not do windows. You have insisted upon this for years."

"I'm a new man. Windows are my business. I'll lick them clean if I have to."

"No," said the Master of Sinanju.

"What do you mean, no?"

"There are other duties she performs that you cannot."

"Like what? Stinking up the back wing with cigar smoke. How come you tolerate it?"

"It is a harmless habit."

"She might set the house on fire."

"Thus far, she has not. If she does, I will reconsider your request."

"I don't get it," said Remo.

"You are too young to get it." And with that, the Master of Sinanju reached out in the wavery light and touched the side of the fish tank he had been contemplating.

It winked out like a TV.

Remo gaped at the tiny white dot in the center of the abruptly black rectangle. "Huh?"

"The Fish Channel," said Chiun. "It is very soothing. Especially when considering complaints of no merit."

With that, the Master of Sinanju padded from the fish cellar, saying, "We will have Arctic char this evening. With jasmine rice. In celebration of the successful completion of your assignment in extinguishing the wicked general so that no one sees our hands."

"I ripped his freaking head off."

"Good. No one would suspect the hand of Sinanju behind such a clumsy and barbaric act. You did well."

"I was planning to strike the breath in his lungs. But I kept thinking of that fishwife of a housekeeper and lost it."

"Visualization is a good technique. Visualize success, and success follows."

"Right now, I visualize a hanging."

As he watched the Master of Sinanju pad up the stairs to the house proper, Remo muttered to himself, "Grandmother Mulberry... I'll bet my next three meals that's an alias."

**6**

It was a stupid assignment.

"Oh, come on," Tammy Terrill complained to her news director, Clyde Smoot, over the din of Manhattan traffic blare and squeal coming through the office window.

"Slow news day, Tammy. Check it out."

"A guy drops dead in midtown traffic, and you want me to cover it?"

"There's some funny angles to this one."

Interest flicked over Tammy's corn-fed face. "Like what?"

"People said they heard a humming just before the guy keeled over. That smells like an angle to me."

"No, it *sounds* like an angle."

Smoot shrugged. "An angle is an angle. Dig up what you can. It's a slow news day."

"You already said that," Tammy reminded.

"Then why are you standing there listening to me repeat myself? Do your job."

Grabbing her cameraman, Tammy blew out of the studio of WHO-Fox in downtown Manhattan. It was a stupid assignment. But that was what the career of

Tammy Terrill had come down to. Covering stupid assignments for Fox Network News.

In a way, she was lucky to be in broadcast journalism. Especially after she had been unmasked in national TV as a faux Japanese reporter.

It wasn't easy being blond and white in TV news in the late 1990s. Everywhere Tammy turned, there was a Jap or a Chinese reporter, perky and stylish, stepping on her blond coif in their scramble to be the next Cheeta Ching–style superanchor. And Tammy wasn't the only WASP left out in the cold. If you were white-bread, you were toast.

Tammy had decided that she wasn't going to let her all-American looks get in the way of her career. Asian anchorettes were the big thing. Her grandmother had been one-sixteenth Japanese, and so with the aid of a friendly makeup man, she had turned Japanese. For on-camera purposes only.

It got her in the door and on the lower rung of network anchor. Until that dark day under the hot lights when her slinky black wig came off, and Tamayo Tanaka was exposed as a blond fraud.

"So much for Plan A," Tammy complained to her agent after she was canned.

"No sweat. You come back."

"As what? A Chinese reporter? I can't claim to be one-sixteenth Chinese. It would be lying. Worse, it would be falsifying my résumé—grounds for dismissal."

"Pretending to be one flavor of black-haired, almond-eyed journalist is as legit as another. But this time you come back blond.''

Tammy frowned. ''As myself?''

''Why not?''

''Blondes don't cut it in this business anymore.''

''Times change. Look, it's been nine months. A lifetime. Even Deborah Norville got a second shot at fame.''

''I won't do one of those hard-news shows,'' Tammy flared.

''Look, I think the Asian-anchorette trend has peaked. In the last year alone, Jade Chang, Chi-chi Wong, Dee-dee Yee and Bev Woo have come on the scene. It's oversaturation city.''

''Bev Woo. She's been around forever.''

''You're thinking of the old Bev Woo. There are two of them now. Both up in Boston.''

''Is that legal?''

The agent shrugged. ''It's great publicity.''

''So I come back as myself?'' mused Tammy.

''Sort of. Tell me, what's 'Tammy' short for?''

''Tammy.''

''Hmm. Let me think. What would 'Tammy' be short for. Tam. Tam. Tam. Tamara! From now on, you're Tamara Terrill.''

Tammy frowned. ''Sounds Japanese.''

''It's Russian, but we won't emphasize that. And if it doesn't work, next time you can be Tamiko Toyota.''

''Are you crazy? I'd come across like a walking

product-placement ad. What about my journalistic integrity?''

"Don't sweat it. I already got the ball rolling."

"Where?" Tammy asked eagerly.

"Fox."

"Fox! They're a joke. Half their newscast is UFO stories and Bigfoot sightings. It's scare news."

"That's just to bolster 'X-Files' ratings. It'll pass. See a guy named Smoot. I told him all about you."

"Except that I used to be Tamayo Tanaka...."

"No. I told him that, too. He thought it was a brilliant career move, except it didn't quite pan out."

"Pan out! I fell flat on my pancake makeup!" Tammy muttered.

THE FOX INTERVIEW went too well.

"You have the job," said News Director Clyde Smoot.

"You didn't ask me any questions," Tammy had complained.

"I just needed to see your face. You have a good camera face."

Except that in the six weeks Tammy had been working at Fox, her face had yet to be seen. Instead, they sent her scurrying here and there chasing down rumors of saucer landings and haunted condos. None of it ever aired.

"Don't worry. You'll break a story soon," Smoot reassured her.

As the cameraman wrestled the news van through

Times Square traffic, Tammy held no hope that this time would be the charm.

"Always a reporter, never an anchor," she muttered, her chin on her cupped hands.

"Your day will come," the cameraman chirped. His name was Bob or Dave or something equally trustworthy. Tammy had learned a long time ago never to get attached to a cameraman. They were just glorified valets.

Traffic had gotten back to normal at the corner of Broadway and Seventh Avenue. Cabs and UPS vans were rolling over a silver-spray-painted body outline.

"Stop in front of it," Tammy directed.

"We're in traffic," Bob—or Dave—argued.

"Stop, you moron."

The van jolted to a stop, and Tammy stepped out, oblivious to the honking of horns and blaring and swearing.

"Looks like he fell on his face," she said.

"Get in quick!" the cameraman urged.

Tammy looked around. "But what made the humming?"

"Forget the humming! Listen to the honking. It's talking to you."

Frowning, Tammy jumped back in and said, "Pull over."

On the sidewalk, Tammy scanned her surroundings.

The cameraman lugged his minicam out of the back and was getting it up on his beefy shoulder.

"They say that if you stand on this corner long

enough, anyone you could name will walk by. Eventually."

"I saw Tony Bennett walk by my apartment last Tuesday. That was my thrill for the week."

"The guy was struck down about this time yesterday. Lunchtime. Maybe someone walking by saw it."

"It's a thought."

Tammy began accosting passersby with her hand microphone.

"Hello! I'm Tamara Terrill. Fox News. I'm looking for anyone who saw the guy who plotzed in the middle of traffic yesterday."

There were no takers.

"Keep trying," the cameraman prodded.

Tammy did.

"Hello. Did someone see the guy drop dead? Come on, someone *must* have seen something. Anyone hear a weird humming here yesterday?"

A discouraging half hour later, Tammy gave up.

"Why not try that traffic cop?" the cameraman suggested.

"Why?"

"Because this is his beat," the cameraman said tiredly.

Officer Funkhauser was only too happy to cooperate with Fox Network News.

"I heard the humming just before the guy plotzed," he said.

"Was there anything suspicious about his death?"

"Between you and me, his eyes and brains got eaten out."

"That wasn't in the papers."

"They're keeping it quiet. But that's what I found. Just keep my name out of the papers."

"What *is* your name?"

"Officer Muldoon. That's with two *O*'s."

"See anything odd or out of place?"

"Just the dead guy."

"Any police theories you can share with me?"

"My experienced eyes say a Mafia hit," Officer Funkhauser said flatly.

"If it was a hit, there had to be a hit man. See anything or anyone who might have been a hit man?"

"No. Just ordinary people. Unless you consider the street vendor."

"Wouldn't that be a good hit-man disguise?"

"Maybe. He was giving away candy samples."

"What'd he look like?"

"Tall. Thin. Wore a Charlotte Hornets cap and team jacket."

"Isn't that kinda strange? A Hornets fan in the Big Apple?"

"It's New York. Nothing is unusual here."

"Point taken," said Tammy. "Thanks. You can go now."

The officer went back to directing traffic. Tammy went back to accosting the lunch crowd.

"Anyone who saw the death here yesterday gets to be on TV," she announced.

Faces brightened, and suddenly Tammy was surrounded by helpful citizens crying, "I saw him! I saw him!"

"I did, too. He was short and fat."

"No, tall and bean-poley."

"Actually, it was a woman."

"Forget it," said Tammy, disgusted with her opportunistic fellow men.

"I guess we pack it in," she told her cameraman dejectedly.

"You discourage easy."

"It's a discouraging game. I've been in it over two years and I'm not rich and famous yet."

"Life's an ordeal and then you fall into a pine box," the cameraman commiserated.

At that moment, Tommy's steely blue gaze fell on a light pole.

"What's that?"

The cameraman looked up. A thick clump of orange-and-black matter hung from the streetlight hood. It made him think of some kind of fungus, except pieces of it crawled along the surface.

"Bees. They're swarming."

"That's what I thought. Bees hum, don't they?"

"Actually, they kinda drone."

"The cop said the suspect hit man was wearing a Charlotte Hornets cap...." Tammy mused.

"He didn't say 'suspect hit man.' That was your idea."

"Shut up! Shoot that light pole."

The cameraman shrugged and hefted his minicam onto his shoulder while Tammy chewed her red lower lip and said, "It's too much of a coincidence."

"What is?"

"That the hit man would be wearing a Hornets cap on the same site where bees were swarming."

"We don't know those bees were here yesterday."

"We don't know they weren't. And there's nobody here to say different."

The film shot, Tammy rushed the cameraman back into the van. She got her news director on the cell phone.

"Nice linking," Clyde said.

"Is it a story?" asked Tammy.

"Check out the medical examiner."

"Does this mean face time?"

"Get a shot of the eyeless dead guy, and I guarantee it," Tammy was promised.

As the van lumbered through crosstown traffic, Tammy was musing, "Do bees eat things?"

"Everything eats things."

"No, I mean like meat."

"Depends on the meat if they do."

"I wonder if bees could eat a man's eyes out."

"That kind of meat I don't think so. And weren't you raised on a farm?"

"I didn't pay too much attention to farm stuff. I was too busy trying to get out of the flatlands."

"I've heard of dragonflies sewing people's mouths shut, but not bees who eat eyes."

"Who cares about bugs anyway?"

"I don't know. Sounds like a Fox story to me—killer bees eat man's eyeballs."

Tammy snapped her fingers. "Killer bees. Wasn't that a big story about ten years ago?"

"Sure."

"Killer bees. They were down in Texas or something. Whatever happened to them?"

The cameraman made a nonchalant face. "Search me. I guess they died out."

"Well, they're back and if my theory is on the money, they're going to be the story of the century."

"What theory?"

"Mind your driving. I'm still working on it."

**7**

"Tamara Terrill. Fox News. I'm here to see the medical examiner."

"He's conducting an important autopsy right now," the desk guard said, looking up at the electric sight of the blond newswoman towering over him, her chest puffed out to its greatest expanse. It was a noteworthy chest.

"Great. Stiffs make wonderful TV. C'mon, Fred."

"It's 'Bob,'" the cameraman said.

"Hey, you can't—"

"Shoot us, and we'll shoot back," the cameraman said, turning the harsh glare of his minicam light on the guard.

That was enough to get them into the building.

It was a maze of bone-colored brick, with toe-tagged bodies on rolling carts and formaldehyde aroma. The cameraman happily shot every hanging ice-cold hand and blue tagged-toe he could.

"We don't need that stuff," Tammy snapped.

"If we don't, I can sell it as stock footage to the 'X-Files' people."

The M.E. was bent over a dead man lying inert on a white porcelain autopsy table. It looked as if it had been hosting corpses since before the days of Prohibition. The M.E. didn't look up.

"I am busy here."

"You the medical examiner?" Tammy asked.

"Please douse that light."

Tammy snapped her fingers. The light went off.

"Tamara Terrill. Fox News. I'd like to talk to you about the dead man you autopsied yesterday."

"I autopsied many dead men yesterday. This is New York, after all."

"This dead man had his eyes eaten out of his sockets," Tammy explained.

"Yes, I am familiar with that case."

"In your expert medical opinion, could killer bees have done that?"

The M.E. snapped out of his professional trance and looked up at Tammy for the first time.

"Bees?"

"Killer bees. From Brazil."

"Why do you ask about bees?"

"There's a swarm of them attached to the light post over the crime scene."

"And why do you call it a crime scene, may I ask?"

"We'll get to that. Answer my question and I'll answer yours."

"I did not perform the autopsy on Doyal Rand, I confess."

"Oh. Well, I need to talk to the guy who did."

"I am sorry to disappoint you, but you cannot do that."

"You don't know how determined I am."

"I am sure you are quite capable, but the man in question happens to be the man I am presently autopsying."

Tammy blinked and said, "What?" and then added, "What did you say?"

"I am the new medical examiner. My predecessor lies here on this slab."

Tammy walked up, looked at the dead face and asked, "What happened to him?"

"He was found dead in this very room this morning."

"What killed him?"

"That, I am attempting to ascertain."

"Could it have been killer bees?"

"Killer bees, as I recall, are not normally fatal unless one is stung by great numbers of them."

"Was this guy stung at all?"

"It is a thought." And the M.E. went back to his duties.

Tammy watched.

The M.E. was speaking into a microphone suspended before his face on a flexible snake.

"Subject is a white male 180 centimeters tall and weighing seventy-seven kilograms. There are no discernible marks or contusions visible on the body...."

"Are you getting this?" Tammy hissed to her cameraman.

The man rolled tape.

The M.E. was saying, "The throat and tongue appear swollen, and there is evidence of cardiac arrest.

Lividity is normal, and rigor has not yet commenced."

"What's that?" Tammy interrupted.

The M.E. looked up. He saw Tammy's gesturing finger, and his eyes jumped to the spot on the dead man's shoulder where she was pointing.

Taking up a magnifying glass, the surviving M.E. examined the mark.

"Looks red," Tammy said helpfully.

"I can see that," the M.E. snapped.

"A moment ago, you were saying there were no marks."

"Hush!" the M.E. said.

With a tweezer taken up from a stainless-steel tray, he brushed at a tiny dark dimple embedded in the center of the red mark.

"Odd."

"What?"

"It appears to be insect fragments."

"A bee! Could it be a bee?"

"They appear to be too small for that."

"Oh," said Tammy, deflating.

Carefully, the M.E. scraped the fragments into a waiting envelope. He carried them over to a microscope, deposited the fragments onto a glass slide and inserted it into the microscope.

Bending over, he peered within.

"Can I see?"

"No."

"Okay, can you tell me what you see?"

"I see the crushed remains of a very small insect."

"A killer bee! It's got to be a killer bee!"

"I am no specialist, but bees don't grow to this size. It cannot be a bee."

"It's gotta be a bee. If it's not a bee, I have no killer-bee story. I need a killer bee for my story."

"It is not a bee of any kind," the M.E. said, straightening. "But this is very strange. I don't know what kind of insect could inject a man with fatal consequences."

"A wasp, maybe? Could it be a killer wasp?"

"No."

"How about a hornet? The alleged hit man was wearing a Charlotte Hornets ball cap."

The M.E. looked at Tammy Terrill as if she were not quite sane. "What are you babbling about, miss?"

"Nothing. Aren't you going to test the body for bee venom?"

"I will examine the tissues for foreign toxins, of course. But I don't expect to find bee venom. And now I must ask you to leave this building."

"You're welcome," Tammy said frostily.

OUTSIDE, SHE SNAPPED open her cell phone and got her news director.

"I think I have a story, Clyde. Listen to this...."

At the end of it, Smoot was skeptical. "Killer bees are passé. Strictly seventies."

"I think they're back. Put me on the air, and let's see where this goes."

"You're on. But first get to the library."

"What's there?"

"Books on bees. Do your research. I want this story backed up by hard facts."

"I have film and a chain of coincidences. What do I need facts for?"

"Facts," the Fox news director said, "will keep the snowball rolling down the happy hill. And the longer it rolls, the bigger it will be."

"Not as big as I will be," Tammy breathed, clicking off.

**8**

"Her name is Grandmother Mulberry," said Remo into the pay phone at the Vietnamese market around the corner from Castle Sinanju.

"First name?" asked Harold Smith.

"That's all I have. I think it's an alias. And dollars to doughnuts she's an illegal. I want her deported. Preferably to the dark side of the moon."

"What will the Master of Sinanju say?"

"This time, for once, I don't freaking care. He can storm around like Donald Duck, screaming like Chicken Little and make my life generally miserable. I want the old bat out of my hair and my life."

"One moment, Remo."

Harold Smith was at his Folcroft desk. The buried amber monitor was active. Tapping the illuminated capacity keyboard with his thin gray fingers, he input "Mulberry" and executed a global search of his data base.

He was expecting no results from such meager data, but Smith's gray right eyebrow involuntarily jumped as something popped up. He read it through the lenses of his rimless glasses.

"Remo, I believe I can confirm 'Grandmother Mulberry' is an alias."

"I knew it! What's her real name?"

"According to this, Grandma Mulberry was an historical or possibly mythical person in old Korea. She was left stranded by the closing of the tides over a stone bridge to an island, her fate unknown."

"How long ago did this happen?"

"An estimated five hundred years ago."

"Well, the old bat looks old enough to be that Grandmother Mulberry," Remo said sourly.

"I suspect Master Chiun is playing a joke on you."

"How about if I get you her fingerprints?"

"If she is illegal, they will be useless," Smith answered. "And if she is legal, she cannot be deported."

"What if she's a North Korean spy?"

"That is a farfetched theory."

"I'll grasp at any shaky straw at this point."

The Nynex computer operator asked Remo for another dime, and he deposited the coin.

"Why are you calling from a pay phone?" Smith asked.

"So nobody knows it's me dropping a dime on the old bat."

"We may have to live with this woman until Chiun decides otherwise," Smith said.

"That's easy for you to say. You don't have to live with her."

"She calls me Sourpuss when I answer," Smith said.

"It's better than being a pussy-willow-faced pillow-biter," Remo growled.

"What did you say, Remo?"

"Never mind. Look, I'm going stir-crazy here. Got an assignment for me? I'll happily squash any terrorist or mafioso you care to finger."

"There is nothing on my desk at the moment."

"Are there riots anywhere? Send me to the worst section of Washington, D.C. I'll clean up the crack houses and paint them any color you want."

"Local law enforcement will handle Washington, D.C."

"Not from what I read. The town is practically a Third World hellhole, and no one can do anything about it."

Smith sighed like a leaky radiator valve. "If you stay on the line, I'll see what my system comes up with."

A dollar-fifty in change later, Smith's voice came back on the line.

"Remo, a man was killed yesterday in a bizarre fashion."

"It would have to be real bizarre to impress me. I've seen bizarre. I've done bizarre. What's your definition of bizarre?"

"He collapsed while crossing Seventh Avenue at Times Square and was found with his eyes and brains consumed by some as-yet-unknown agency."

"Sounds like the IRS to me."

Smith's voice actually winced audibly. "That is not funny."

"But it's true. You've been audited. Okay, it's bizarre. Where do I start?"

"I want you and Chiun—"

"Whoa! Where does Chiun fit into this?"

"The medical examiner who autopsied the victim died himself under strange circumstances. Chiun is an expert on exotic deaths, especially poisons. His knowledgeable eye might be useful."

"As long at that Korean battle-ax doesn't tag along," Remo growled, looking over his shoulder at Castle Sinanju.

"See that she does not," said Smith, and hung up.

RETURNING HOME, Remo broke the news to the Master of Sinanju.

"Smith's got an assignment for us."

"You go. I am busy."

Remo saw that the Master of Sinanju was sorting teas. Oolongs and Pekoes and greens in tin containers were arrayed about him on the floor. Chiun carefully opened and sniffed each container, disposing of stuff that had gone bad. He reminded Remo of King Croesus counting his wealth.

"Smith says you're needed on this one."

Chiun looked up, delight touching his wrinkled countenance. "Emperor Smith said that. Truly?"

"Yeah. A guy was killed somehow. When they found him, his brains and eyes were missing. Then the guy who did the autopsy died under mysterious circumstances."

"Someone does not wish the truth to be discovered."

"What truth?"

"The truth which we will soon discover."

"Smith said the second guy died of poison. You know about poisons. That's why your help is needed here," Remo explained.

The Master of Sinanju rose to his feet, a golden puffball with rose-stem limbs.

"I go where my emperor bids me to go," he intoned, his visage suffused with a golden pride.

"You go where he says because it keeps the gold flowing."

"Do not be crass, Remo."

"I call them as I see them."

"That is the motto of the crass."

THE MEDICAL EXAMINER in Manhattan examined Remo's Department of Health credentials, eyed the Master of Sinanju with a mixture of dubiousness and, nodding respectfully, he said, "I have not yet determined a cause of death."

"For which one—the victim or the guy who autopsied him?"

"Either. Come this way."

The two dead men occupied adjoining refrigerated drawers. Dr. Schiff—his card read Norman Schiff—pulled out the body of Doyal T. Rand first, and the Master of Sinanju bustled up to examine it critically.

"For all intents and purposes, this man's head has

been emptied of all organic matter except for the skull bones," Dr. Schiff explained.

"What would do that?"

"This is so far into the realm of the unknown that I wouldn't venture a guess. But the brain matter showed signs my predecessor ascribed to having been thoroughly chewed."

"Chewed?"

"Chewed."

"Something ate his brain?" Remo asked.

"It would appear so."

The drawer rolled shut. Out came the cadaver of the chief medical examiner for Manhattan until that morning.

"I have found what appears to be an insect bite on Dr. Quirk's shoulder."

Chiun peered at the bite site and said, "A bad bee did this."

"Insect parts were found, but they were too small to support the bee theory."

"It was a very small bee," Chiun said.

Dr. Schiff frowned fiercely. "I am in contact with one of the most renowned entomologists in the country, and he says no bee that small exists in nature. Therefore, it was not a bee."

Chiun asked, "Where is the corpse of the bee?"

"Follow me."

They were shown the microscope, and it was turned on.

"Without this contraption for the blind," said Chiun.

"Beg pardon?"

"I prefer my naked eyes."

"But you will not be able to see anything."

"Do what he says," suggested Remo. "He's the big cheese in his speciality."

"What is your specialty, might I ask?" Schiff inquired of Chiun.

"Death," said Chiun in a chilly tone.

Shrugging, the M.E. shut off the microscope and extracted the slide. He handed it to Chiun, who lifted it to the light.

Chiun subjected the slide to the critical acuity of first one eye, then the other. Remo leaned over, but Chiun faded back, hissing, "You are in my light, oafish one."

"Sorry," said Remo, stepping around to the other side.

"I see bug parts," said Remo.

Chiun nodded. "Yes, these look like the parts of a bug."

"Of course," said the M.E., who was astonished that these two could discern this with only their unassisted eyes.

"Bee parts," Chiun added.

"No bees are so small," the M.E. insisted. "I have this on the highest authority."

"Who's that?"

Dr. Helwig X. Wurmlinger, the renowned entomologist."

"Renown does not equal correctness," sniffed

Chiun. He eyed Dr. Schiff. "Do you know the name of the finest assassin in the world?"

"I do not."

"Or his title?"

"Of course not. Therefore what?"

"He is not renowned."

"That makes him perhaps more, not less great," said the Master of Sinanju, handing the slide back and leaving the room in a rustle and swirl of kimono skirts.

Outside, Remo turned to Chiun and asked, "So, we got nothing?"

"On the contrary. We have something terrible."

"What's that?"

"The bee that is not."

And that was all Remo could get out of the Master of Sinanju.

**9**

The New York Public Library near Bryant Park was a lot bigger than Tammy Terrill expected it to be. She immediately got lost among the bewildering maze of book-laden shelves.

"Where's the bug department?" she asked a librarian.

The woman looked up from reshelving a cart full of books. "The what?"

"Uh, the department of insects?"

"Try biology."

"Is that near here?"

Her tone and face were so helpless that the librarian broke down and escorted Tammy to the biology section and indicated a row of fat books so long Tammy blurted, "I didn't know there were that many books in the world!"

"Insects outnumber people by billions. In fact, if you could place every ant on earth on one side of a balance scale and every human being on the other, ants would outweigh mankind."

"Ooh. Neat factoid. You must watch the Discover Channel *constantly.*"

"No," the librarian said frostily, "I *read.*"

"I read, too. TelePrompTers. Sometimes AP wire stories when I absolutely have to."

"I'll leave you to your digging," the librarian said.

Her eyes widening, Tammy grabbed the woman by her skinny arm. "Wait. I only need to know about bees."

"Bees?"

"Killer bees."

The librarian walked the length of the long rows of shelving and, without seeming to look at the spines, stopped and indicated an upper section of shelf.

"Here," she said.

"You really know this shelf, don't you?"

"I *work* here," the librarian returned, and walked off, trailing a faint scent of lilac.

There were a lot of bee books, Tammy found. Two on killer bees alone. Both were titled *The Killer Bees,* but they were not the same book. The author names were completely different. Tammy wondered if it was legal for two people to write a book on the same subject with the same title and decided because they were books, nobody probably read them much and by this time nobody really cared. Reading was so pre-MTV.

She took the books off the shelf and saw they were pretty old—mid 1970s. It gave her a weird chill to think that she herself was as old as an actual book. And vice versa.

The upside was that the prices were really, really cheap.

At the checkout line, they wouldn't accept Visa. Or Discover, Tammy found.

"Miss, I need to see your library card," a prim woman told her.

"Oh, I don't have that one. Must have maxed it out. Will you take a check?"

They wouldn't take checks. Or cash, either.

"You'll have to apply for a card. Or read them here."

Tammy still didn't quite get it, but figured if they were stupid enough to let her read the books on the premises, why should she bother to buy?

At a desk, she skimmed through both books, absorbing factoids by the score. This was how she did most of her research. Tammy had discovered long ago, you didn't need much to get through for a three-minute stand-up report. A necklace of names and facts usually carried the segment.

While skimming, she committed dozens of interesting facts to memory.

Bees, she learned, were very, very important. They gathered the pollen grains that fertilized all plants on earth. Without bees, flowers couldn't reproduce.

"Great! A sex angle."

Bees were good insects, because they fertilized food plants. And they made honey. Another good, beneficial thing.

"Ooh, a diet angle. It's getting better."

Then she got to the juicy stuff.

The proper name was Africanized killer bee. That presented an image problem, but that would be up to

Fox standard practices whether or not to identify killer bees by race.

Early on, she read that there was no known geographic or climatic barrier that would prevent the spread of the killer bee into North America. That one she wrote down because it was an actual quote and she wanted to get it right in case someone actually checked. It sounded perfect for her lead.

Killer bees, Tammy further discovered, injected a neurotoxin that was more deadly than the simple toxin of ordinary honeybees. They were also unusually aggressive and easily provoked.

"More people succumb each year to bee stings than to snakebites," she muttered, moving her lips with each enunciated word.

"Deadlier than a rattlesnake!" she cried, instantly coining a new lead.

"Shh!"

Tammy ignored the other browsers at their tables. She wondered how libraries made money. Everyone seemed to be reading, not buying.

She was surprised to find that bees were kept in apiaries.

"Wonder where apes are kept. In honeycombs?"

She shrieked a resounding "Eureka" when she came to an illustration in the version of *The Killer Bees,* copyright 1977, that showed a projection graph of killer-bee migration that predicted they would reach New York by 1993.

"Perfect!" she added, rushing off to make a photocopy.

Leaving the library, clutching her notes, she found her cameraman eating a hot pretzel with mustard at a vending cart.

"I got everything I need," she said, waving her notes in his slowly chewing face.

"Except a talking head of an expert," the cameraman reminded.

"Expert what?" asked Tammy.

"On bugs, natch."

"Oh, damn. Where do I find one of those?"

"That's what news directors are for. Ask yours."

CLYDE SMOOT, news director of WHO-Fox, listened patiently to Tammy's breathless recitation of factoids and said, "You're on to something."

"I knew it! I knew it!"

"But you need a talking-head expert," he added.

"Told you so," the hovering cameraman said.

"Where do I find one?" Tammy asked.

"In the Fox research library," Smoot said.

"We have one of those?"

"For paranormal stories, absolutely."

And crooking a finger, Smoot motioned Tammy to follow him.

In a room marked Storage, he flicked a light switch and rummaged through shelves of black videocassettes. Finding a certain one, he popped it into a deck and fast-forwarded it to the end.

"Isn't that Fox Mulder?" Tammy asked, squinting at the off-color image.

"Yeah."

"Since when is an 'X-Files' episode considered news research?"

"Since it's the killer-bee episode."

"They did one?"

"Here's the end credit." Smoot slowed the tape down. Eerie music floated through the air, and he hit Pause.

"What's that?" Tammy asked.

Smoot laid a finger on a jittery line in the end credits and read it aloud.

"'Special thanks to Helwig X. Wurmlinger, special consultant.'"

"On what?"

"If this were the poltergeist episode, I'd say poltergeist. But it's the killer-bee episode, so it's gotta be—"

"Killer bees!" Tammy cried joyously.

"There you go. Call the 'X-Files' production office in Toronto, and they'll point you in the right direction."

"Shouldn't I air a preliminary report first?"

"With stuff from stuffy old books and morgue shots? No way. We need a talking head for credibility."

"Oh, all right…"

At her desk, Tammy worked the phone.

"I'm doing a story on killer bees," she explained.

"They're old hat," the "X-Files" production office told her.

"My story will prove they've hit New York. A guy's already plotzed with his brain eaten out."

"Damn!"

"What's the problem? You're way down there in Canada."

"Canada is up. And we already did a killer-bee episode. We can't do another. We're already in secondary syndication."

"Tough break. Now, how about Wurmlinger's address?"

"All my Rolodex has is a telephone number."

"Shoot," said Tammy.

After hanging up, Tammy immediately dialed the number of Helwig X. Wurmlinger.

"Hello?" a low, buzzing voice said.

"Is this Earwig Wurmlinger?"

"It is not. And I cannot talk to you at present."

"This is for TV."

"I will have no statements until I have examined the victim."

"Which victim?"

"Why, the deceased medical examiner, of course."

"I saw the autopsy. They think it's bee poison."

"Toxin. Bees produce venom. Poison is another secretion entirely."

"How about I meet you at the New York morgue?"

"Impossible."

"Why?"

"Because I am about to catch a flight for Los Angeles and the L.A. County morgue."

"But the New York morgue is here in Manhattan," Tammy protested.

"I do not know what you are talking about, but the stricken medical examiner is in Los Angeles."

"Are we talking about the same M.E.? Died of a bee sting?"

"A *suspected* bee sting. After autopsying a person who appeared to have succumbed to the same malady."

"There are killer bees in L.A.?"

"I deal in theories," Helwig X. Wurmlinger said stiffly, over what Tammy realized was a background buzzing.

"And I deal in coincidences," exulted Tammy. "I'm on my way to L.A. See you there."

Turning to her cameraman, she said, "It's a bicoastal story. Can you believe it? Bicoastal. My story has gone nationwide, and I haven't even been on the air yet!"

**10**

On the flight to Los Angeles, Remo found he had time on his hands.

The flight attendants were ignoring him as if he didn't exist. There was only one exception.

"Don't I know you?" asked a fleshy blonde whose lips were so red they were almost black.

"Search me."

"You look familiar to me," she said as she lowered his seat-back tray and laid down a monogrammed napkin.

"All stewardesses look the same to me," Remo said truthfully.

"How's that?"

"Hungry for love."

"I'm happily married," the blonde said disdainfully. Her name tag said Lorna. Her eyes went to Remo's thick wrists. Recognition bloomed in them.

"I know you! I served you on a Detroit flight a few years ago." Then, memory clarifying, she blushed a beet red. "Oh."

"Don't tell me," said Remo. "You tried to sit on my lap while I was standing."

"I—I wasn't married then," she stammered. "Would you like a refreshment, sir?"

"No," said the Master of Sinanju, who was indifferent to stewardesses.

"And you?" she asked of Remo.

"Mineral water."

As she poured mineral water into a short plastic glass, the stewardess said, "I want to apologize for my behavior."

"Apology accepted."

"I don't know what possessed me. I never tried to sit in passengers' laps, married or not."

"No problem. I put it behind me a long time ago."

"Did you age or something?"

"No."

"Lose weight?"

"No," said Remo, taking the glass. "Why?"

"It's just...I don't know what I saw in you." Her fingers flew to her mouth. "Oops. That just came out."

"Don't sweat it," Remo said sourly as the flight attendant bustled on to the next row.

In his seat, Remo's face darkened in cast.

"What troubles you?" asked Chiun.

"I don't know... I think I'm starting to miss stewardesses falling all over me."

"Stop eating malodorous carnivorous fish, and they will return to their former predatory ways."

"I wonder if I'm going through a midlife crisis."

"Not unless you are planning upon dying young,

and if you are, I would consider advance warning a boon, for I must train your replacement."

Remo grinned. "No one could ever replace me, right?"

"No one could ever replace you," the Master of Sinanju agreed.

Remo's grin widened.

"Without my guidance and assistance," Chiun added. "And of course I would mourn. For a time. Not long. Enough to be seemly. Too much mourning would be unseemly. I will not mourn long. Only a prescribed interval."

"Can it, Little Father."

Chiun resumed his examination of the sleek aluminum wing, which he feared might fall off. It was a longtime phobia. It had never happened, but as Chiun was forever reminding Remo, aircraft fell out of the sky constantly. At least three per season—which was too many.

Remo remembered what the Master of Sinanju had said at the Manhattan morgue about the cause of death of the late medical examiner.

"Hey, Chiun. When is a bee not a bee?"

"When it is not," Chiun said flatly.

"Care to elaborate?"

"My wisdom would be wasted upon small minds."

"Bees are bees."

"Except when they are not."

"I saw a bee. A very tiny bee."

"And you do not question what your eyes see?"

"Hardly ever."

"Then you saw a bee."

"What did *you* see?"

"A not-bee."

"Is that anything like a knothole?"

"I will not answer your riddle because it has no answer," Chiun said elliptically.

"Suit yourself. I'm going to catnap. It's a long way to L.A."

"With you snoring at my side, an eternity," Chiun sniffed.

But Remo dropped off to sleep anyway.

He dreamed of stewardesses dressed in bumblebee uniforms. They kept trying to sting him with their fingernails.

## 11

Los Angeles County Deputy Coroner Gideon Krombold was certain of his diagnosis.

"Dr. Nozoki succumbed to anaphylactic shock," he was saying.

"I concur," said his visitor. He was long of body, with the pinched, inquisitive face of a locust. His features twitched. Dr. Krombold thought Helwig X. Wurmlinger was twitchy because he was used to dissecting insects, not humans. But as his dark eyes lifted from a cursory examination of Dr. Nozoki's undraped body, his face continued to twitch. The man clearly suffered from a nervous tick.

"The cyanosis, facial mottling, constricted windpipe and other symptoms all point to toxic systemic shock induced by hypersensitivity to a bee's sting. In other words, death by anaphylaxis."

"Did you discover the ovipositor?"

"No. There is a puncture wound. But no stinger."

"Show me," said Helwig X. Wurmlinger, his left eye twitching to the right. His mouth twitched in the opposite direction. He wore glasses whose lenses were as thick as ice pried off a midwinter sidewalk.

They distorted his tea-colored eyes into the swimmy orbs of a frog.

Dr. Krombold lifted a dead gray arm and turned it so the elbow was visible beneath the overhead fluorescents.

"Here."

Wurmlinger took off his glasses, and his eyes jumped back to normal size with a speed that was unnerving.

He used one lens like a magnifying glass to inspect the dead man's elbow.

"I see a puncture wound consistent with a bee's sting, but there is no barb."

"Maybe he scraped it out," Dr. Krombold suggested.

"It is possible. That is the recommended procedure. But typically, those who are allergic to the toxins of *Apis* fall into respiratory distress very quickly. He would have to have had great presence of mind to have removed the stinger before collapsing." Wurmlinger replaced his glasses and regarded Dr. Krombold with his froggy orbs. "Was there any evidence of a tool in his hand when he was found?"

"No."

"Any sign of disarray?"

"No. In fact, he was found seated in his chair."

"Wearing long or short sleeves?"

"Long."

"Odd. A lone bee rarely stings though clothing."

"But one *could,* am I not correct?"

"It is possible. The bee in question might have

entered via a sleeve by accident and, becoming trapped, grew enraged. Was a bee found?''

"No."

"Peculiar. No sting and no dead bee. Bees die after they sting, for the barbs prevent the stinger from being withdrawn from human flesh. The effort required for the bee to disassociate itself from its victim literally disembowels it. There should be a dead bee. It is inescapable.''

"I had Dr. Nozoki's office vacuumed. No dead bee was found."

Dr. Wurmlinger's face twitched in every direction conceivable. "Peculiar. Most peculiar," he murmured.

"Maybe it flew away and died under something," Krombold offered.

Wurmlinger shook his head firmly. "Upon losing its sting, the bee suffers immediate distress. It cannot fly and can barely crawl. This is much the same as losing a leg. It could not have gotten far.''

"Well," Krombold said helplessly, "there was no bee."

"There was no bee *found*," Wurmlinger corrected.

"True." Dr. Krombold cleared his throat. He was becoming uncomfortable with this pedantic entomologist. "Would you like to see the other victims?''

"No. I would prefer to see the contents of their thoraxes.''

"You mean stomachs."

"Yes, yes. Of course.''

"This way, Dr. Wurmlinger.''

In a laboratory, Dr. Krombold sorted through several blackish green piles of organic matter—the partially-digested stomach contents of Perry Noto, his wife, Heather, and their chef, Remy.

Wurmlinger was as methodically creepy as a night crawler, Krombold thought after watching him pick through the stomach contents and take tiny bits of insect matter to a waiting microscope for study.

Krombold had to leave in the middle of it, but Wurmlinger seemed as happy as a dung beetle in shit.

"I'll wait for you in my office," the deputy coroner said, closing the door after himself.

Wurmlinger nodded absently.

Dr. Krombold wasn't in his office very long when a blond woman with the energy of a hyperactive Ritalin candidate stormed in.

"Are you the coroner who died?"

"Obviously not. That was Dr. Nozoki. I'm Dr. Krombold. Gideon Krombold. Who are you?"

"Tamara Terrill, Fox News." She called over her shoulder. "Joe, get in here!"

"The name's Fred," said a man with a minicam for a face—or so it seemed to Krombold on first impression.

"Has Dr. Wurmlinger got here yet?" Tammy Terrill demanded.

"Yes. But he's busy."

Tammy showed him her portable mike. "I'll talk to you first. Tell me everything."

"You have to be more specific than that."

"No time. Just spill your guts, and we'll edit them in the studio."

Dr. Krombold blinked.

"I'm talking about the killer bees. I know they're out here," Tammy prodded.

"Nonsense. Dr. Nozoki succumbed to an ordinary bee sting. The others—"

"Tell me about the others," Tammy interjected.

"I haven't yet finished telling you about Dr. Nozoki."

"This is TV. We can't dwell on stuff. People lose interest. Especially our audience."

"You know," Dr. Krombold said, picking up his desk telephone, "I think it would be best if you two left the building. I have not consented to an interview."

"Too late. Once you're on tape, the only way not to look bad is to go with the flow."

Dr. Krombold jumped from his seat and pointed an angry finger at the minicam lens that was recording his complexion going from florid to brick red.

"Turn that thing off!" he blazed.

It was spoken in anger. Krombold probably never expected an instant response, never mind compliance. But he got both.

The cameraman let out a strident yell, screamed and the minicam hit the yellowed linoleum with a bang. The light fizzled out.

Tammy shouted down at the man, "What the hell are you doing, you clumsy—!"

The cameraman was on his back, going into convulsions. He gasped, the gasping turning to a wheezing with his face becoming as mottled as wine sprinkled on satin.

"What's wrong?" Tammy demanded.

"B-b-b-b-bee!" he managed to say.

And up from between where his fingers were clutching his belly crawled a fat, fuzzy black-and-yellow insect. With a nasty *ziii*, it took to the air.

"Killer bee!" Tammy screeched, picking up a chair. "It's a killer bee. Damn, and it's not on tape."

"Don't become excited!" Dr. Krombold said. "Please calm down. It has stung your cameraman. It's only a matter of moments before it dies a natural death."

"I'm not letting it sting me," Tammy shrieked.

"Be still. Don't attract its attention," Krombold urged, coming around from behind his desk. "It will die soon. And it can't sting again. It has lost its sting."

"Tell that to the damn bee," said Tammy, trying to whack it with the chair.

The bee didn't die. It buzzed around but Tammy kept it at bay with her chair.

Finally, it took up a position atop a file cabinet and turned around completely once, then sat there looking at them with its many-faceted eyes.

"Grab a rolled-up newspaper," Tammy hissed, holding the chair between her and the intent bee. She knew that chairs were the best defense against knives. She figured a bee was just a tiny blade with wings.

"No need," Krombold assured her. "It is dying."

"You positive?"

"Bees can only sting once. Then they die. Dr. Wurmlinger said so."

"Well, he's the expert, right?"

Slowly, carefully, Tammy set the chair down.

She knelt over Bob or Ted or whatever his name was and shook him vigorously.

"Get up, you slacker."

The cameraman just lay there. His eyes were swelling shut.

"Hey, I think he's sick."

Dr. Krombold jumped to her side. His expert hands went to the man's throat, felt for a pulse, opened one eye and then the other and tested the open mouth for the warm breath of respiration. He found none of those signs of life.

"This man is dead," he said.

"I knew it! I knew it was a killer bee." And grabbing up the fallen minicam, she trained it on the bee.

"Smile for America, you little monster. I got you now."

The harsh light fell upon the bee. In response, it lifted its wings and launched itself at Tammy.

Venting a shriek, Tammy then launched the minicam at the bee, praying the tape would survive a second jolt.

Bee and camera collided in midair. The camera hit the floor for the second time.

This time, the bee came roaring back. It flew straight up into the air and attempted to dive-bomb

Tammy. She slithered out of the way, grabbed up a newspaper and made it into a tight, hard roll.

"I'll teach you, you little bugger!" she screamed.

Her first swipe missed. The second, coming on the backswing, knocked the bee clear out into the hall. It landed on the black-and-white diamond-pattern linoleum of the hall with a distinct but tiny clink.

"Where did it land?"

Dr. Krombold eased out into the corridor. "I can't see it."

Then the bee crawled onto a white diamond from a black one.

"There!" said Tammy, descending on it with blond fury. The newspaper smacked it hard.

"Got it!"

But the bee wasn't dead yet. It continued to crawl.

Tammy hit it again.

Smack.

She hit it twice more and, when it still wouldn't die, unfolded the paper and dropped it square on the stubborn bee. Amazingly, the paper marched along the floor, pulled along by the still-not-dead insect.

"What does it take to kill you?" Tammy complained.

This time, she stomped on every crumpled inch of the newspaper with both feet.

"I think I got it this time," she panted, stepping back.

"It's dying anyway," Krombold said.

When Tammy lifted the paper, the bee was still intact. It just hadn't moved much.

"I fixed its fuzzy ass!" Tammy chortled.

The bee then resumed its painful crawling.

Before Tammy could descend on it again, it crawled under a closed door. The funereal black letters on the frosted panel said Togo Nozoki.

"Damn, that is one ferocious bee," she panted. "No wonder they're feared from Brazil to Mexico."

"It looked like an ordinary bumblebee to me," Krombold allowed.

"That shows how much *you* know," Tammy snorted. "That was a killer bee. An Africanized killer bee. Loaded with neurotoxins and other poisons lethal to people."

Dr. Krombold frowned. "I must be mistaken...."

"About what?"

"I think we should bring Dr. Wurmlinger into this."

"Now you're talking!"

**12**

Dr. Helwig X. Wurmlinger was no different from any child who went through a normal bug period. He just never grew out of his.

There was no insect on earth he didn't know, but he specialized in what others called pests. He was the leading authority on the social life of fire ants, on scuttle-fly dispersal and migration patterns of the corn borer.

He knew whiteflies from gypsy moths, and could tell the summer temperature from the pitch of the cicadas chirring in the trees.

It was true that not all of the multitudinous species of insects on earth had been cataloged and classified. But Wurmlinger was the first to identify every insect of his native Texas, the state with the greatest diversity of insects in the United States. He could at a glance distinguish an ant thorax from that of a wasp, although they were in fact closely related. He could tell the forelegs of a praying mantis from the hind legs of a grasshopper and separate wartbirt from field crickets.

And after three hours of methodical sorting and classifying, he came to one inescapable conclusion:

the owners of La Maison Punaise had not ingested any portion of any species of bee known to man.

He rendered his expert opinion when Dr. Krombold returned with a rather breathless-looking young blond woman in tow.

"The victims in question didn't die from ingesting bee parts or associative glands or toxins," he said.

"Forget them!" the blonde snapped. "We got a killer bee cornered in an office. It just murdered my cameraman."

"How do you know it's a killer bee?" Dr. Wurmlinger said, twitching in curiosity.

"It zapped my cameraman, and he died just like that!" Tammy snapped her fingers once. "It's a damn shame he didn't have the presence of mind to point the lens back on himself. It would have made great pictures. Death by killer-bee sting."

"No, you misunderstand me. How do you know it was an *Apis mellifera scutellata?*"

"A what?"

"Bravo bee, or so-called killer bee."

"It looked like one. It was big and yellow and fuzzy."

"Africanized killer bees are not distinguishable to the naked eye, and they are not in any way or shape fuzzy," Wurmlinger noted.

"This one was."

"I would like to see this bee with my own eyes."

Dr. Wurmlinger was led to the locked door of the office that formerly belonged to Dr. Nozoki. He gave the dead cameraman a sidelong glance and, evidently finding him less interesting than a live bee, ignored him.

"I have the key," Dr. Krombold offered.

"Is this safe?" Tammy asked. "Maybe we should spray some Raid under the door."

Wurmlinger visibly flinched. "No doubt the bee is dead by now," he said.

Dr. Krombold unlocked the door and pushed it open gingerly.

"There is nothing to be afraid of," Wurmlinger assured him.

Tammy had retrieved her minicam and had it up on her shoulders. The light was burning hot, but the protective glass was broken, exposing the hot bulb. Faint vapor curled out from it.

Dr. Krombold went in first and looked around. His puzzled gropings caused Tammy to say, "It crawled in, remember? Look on the floor."

Dr. Krombold did. "I see no bee," he reported.

Thereupon, Wurmlinger entered and gave the room the benefit of his practiced eye.

There was no bee on the floor. Nor was there a bee, dead or otherwise, under the heavy mahogany desk. He looked in other places. Behind a trio of beige filing cabinets. In the wastepaper basket. Even at the base of a human skeleton suspended from a chain on some kind of dull metal standard.

The brownish white bones, held together by steel wire, rattled.

"No bee."

Tammy had slipped into the room. She directed the

hot beam all over, saying, "This ought to flush the little bugger out."

"It is no doubt dead by now," Wurmlinger insisted.

"I'll believe it when I see its fuzzy dead behind."

Wurmlinger started and gave Tammy a goggly look. "You say the bee was fuzzy?"

"Very. It looked like a tiny black-and-yellow mitten."

"You are describing the common bumblebee."

"There was nothing common about this guy. He had more lives than Felix the Cat."

"Bumblebees are not aggressive by nature. They rarely sting."

"That one stung. We all saw it."

Wurmlinger frowned. "It could not be the morphologically similar male drone honey bee. They are not equipped by nature with a modified ovipositor, or stinger. It is impossible for it to sting. Nor do drones possess venom sacs. The drone can neither sting nor inject poison, possessing neither biological apparatus. Yet bumbles are not violent."

"Find that bee, and you'll see different," Tammy insisted. "It's vicious."

This time, everyone searched except Tammy. She was busy working her minicam. She rolled tape as she blazed light in every direction.

In the end, they were forced to give up. There was no sign of the bee or its tiny furry corpse.

"It is very puzzling," Wurmlinger murmured.

"Maybe it crawled back out," Tammy suggested.

Wurmlinger shook his head. "Impossible. It should have been in its death throes after all that happened."

"Tell that to the damn bee," grunted Tammy, dousing her minicam.

At that moment, a man poked his head in the open office door and Tammy did a double take. He had pronounced cheekbones and extremely deep-set eyes. One hand held the door, and it was backed by a wrist like a two-by-four.

"Do I know you?" Tammy blurted.

"Were you ever a flight attendant?" asked the man with the very thick wrists.

"No."

"Then probably not."

The man showed his ID card and said, "Remo Teahan. Center for Disease Control. This is Bruce Rhee."

Tammy took one look at the elderly Asian who entered next and said, "I know you, too!"

"Remo, it is Tamayo Tanaka," the Asian flared in a familiar voice.

Remo looked more closely. "Oh, yeah. I didn't recognize her without the phony Japanese makeup. I thought they drummed you out of network news when your Geisha wig fell off on camera."

"I'm with Fox now," Tammy said defensively.

"Then I was right. Drummed out."

"Hey, we're the cutting edge in the next century news. All the Generation Xers watch us instead of those stuffy bleeding ponytails on the majors."

"Wait'll you turn forty," Remo warned.

Tammy shook her blond head stubbornly. "Never happen."

"We're looking for Dr. Wurmlinger."

Wurmlinger actually raised his hand. "I am he."

"Gotta talk to you. In private."

"And this is about what?"

"We're looking into these bug killings. We think there's more to it than bee stings."

Unnoticed by everyone, a pair of feelers emerged from the right eye socket of the hanging skeleton specimen. They quivered.

Remo went on. "This is starting to look like a serial killer bee is on the loose."

"Serial killer bees! What a great lead," Tammy rejoiced.

"Shut up," said Remo, who was making up his theory for the sake of cutting through objections.

"Are you suggesting a serial killer is employing bees?" asked Dr. Krombold.

"Maybe," said Remo, who was suggesting no such thing.

The bee's entire head emerged and looked at Tammy with its compound eyes like black bicycle reflectors.

"This is the story that will make my career," she was saying. "I can hardly wait to tell the world. Never mind my generation. Just call me Blond Ambition."

At that, the bee launched itself toward Tammy. It landed atop her hair, crimped its plump abdomen and inserted its vicious little stinger into the exact apex of her skull.

"Ouch!" she cried, smacking the top of her head. Too late. The bee slipped past her snatching hand.

Then realization hit her. She began doing a syncopated version of the *macarena.*

"I've been stung! Oh, my God, I've been stung! And I'm going to die. God, I'm going to die. I can feel myself dying."

Remo stepped in, both hands coming together. He had the bee between his hands.

*Slap.*

"Got him!" said Remo.

"No, you did not," said Chiun, his hazel eyes sweeping the room. He brought his nails up into a defensive posture, turning with each sweep and tumble of the bee's flight.

"I had him," Remo insisted.

"You missed."

"I can't miss. I had him dead to rights."

In a corner, Tammy was searching her hair, trying to locate the site of the bee's attack. "Someone help me. Somebody suck out the poison."

"That is for snakebite," Wurmlinger said, completely unmoved by events.

"What do you do for bee stings?"

"You have not been stung," Dr. Krombold assured her. "That is a drone honey bee. It is stingless."

Then the bee proved him wrong by alighting on his hand and stinging him viciously. Krombold let out a snarl.

"I have been stung," he announced, more in annoyance than anger.

"Are you allergic to bee stings?" asked Wurmlinger, coming over and taking his hand.

"No. I have been stung many times without incident."

Wurmlinger used his eyeglass lens on the sting site. "I see no barb."

"I can assure you I was stung. It was quite painful."

Then Krombold started to turn red in the face and wheeze.

"You are going into anaphylactic shock," Wurmlinger said disappointedly. "This is impossible. You couldn't have been stung."

Dr. Krombold nodded his agreement with Wurmlinger's professional diagnosis of anaphylactic shock but shook his head vigorously at the sting assessment.

Clutching his throat, he lumbered to a wooden chair and sat down, where he went into urgent respiratory distress and then cardiac arrest. With a final convulsive shudder, he deflated like a burst football.

"Is he dead?" Tammy gasped from her corner.

Remo and Chiun, swiping at the airborne bee, were too busy to reply. Wurmlinger strode over to the coroner and examined him with clinical disapproval.

"Yes, he is dead."

"Why aren't I dead?" asked Tammy in a funny, low-to-the-floor voice.

"You are not allergic."

"But he said he wasn't allergic, and look at him."

The weird low quality of her voice brought all heads turning her way.

Tammy had stood herself on her head in a corner. She was supporting her body with her flat-to-the-floor hands.

"What are you doing?" asked Remo.

"Standing on my head."

"We can see that. Why?"

"So the bee poison in my scalp will drain out," Tammy explained.

"That will not work," Wurmlinger said.

Abruptly, Tammy somersaulted to her feet. She grabbed Wurmlinger by his smock lapels. "I'll pay you to suck out the poison! I'll put you on TV. I'll do anything."

If the prospect of a blank check with Tammy Terrill's name on it interested Helwig X. Wurmlinger, he gave no sign. After a twitchy pause, he pulled free and returned his attention to Remo and Chiun.

They had the bee surrounded. It was describing loops, turns, chandelles and other aerial acrobatics over their heads. Remo kept trying to catch it between his hands while the old Korean was clearly attempting to slice it in two with extended fingernails. They were good techniques, but they failed utterly.

The bee was swifter than any drone Wurmlinger had ever before seen. And it seemed to be getting faster by the second. It would hang like a bumble in one spot, as if baiting the pair to strike. Then as hands blurred toward it, it would drop or dart or pirouette out of range. It was very striking. The bee showed signs of intelligence. There was certainly cunning and forethought, at least.

"Do not kill that bee!" he sputtered.

"Why not?" asked Remo, switching to his fists. He let fly as if to sucker punch the bee from behind.

"That is no ordinary bee."

"No fooling," said Remo.

"It appears to be intelligent."

"Well, it is fast."

The bee swooped. Spinning, it dive-bombed Remo. Remo feinted. The bee barrel-rolled out of the way. Recovering, Remo backhanded it smartly.

The bee was nimble. It came close to escaping, but it flew out of harm's way into harm's way. A slashing fingernail like a thin ivory dagger caught it.

Helwig Wurmlinger heard the tiny clip as one of the bee's wings came off in midair.

Buzzing, the bee dropped, fought to regain airspeed and struck the floor.

Landing on its feet, it spun in a frantic circle as if seeking escape. The skirted figure of the old Korean got between it and the door. Remo stepped up behind it.

"We got you now, you little bastard," Remo growled.

"Don't hurt it," Wurmlinger urged.

"It tried to kill us," Chiun hissed. "It must die."

As if the bee understood every word, it suddenly took off. Remo dropped one Italian loafer in its path. It scooted around it. Remo repositioned his foot, blocking it again.

Each time, the bee moved around it.

Helwig Wurmlinger watched in slack-jawed fascination. Bees, he knew, moved in random patterns. They didn't move toward goals, except toward their hives or food sources.

This bee appeared to be moving toward the dropped minicam, whose light was still blazing through its broken protective lens.

"Peculiar," he said.

Chiun indicated the bee's fuzzy black-and-yellow thorax with a long fingernail.

"Behold, the face of death," he intoned.

Wurmlinger bent at the waist and blinked at the yellow markings on the black thorax. They formed a pattern he had seen before. On moths. It was a tiny but very symmetrical skull, or death's-head.

"I have never seen a death's-head marking on a bee before," he breathed.

"Take a good look," Remo growled. "You won't see it again."

Helwig Wurmlinger started to protest. Before the first word could take shape, the bee gave a last convulsive effort and leaped over Remo's blocking shoe.

And jumped into the hot bulb.

With a sputtery sizzle, it died.

The smell that arose with the tiny grayish black mushroom cloudlette stank amazingly for such a small thing.

Wurlinger pinched his long nose shut with his spidery fingers and said, "It committed suicide."

"Bull," said Remo.

But the cold voice of the Master of Sinanju cut the room with a brief intonation. "It is true. The bee killed itself."

Remo made his voice scoffing. "Why the hell would a bee up and kill itself?"

"Because it is not a bee," returned the Master of Sinanju cryptically.

**13**

"Bees," Remo Williams was insisting, "do not commit suicide."

"That one did," Chiun retorted.

Tammy Terrill decided to put in her two cents. She hadn't resumed her standing-on-her-head position after she failed to gain Dr. Wurmlinger's assistance.

"Hey, they commit suicide every time they sting someone, don't they?"

"It's not the same," Remo said. "And you stay out of this."

"I will not," she said. Then, apparently remembering that she had been stung, suddenly turned the color of yesterday's oatmeal.

"Oh, my God. Am I still dying?"

"Die in seemly quiet if you are," Chiun hissed.

"Let me examine you," Dr. Wurmlinger said.

"Will you suck the poison out?" Tammy asked anxiously.

"No," Dr. Wurmlinger answered.

Tammy sat down, and Wurmlinger began massaging her blond head with his spindly fingers.

"What are you doing?" she challenged.

"Feeling for the bump."

She winced. Her scalp winced, too. "It hurts."

"The sting of a bee is painful, but of short duration," Wurmlinger told her.

As he quested about among Tammy's roots, Remo and Chiun continued their argument.

"No bee in its right mind would commit suicide," Remo was saying. "They're not intelligent. They don't think like we do. That's why they sting. They don't know they're killing themselves by stinging people."

"That not-bee deliberately ended its life," Chiun insisted.

"Why would he do a thing like that?"

"To avoid capture and interrogation at our hands."

"Not a chance in hell, Chiun."

"I am afraid I must agree with you," Wurmlinger commented, fingering Tammy's roots aside to expose a reddish swelling.

"Which one of us?" asked Remo.

"Both."

"See?" Remo said to Chiun. "He's an expert. He knows about bees."

Chiun stiffened his spine. "He knows about bees, not about not-bees. Therefore, he does not know what he is talking about."

"He's an etymologist," Remo argued.

"Entomologist," corrected Wurmlinger.

"What's the difference?"

"Entomology is the study of insects. An etymologist studies the roots of words."

"I stand corrected. Now correct *him*," said Remo, pointing to Chiun.

But Wurmlinger had already focused the entirety of his attention on the site on Tammy's skull where a reddish bump was rising, angry and dull. It was at the exact top, along the depressed sagital crest.

"Ah."

"Is the stinger still in there?" Tammy moaned.

"No, there is no stinger."

"Is that good or bad?"

"You are in no danger," Wurmlinger said.

"How can you be sure?"

"Because you are breathing normally, and the wound did not penetrate your skull."

"Why not?"

"Because it is exceedingly thick."

Tammy, her eyes rolled up as if she could somehow peer over the top of her own head, made a notch between her pale brows and asked, "Is that good or bad?"

"It's not usually considered a compliment to be thick of head, but in your case, it has saved your life."

"What about the poison?"

"I see no sign of venom or infection."

"Suck it anyway."

"No," said Wurmlinger, stepping back in disgust.

Tammy's eyes flew to Remo. "Suck me."

"Bite me," said Remo.

Tammy's blue eyes flared. "Hey, that wasn't nice!"

"It's called tit for tat," returned Remo, who then resumed his argument. "That bee was just a bee, only more stubborn than most bees. You know about being stubborn, Chiun. Not to mention mule-headed."

Chiun's almond eyes squeezed down to knife slits. "You are the stubborn one."

Remo addressed Dr. Wurmlinger. "You're the bee expert. Are they naturally suicidal or not?"

Rudely, Wurmlinger walked between them as if they weren't there and got down on one knee next to the minicam. A faint curl of fading smoke was still wafting upward from the broken bulb. Wurmlinger found the Off switch and doused the light.

"This is most peculiar," he said after a moment.

"What is?" asked Remo.

"I see no remains."

"Of what—the bee?"

"Yes. There are no bee remains."

"He got zapped," Remo contended.

"There should be some matter remaining."

They all gathered around the minicam, which was still emitting a wisp of what looked like cigarette smoke.

Tammy grabbed her nose. "Smells like burning garbage."

"Smells like fried bug to me," grunted Remo.

"A bee is not a bug," Wurmlinger said, grimacing as if suffering a personal insult.

"It is a not-bee," said Chiun. "Why will no one accept my words?"

"I am not familiar with that species," Wurmlinger

muttered. He was on his knees now and sniffed around the lamp with his eyelashes held before his sharp nose.

Wurmlinger poked and prodded and attempted to scrape some smoky residue from the flash reflector, but all he got was thin black soot.

Frowning like a twitchy bug himself, he climbed to his long, spindly feet.

"There is nothing left," he said in a small, disappointed voice.

"It was a very thorough suicide," said Chiun.

"The bee did not immolate itself," Wurmlinger explained, snapping out of his mental fog. "It merely sought a light source it mistook for the sun. You see, bees navigate through sighting the sun. Any bright light in an indoor setting will confuse them. He sought escape. The light drew him. And, sadly, he perished."

"Better luck next bee," said Remo, who then drew the Master of Sinanju aside and said, "Cover me. I'm going to call Smitty."

"Do not tell him about the not-bee."

"Why not?"

"Because that is my discovery. I do not want you hogging all credit."

Remo looked at the Master of Sinanju dubiously. "Chiun, the not-bee theory is all yours."

"See that it is," said Chiun, who then turned his attention to the shambles that was the office.

As Remo slipped out the door, the Master of Sinanju was poking about the room with all the focused concentration of an Asian Sherlock Holmes, searching for clues while Tammy piped up with a question:

"How can bees have sex? Don't their stingers get in the way?"

Wurmlinger's voice brightened with interest.

"The male bee," he said, "invariably dies in the act of procreation."

"Cool beans," said Tammy.

**14**

Dr. Harold W. Smith was a logical man. He lived in a world that, despite testing his sense of order, ultimately made sense. Or, sense could be made out of it.

Smith had grown up during the Great Depression, although to a family of means. It had been a dark time, and Smith hadn't escaped the meanness and frugality. Nor had the following decade, with its global war, been any better. Nor had the 1950s and the Cold War been a golden age, as some nostalgic writers liked to purport.

But in retrospect, all of those times made sense to Smith. He first began to notice the world going out of kilter in the early 1960s. Over the course of that decade, things began to shift. At first, it was subtle. Much of it eluded him for a long time.

Then one day, during the Vietnam conflict, Smith was watching the television, and nothing he saw made sense. Not the long-haired, bearded protesters trying to levitate the Pentagon with the dubious power of their minds. Not the smug politicians determined to prosecute an undeclared war with doubtful aims. Not the veterans of a prior Asian war, still scarred by conflict, yet willing to encourage a new generation to follow a doomed path.

Eventually, he adjusted. Not easily. After a while, Harold Smith came to a realization that helped his peace of mind. And it was this: any man blessed with sufficient years will ultimately outlive his time.

Smith's time had been the era of big bands and patriotism. He had had the misfortune—or the luck—to outlive the comfortable social context of his formative years.

Still, he liked for things to be logical.

Smith was having trouble following Remo's telephone report. Maybe it was because he had just received a wire-service report that the publisher of the *Sacramento Bee* in California had succumbed to a bee sting. There were no other details, only that the man had been found in his office dead. It was a very bizarre coincidence. But Smith had dismissed it as just that—coincidence.

And now Remo was telling him things that cast doubt on that very logical conclusion.

"We lost another coroner," Remo was saying.

"I know."

"No, I think you're a coroner behind."

"I understand that the medical examiner who performed the autopsy on the medical examiner who autopsied Doyal T. Rand has died," Smith said.

"That was a medical examiner. I'm talking coroners now."

"Remo, where are you?"

"L.A."

"Where Dr. Nozoki succumbed to a bee sting," said Smith.

"That was yesterday's news. Today's news is that the guy who took over his job bought it, too. A killer bee got him."

"Are you saying that another coroner has died mysteriously?"

"Nothing mysterious about it, Smitty," Remo said patiently. "We came in just after it happened. A bee got him. Then it attacked a cameraman and then it attacked a dip of a TV reporter named Tammy Terrill. But she survived. Then it got Dr. Krombold. He's dead. It tried to get us, too."

"A killer bee, you say?"

"No, that's what Tammy says. Chiun says it's a not-bee."

"A what?"

"Uh-oh. I wasn't supposed to say that. It's Chiun's big secret. He called it a not-bee. In other words, it ain't a bee. And you didn't hear that from me."

"If it is not a bee, what is it?"

"Wurmlinger says it was a garden-variety drone honey bee. But we saw it sting one guy to death, so that can't be."

"Why can't it be a drone, Remo?" asked Smith, struggling to follow Remo's illogic.

"To bee or not to bee," said Remo.

"Excuse me?"

"Nothing. According to Wurmlinger, who was with us the entire time, drone bees can't sting. They don't have the equipment. Therefore, it's not a killer bee. But it had these weird markings on its back, kinda like a death's-head.''

''There is a moth called the death's-head moth, but it is not poisonous in any way,'' Smith said slowly.

''Well, I saw the world's only death's-head bee, and it's vicious as a pit bull with wings.''

''I am very confused, Remo,'' Smith confessed.

''Join the club.''

''Who is Dr. Wurmlinger? Another coroner?''

''No. He's an etymologist.''

''You mean an entomologist.''

''Whatever a bug expert is, that's him. He's looking into the bee deaths. He says the bee that was trying to kill us isn't a killer bee. But we saw it kill. In fact, it tried to murder us all before it committed suicide.''

''Bees do not commit suicide,'' Smith said flatly.

''I agree with you there. But Chiun swears it did. We had it trapped on the floor, and it ran into a hot electrical bulb and went blooie!''

''It was probably attracted to the bulb. Sometimes bees mistake ordinary ceiling lights for the sun and fly into them repeatedly.''

''This one only got one shot. And that's what Wurmlinger was saying. It mistook the bulb for the sun. Only it bothers him that it went straight for it. Bees are supposed to bumble. Or meander or something. They don't do straight lines.''

''The bee made a beeline for the bulb,'' said Smith.

Remo's puzzled voice brightened. ''That's right. They do call it a beeline, don't they?''

"They do." Smith was tapping the rubber end of a yellow No. 2 pencil on his desk absently. "Remo, how did Wurmlinger escape the bee's attack?"

"Good question. While we were here, the bee never bothered him."

"That seems strange."

"Well, he's a bug expert. Maybe he wears Deet instead of Mennen Skin Bracer."

"Let me look Wurmlinger up."

"Feel free. He and Chiun were busy arguing about bees."

Smith input the name "Wurmlinger," and up came a series of newspaper and magazine articles on Wurmlinger and his works.

"Helwig X. Wurmlinger is chief apiculturalist at the USDA's Bee Research Laboratory at Beltsville, Maryland. He specializes in pests, particularly the African killer bee. He has done significant work in the field of insect genetics. The man has a reputation for eccentricity," Smith reported.

"You ask me, he looks like he crawled out from under a rotten log."

"Excuse me?"

"Buggy. He's definitely buggy."

"He maintains a private laboratory in Maryland. You say he is still there in Los Angeles?"

"Yeah, they called him in over those restaurant poisonings."

"While he is preoccupied, go look at his lab."

"Why?"

"Because," said Harold W. Smith, "he is telling

you that a stingless bee is responsible for a new string of stinging deaths. Wurmlinger is one of the nation's leading apiculturists. He cannot easily be wrong. Perhaps he is deliberately misleading you.''

"You mean he's involved in this?''

"It is possible.''

"What's possible?''

"That Dr. Wurmlinger is some new kind of serial killer.''

"A serial killer who kills with bees?''

"We know that bee stings are implicated in every death in the present chain of deaths, although in the case of Doyal T. Rand, it's far less straightforward.''

"And we don't know that a bee *didn't* do him,'' Remo said.

"No bee could devour a man's brains and eyes.''

Smith gave Remo the address of Dr. Wurmlinger's laboratory near Washington, D.C.

"Be careful,'' Smith admonished. "You and Chiun are not immune to bee stings.''

"I'll *bee* seeing you,'' said Remo.

When the line went dead, Smith took another look at the report out of Sacramento. The publisher of the *Sacramento Bee,* Lyndon D'Arcy, had been found dead at his desk. There was no obvious cause of death, but a bee had been discovered flying around his office. Once the door had been opened, the bee had flown out.

There was no description of the suspect bee.

Smith wondered if it might have been a bumblebee and set about looking into it.

As he worked, he wondered if perhaps he shouldn't have sent Remo and Chiun to Sacramento, especially since they were already in California. Too late now.

WHEN REMO FOUND the Master of Sinanju, Chiun was arguing with Wurmlinger over something clutched tightly in his old-ivory-and-bone fist.

"I demand you surrender that to me," Wurmlinger was saying in an agitated voice.

Chiun presented his back to the tall entomologist. "I found it. It is mine."

"You have no right, no authority to keep it. I am here in an official capacity, at the behest of the Los Angeles County Coroner's Office."

"Finders keepers," intoned Chiun.

"What is it now?" asked Remo.

Hearing this, Chiun moved to Remo's side. "Tell this elongated cretin that he has no right to what is not his."

"Okay. What's going on here?" Remo demanded.

Wurmlinger pointed a shaking-with-rage forefinger in the old Korean's direction. "He has confiscated evidence in a crime," he spluttered.

"What did you find, Little Father?"

"Look."

And the Master of Sinanju opened his antique ivory claw. Nestled in the withered palm was a tiny-veined bee's wing.

Remo studied it a moment. "That come off the killer bee?"

"The correct term is 'Bravo bee,'" Wurmlinger

interrupted. "'Killer bee' is press invention. And I demand the right to examine that artifact," he said tightly, his long, bony mandibles clicking with each enunciated syllable.

"If Chiun found it, it's his," Remo countered.

"Are either of you qualified to judge insect parts?"

"Maybe yes. Maybe no. But like he says—finders keepers. Come on, Little Father. Let's go."

Chiun preceded Remo out the door of the deceased Dr. Nozoki's office.

"Where are you going?" Wurmlinger called after them, his fists shaking at his sides.

"None of your beeswax," said Remo. "You stay here and tell the next coroner in line what happened here."

"You cannot leave me alone with these deceased persons. You are both witnesses."

"You carry our water for us."

"And I'm here, too," Tammy Terrill piped up.

Wurmlinger looked at Tammy as if she were a particularly uninteresting specimen. Tammy didn't notice.

"Tell you what," she said, hoisting her Fox minicam on her shoulder. "I'll interview you, and then you can interview me. We can be cointerviewers. I usually don't do this, but I'm part of the story, too, and I'm grabbing for all the face time I can hog."

Dr. Wurmlinger groaned deep in his long throat. It was a pitiable, almost unearthly sound.

"First, ask me how I got into broadcasting...." Tammy chirped.

**15**

On the way to their rental car, the Master of Sinanju noticed the lingering bee. It was hovering in the top of a eucalyptus tree, but dropped lower as they passed it.

"Behold, Remo. A spy."

Remo followed Chiun's indicating finger with his gaze. It was a fat bumblebee, hanging there in place like a miniature helicopter. Its jeweled eyes seemed to be regarding them.

"Looks like an ordinary bee to me," Remo grunted.

"It resembles the nefarious not-bee."

"It's a bee. An ordinary bee."

Chiun frowned darkly. "Let us see if it follows us, then."

"Why would it do that?"

"If it is a lurking spy, it will naturally follow us. For that is the mission of a spy."

"Not a chance."

They found their car in the lot. Remo slid behind the wheel, while Chiun got into the passenger seat. It was a cool spring day, so Remo rolled down his window instead of turning on the air conditioner.

"No," said Chiun.

"No, what?" asked Remo, turning.

"No, we do not want the not-bee to accompany us."

"Why would it do that?"

"Because it harbors ulterior motives," said the Master of Sinanju.

Shrugging, Remo reversed the window control, and the glass hummed back into place. A moment later, Remo heard the tiny but distinct click. He turned.

The bumblebee—he couldn't tell if it was the same one that followed them out—was hovering outside his driver's-side window on whirring wings.

"That's funny," muttered Remo.

"There is nothing funny about it."

Then the bee banged its metallic-looking face against the glass. It bounced off. Hovering, it tried a third time. The glass defeated it. Every impact resulted in an audible click like a ring stone against glass.

"Maybe it's upset over something," Remo said slowly.

"Bees are attracted to the color blue," Chiun suggested. "This is well-known."

Remo looked at Chiun's amber kimono, and his own black-and-white clothing.

"We're not wearing blue. The car isn't blue, it's maroon. Nothing blue in here."

"Yet the bee-that-is-not attempts to gain entrance to our conveyance."

"Maybe he's seeing his own reflection in the window and thinks it's another bee. One he doesn't like."

At that point, the bee gave up on Remo's side and zoomed around to Chiun's window. As it passed before the windshield, it showed its fuzzy thorax with a black-and-yellow dappling that made them sit up straighter in their seats.

"Did you see what I just saw?" muttered Remo.

Chiun nodded. "Yes. A death's-head."

"Guess there's more than one of the little devils...."

"Leave this place, Remo," Chiun hissed. "Now."

"Why?"

"So that we may see if it follows."

"Not a chance in hell of that happening," said Remo, keying the ignition.

Backing out of the lot, Remo took the San Diego Freeway back to LAX. The bee followed them as far as the lot, whereupon Remo accelerated, leaving the tiny black-and-yellow nuisance behind.

"Lost it," he said, grinning.

"There are other bees," said the Master of Sinanju cryptically.

"Or not."

RETURNING THE CAR to the airport rental lot, Remo and Chiun walked to the main terminal.

From time to time, Chiun turned without breaking stride, making a complete walking circle, as if to check for trailers.

"See anything?" asked Remo.

Chiun shook his bald head. "No bees."

"Anything else?"

"No not-bees, either."

"What the hell is a not-bee?"

"That I do not know. But I possess the wing of a not-bee. Perhaps Emperor Smith can enlighten us."

There was a Federal Express collection box in the terminal. It gave Remo an idea.

"Let's FedEx it to him."

"Good idea," said Chiun, surrendering the bee's wing to his pupil.

Remo dumped it into a FedEx mailer and addressed it to Harold Smith at Folcroft Sanitarium, Rye, New York.

When he turned, he saw a bumblebee hover outside, on the other side of a plate-glass window. It hovered low enough that the fuzzy death's-head marking on its back was discernible.

"That can't be the same bee," Remo said.

"It is a not-bee," Chiun declared.

"Whatever it is or isn't, it can't be the one we lost back in the city."

Chiun's hazel eyes grew sharp. "Remo, he was watching you all along," he hissed.

"So what?"

"He saw you inscribe that package to Emperor Smith. The address of Fortress Folcroft is now known to outsiders."

"Oh, come off it. A bee that can read! What's he going to do? Hop a flight to New York State and sting Smith?"

"It is not impossible...." Chiun breathed.

"It is ridiculous," said Remo. "Let's find our gate."

The bee followed them as far into the terminal as there were outside glass windows.

At their gate, they stood watching the planes take off and land. Their jet was at the gate, being serviced. A food-service truck moved into place on the opposite side of the 727 where the jetway ramp hugged the open passenger door.

As they watched, the driver opened the top forward part of the truck body over the cab and manipulated a fold-down ramp. The food-service trolleys rolled across this ramp into the food-service door of the aircraft.

It was not particularly interesting, but it was something to look at.

During this procedure, Remo and Chiun spotted the fat bumblebee.

At first, the bee appeared to flit about aimlessly like any other bee. Then it came to their window, hovered there with tiny black eyes that seemed vaguely malevolent. Abruptly, it dived away and swooped toward the open access door, showing the unmistakable skull on its fuzzy thorax.

"Uh-oh," Remo muttered.

"It has boarded our sky conveyance," said Chiun, stroking his wispy little chin.

"Maybe it's just lost."

"It is a spy. It saw that we awaited that aircraft. It seeks to accompany us."

"Wait a minute. Now I sound like you. That's just a stupid bumblebee. It's not even the same bee from the morgue."

Chiun looked at Remo with thin, narrowing eyes.

"Can you be certain of this, Remo?"

"No," Remo admitted. "But bees are just bees."

"But not-bees are dangerous."

They boarded their flight with wary eyes.

They saw no sign of the skull-marked bee as the 727 rolled out onto the runway. As it idled, awaiting clearance for takeoff, Remo said, "I'm going to reconnoiter."

He went to the forward part of the plane, looking for a pillow. He came back with a nice fluffy one and checked the men's room. No bees lurking there.

"You should be in your seat, sir," a flight attendant warned.

"I think there's a bee on board," Remo told her.

"This happens from time to time. They wander aboard. Are you allergic to bee stings?"

"No."

"Then don't worry. Please take your assigned seat."

Over the intercom, the pilot announced, "Final cross-check. Flight crew prepare for takeoff."

"Now, sir," the flight attendant said edgily.

Reluctantly, Remo took his assigned seat.

The takeoff was smooth. The gleaming aluminum wings took to the air, and the rumble of the wheels whining into their wells told them that they had committed to flight.

That was when the death's-head bee popped out of the galley. It flew back into the cabin, hovered in midaisle and seemed to hesitate at the sight of Remo and Chiun eyeing it back.

Then, as if having second thoughts, it retreated into the first-class section.

"I don't like the looks of that," said Remo.

Chiun made a satisfied mouth. "It fears us. Good."

Remo shrugged. "It's just a freaking bumblebee."

Then a scream ripped out of first class.

*"Ahhh!"*

Remo came out of his seat so fast his seat belt snapped in two. Chiun followed, a wraith of silken skirts.

They moved through the first-class cabin and collided with a panicky knot of flight attendants jamming the aisle.

"Back in your seats. Back in your seats, please. We have to land," one was yelling.

"Why?" asked Remo.

"Because the pilot's been stricken. But it's all right. Stay calm. The flight engineer is capable of landing the plane without help. Return to your seat, please."

Beyond the stewardess's worried face, Remo saw through the open cockpit door the pilot convulsing in his seat.

Then the copilot slapped the side of his neck—and just ahead of it danced the fat black-and-yellow honey bee with the death's-head markings, free and unscathed.

"If the flight engineer's out of action, who lands the plane?" Remo asked the stewardess urgently.

"Don't be worried. We've never lost two crew members."

"Answer my question," Remo demanded, shaking the stewardess. "Who lands the plane?"

"No one. There's just the pilot and flight engineer."

Remo set the stewardess aside like a hat rack and moved into the cramped cabin.

The pilot was slumping to one side, completely out of it. The flight engineer had one hand on the yoke. The other was fumbling about among the controls weakly.

But even from behind, Remo could see that he was going into shock.

## 16

The flight engineer was definitely going into shock.

There was no question what was happening to him. He took his free hand off the yoke and grabbed his throat. He began to wheeze. His face turned a smoky reddish hue. He gasped audibly.

"Easy, fella," Remo said, reaching his side. "You got stung by a bee, that's all." Remo kept his voice calm. But the flight engineer was gasping for air now. His windpipe was closing off, like an asthmatic's.

"Stay with me," Remo urged, squeezing the man by the back of his neck to encourage adrenaline production. "The pilot's gone. You're the only one who can land the plane."

The flight engineer started to nod. The nod turned into the shaking that shivered down the length of his body and became a convulsion.

"Easy," Remo warned.

Then he saw the reddish swelling over the carotid artery on the left side of the man's neck. The bee had injected its venom directly into the man's bloodstream. There was no way to save him, Remo knew.

Meanwhile, the plane continued its screaming climb.

"He's out of it," Remo cried to Chiun.

"Where is the not-bee?" Chiun hissed, his eyes questing about the cockpit.

"Forget the bee. Someone's got to land the plane."

"You do it. I will watch the wings for signs of treachery."

"I don't know how to freaking fly a 727!" Remo exploded.

"How hard can this be?" asked the Master of Sinanju. "You have a wheel with which to steer. You know where the ground is."

"I don't know squat about flying a big bird like this."

"Where are the parachutes?" Chiun wondered aloud.

"They don't equip passenger aircraft with parachutes, Chiun," Remo said heatedly.

Chiun blew out his cheeks in indignation. "We have been cheated, for we paid full fare!"

"Never mind that, help me get these guys out of here so I can work."

Chiun bustled forward and took the blue-faced pilot by his shoulder epaulets. He pulled him back into first class, which caused no little consternation among the passengers.

A pale-faced man stood up. "Is this a hijacking?"

"No. We are only going to crash," returned Chiun thinly.

That reassured absolutely no one, although a few people did faint.

Remo slid into the pilot's seat, and drew on the earphones and mouth microphone.

"Pilot to base," Remo said.

"Say again. This is LAX Tower. Repeat message."

"This is TWA flight to Baltimore."

"Say flight number?"

"Let me get my ticket," Remo said, fumbling in his pockets. Then he remembered leaving it in his seat pocket. "Hey, Chiun what's the freaking flight number?"

"It has two zeroes in it."

"Are they in front or back?"

"Back."

"Tower, this is a flight number zero-zero," said Remo, clearing his throat on both sides of the zeroes and hoping for the best. It worked.

"TWA, confirm you are flight 600."

"Confirm," said Remo, making up his lingo. "We have an on-board emergency here."

"Flight 600, state the nature of your emergency."

"The pilot and copilot are dead. It's up to me to land this thing."

"Is this a hijacking?"

"No."

"Are you qualified to pilot a passenger aircraft?"

"No ."

A silence cracked in the earphones. Then in a drained voice, the tower said, "Stay calm, sir. And we will attempt to talk you down."

"Better put a lot of foam on the runway for this one," Remo warned.

"Acknowledge."

The tower ran Remo through the essentials of piloting a big bird. They told him where the throttle was. How to trim flap and deploy the thrust reversers. It sounded easy at first. Then they began piling on the details.

"Look, we need to keep this simple," Remo complained.

"This is the simplest version, sir."

"I need a simpler version. There's a lot of distractions up here."

Just then, another one reared its bulging head.

"Remo, the not-bee has returned," squeaked Chiun.

"Swat it. I'm busy," Remo called back.

The Master of Sinanju stepped around and blocked the door, saying, "Bumblebee-who-is-not, do not dare intrude, for here stands the Master of Sinanju to deal with you."

The bee, if it understood, only grew more determined. It swooped at Chiun's bald head, encountered a sweeping backhand and went corkscrewing away. Striking a bulkhead, it ricocheted, rebounded and came again.

This time, it tried to zip between Chiun's outstretched legs.

Chiun gathered up the hem of his kimono skirt, ripping out a swatch of silk lining. Snapping it between tense hands, he waved it before the bee like an Oriental matador with a too-small cape. The bee bobbed and weaved, but refused to retreat.

"Come, bee. Come to your doom...." Chiun invited.

The bee zigged, then zagged, trying to get past the snapping silk. It made a dive for the space between Chiun's black sandals.

Twisting the swatch into a knot, the Master of Sinanju bent his deceptively frail-looking body, enveloping the bee expertly in a ball of fabric.

The bee hummed and buzzed in frustration.

"I have the culprit," Chiun announced to Remo.

"Good," returned Remo.

The tower was assuring Remo that he would land safely. They were telling him to lay his nose on the main radio beacon. Remo understood none of it in the technical sense. But when the nose was pointing toward the foaming runway, he began to feel a slow surge of confidence.

"Okay, I'm riding the beam," he said, copying the tower's terminology.

"Drop gear."

Remo pulled on the heavy lever that deployed the landing wheels. They rumbled out of their wells.

Remo lined up on the main runway.

"Now ease back. Not too hard on the throttle," the tower instructed.

Remo obliged. There was a sheen of perspiration on his forehead. It came from concentration, not fear. He kept trying to fly by the seat of his pants, the way he drove a car—by feeling every component of the vehicle, and becoming an extension of it. But this was a big, lumbering jet that operated by hydraulics and electrical controls. It was worse than power steering. It was power everything. Remo preferred to be the power in the cars he drove. Here, he was disconnected from total control of the aircraft. It made everything feel wrong.

As the jet dropped lower and lower on its Pacific approach, Remo heard a rare Korean curse emerge from the Master of Sinanju's papery lips.

"What now?" he demanded of Chiun.

"The bee ate through my kimono lining. It is ruined."

"What?"

Then the bee was dive-bombing Remo's head. And the tarmac came rushing up to meet the nose.

"Not now," Remo groaned. "I've almost got this thing on the ground."

The bee dancing before his eyes, Remo slapped at it in sheer frustration. It bounced off the side of his hand, unharmed, and regained its aerial equilibrium.

"What does it take to kill one of these things?" he complained. "Chiun, get in here!"

The Master of Sinanju was in the cabin now. There was hardly any room for him. Chiun made a lunge for the dancing bee.

"I have him."

"Get him out of my freaking hair."

Chiun's fists knocked the bee around the cabin. He was on Remo's right. Then his left. Finally, Remo called out, "You're worse than the freaking bee! Leave it alone!"

"It is trying to kill you."

"I gotta save the plane," said Remo as the rear tires unexpectedly made contact with the blacktop. They barked like stung dogs. The plane bounced, settled, and the barking came again.

Steadily, Remo lowered the nose. It touched down. Then the plane was rolling into the patch of waiting foam.

I did it, Remo thought. I saved the plane!

And he felt a tiny sting over his left carotid artery, and a very cold sensation began to well up inside him.

**17**

At first, it sounded like a tornado.

Gordon Garret heard it as he walked between the corn rows.

The corn was coming up. Last week, there had been a goose-drowner of a rainstorm in this fertile corner of Iowa. That helped some. Not like it was down in the Southwest, where they were suffering from drought. In Texas and those parts, the winter wheat hadn't come up at all. There was a lot of suffering.

Gordon Garret understood suffering. His patch of earth, Garret Farms, had been in Garret hands going clear past the forgotten depression of the 1850s to before the Civil War. There had been a lot of hard times since then. It was a constant battle with corn borers and funguses and the like.

And, of course, there was the weather. Some years, it didn't rain, but it poured. Others, the fertile earth fell apart under the broiling sun. The Great Flood of '93 was still fresh in Iowa minds.

Tornados weren't that common. They happened, sure. But the last thing Gordon Garret expected to hear was the dull roar of an approaching twister.

For a moment, he froze, his boots sinking into the heavy soil. He felt no wind. That was peculiar. There was that dull, distant, freight-train roar, but no breeze.

On either side of him the rows of the new Super Yellow Dent corn—guaranteed to resist corn borers by fooling them into thinking corn smelled like uninteresting soybeans—three months from tasseling, just stood there like so many dull students with their long green-turbaned heads held up off the earth.

But the roar was the roar of a twister. So Gordon shook the fear out of his coveralls and made a dash for the barn.

He ran like the wind, boots crunching dirt. But the roar was moving faster. It *was* the wind.

The roar swelled. Weirdly, it didn't become that full, big-train roar he associated with twisters. It stayed low. Had a metallic kind of sound in it, like heat bees in summer. But this was April.

Flinging a glance over his shoulder, Gordon expected to see a funnel cloud. But there was no funnel. It was a cloud.

What he saw made him stop, stand stock-still and scrunch his seed cap in his uneasy hands.

The low sky was a mass of gray, hazy blackness. It hummed. Weird, that hum. Spooky. Not loud. Just insistent. Angry, maybe. But all hell-winds sound angry.

It looked like a dust cloud, but there was still no wind.

Then it hit.

Like a fury, it hit. The noise was the worst of it. It

came churning in, all rage and viciousness. The fury of it dropped Gordon to his knees. He threw his arms across his flinching face and pushed the front part of himself into the dirt.

A whining buzz roared over and across him. The sound of it assaulted his ears. The sound changed as he cowered for protection in the good earth that supported him.

It chewed and ripped and tore, and it seemed to go on forever in its voracious frenzy.

Then, like a miracle, it passed.

Like a train moving down its assigned track, it had passed on by.

Fearfully, Gordon Garret uncrossed his arms and lifted his body.

The air was settling down. There was no dust, no grit—none of the airborne debris the natural wind stirred up.

Yet green things were falling from the sky. Green, and the smell was the smell of corn-shucking time. A fall smell. Here it was April and the air smelled of autumn.

Gordon looked to his left and to his right. And that deep, cold fear that comes to every farmer in his lifetime settled in his empty stomach.

The corn. The young corn was falling from the sky in tatters. Cornsilk drifted down like thin golden tinsel. The baby kernels were scattered like yellow hail. The green protective leaves were only now coming down on the quieting air. The stalks were gone. Chewed to ribbons as if by buzz saws.

That was what Gordon thought of right off. A million tiny buzz saws. Hungry, vicious buzz saws. They had sickled the new corn into so much fragrant trash.

Climbing to his weak-kneed legs, Gordon turned around on dull, heavy feet like a wooden Indian.

The dust cloud was moving on, having eaten him into bankruptcy.

That was when total understanding took hold of Gordon, and he threw himself to the useless soil and bawled his brains out.

**18**

Remo Williams had been schooled by the Master of Sinanju to dodge bullets, arrows, spears and even thrown rocks. It was not enough, Chiun had told him, on that day many years before when the elderly Korean sullied his pristine hands with an old Police Positive revolver and emptied its chambers at Remo, who successfully—if clumsily—evaded every snarling slug.

"You must learn to evade the flying teeth you cannot see coming," he added after Remo caught his breath.

"How is that possible?" Remo asked, already full of himself because up until that time in his life, only Superman could dodge bullets—and he wasn't real.

"You must learn to feel the breeze the flying tooth pushes before it as it seeks your life," said Chiun.

"Let me get this straight," Remo asked incredulously. "I gotta feel the shock wave coming?"

"Yes."

"Im-freaking-possible!"

But he had learned. Week by week. Month by month. Year after year, Remo had learned how to slow time in his brain and speed up his supercharged reflexes so that a bullet fired at his back, moving ahead of the sound wave of the exploded gunpowder, couldn't catch him off guard.

He learned to feel the approaching shock wave on the exposed surfaces of his skin. The delicate hairs on his forearm became like sensitive antennae. Remo had always thought they were just hairs—remnants of mankind's primitive, hairy ancestry. But he understood they served a sensory function, too.

Later, after he had become attuned to his body hairs, Remo learned to sense the presence of a threatening mind. And to anticipate the firing of the shot or the throwing of the blade before even the attacker had made the decision to kill.

Nothing could touch Remo after that. Not guns, not exploding shrapnel, not anything other than Chiun's own remonstrating fingernail. Remo never learned to evade Chiun's blows.

As the lumbering 727 skidded to a sloppy stop, its wheels awash in fire-dampening foam, Remo experienced a moment of combined fear and shock.

I should have felt the little bastard's legs on my neck, he thought.

I should have felt the stinger pressing into my skin.

And, I'm dead.

Eyes sick, Remo turned to the Master of Sinanju and voiced the fear that was in his mind. "I'm dead, Chiun."

Chiun had stepped in, and his angry eyes were fixed upon the buzzing bee, once more aloft. Remo could hear its tiny, annoying *ziii* sound.

The Master of Sinanju made two claws of his hands and lifted them. His wrinkled features were extremely intent. His concentration was ferocious.

"It's too late," Remo said.

"Never fear. I will capture the dastard!" Chiun hissed.

"That's not what—"

And Chiun brought his palms together in a short blur. His nails intersected. Fingers nested. Palms met with a meaty slap.

The *ziii* stopped abruptly.

Chiun squeezed his hands, grinding them together. A crackly sound came from the thin plane where his palms met.

With a flourish, the hands separated, and what was left of the bee fell to the floor. A black sandal snapped down, grinding the remains into the rubber floor mat.

"You are defeated, bee-who-is-not," Chiun intoned.

"You're too late, Little Father," Remo said thickly.

Chiun shook his aged head firmly. "No. It was too slow. Although it was exceedingly swift for a bee."

Remo stood up. "I got stung."

Chiun flinched. "Where?"

Remo had his hand over the carotid. "Here."

Reaching up, Chiun slapped Remo's hand away and pulled his neck into view by the harsh expedient of dragging down on his pupil's dark hair.

"Let me see."

"Ouch!"

Chiun scrutinized Remo's pulsing carotid artery. "I see a tiny wound. How do you feel?"

"Cold."

"You should feel stupid. To let a mere bumblebee sting you."

"You saw what it did. You saw how fast it was. Even you had trouble catching it."

"I did not allow it to sting me," Chiun spat.

"What do I do?" asked Remo.

"Try standing on your head. If the poisoned blood is drawn from your brain, little will be harmed." Remo's eyes went into hurt shock. "How can you say that?"

"It is easy," snapped Chiun. "For you are not poisoned."

"I'm not?"

"No. There is no redness. Your eyes are clear."

"Maybe I'm immune...."

"Perhaps the bee had already exhausted its venom."

"Guess that's possible, too, but I still feel kinda cold."

"Stupidity. It will pass." Chiun turned about, coaxing Remo to follow with a crooking finger. "Now come. We must leave this wounded bird that you so clumsily wrecked, lest we are discovered by prying eyes."

"Yeah. Okay. We can't afford to answer too many questions anyway."

Passing the first-class cabin, Chiun announced in a loud voice, "Hearken well, for you have been saved by the House of Sinanju. These are your tax dollars at work. Pay your taxes promptly and often. Lest your nation lose our services, and your empire succumb to foreign emperors.''

The passengers looked too dazed to respond. Many were still fumbling with their seat belts or lifting their heads from the between-knees crash-survival position. Nobody appeared injured.

''What happened to avoiding problems?'' Remo asked Chiun.

Chiun dismissed his pupil's objection with a careless wave. ''That was advertising. It always pays.''

Remo tried to open the hatch by hand, but the mechanism was too complicated, so he just kicked it open. The thick hatch jumped outward with a dull sound like a flat bell being rung. It went splat in the foam. That seemed to rouse the flight crew.

At the emergency exits, inflatable escape chutes were deploying, and the first passengers began sliding down the big yellow chutes, under the direction of the flight attendants.

In a very short time, passengers were milling around the tarmac as paramedics and other emergency professionals came and got them.

When the big silver bus came to load the most able aboard, Remo and Chiun were already calmly seated in back.

It was easier to go this way than trying to walk along the wide-open runway system under the sweep and blaze of emergency lights.

At the terminal, an airline representative was waving sheafs of official-looking forms and began trying to get the walking wounded to sign away their rights to sue or receive compensation for their injuries.

Remo took an offered Bic pen and jammed it halfway up the airline rep's left sinus cavity. The man stumbled off, muttering nasally that he was going to sue somebody. That was the end of airline damage control.

From a pay phone, Remo called Harold Smith.

"Smitty, get set for the unbelievable."

Smith sighed. "I deal with the unbelievable on an almost daily basis."

"We were tailed from the coroner's office," Remo said.

"Yes?"

"The tail sneaked aboard our flight. We saw him go through the food-service door. Once the plane was in the air, it murdered the pilot and copilot. We would have crashed, but I took the controls and landed the plane."

Remo's voice lifted on a note of pride toward the last. Smith brought it crashing down with his incredulous "You? Flew a jet plane?"

"The tower kinda helped out," Remo admitted.

"The plane crashed," Smith said.

"Crash-landed," said Remo. "It was a crash landing, not a crash. Nobody died."

"Except the pilots," Smith corrected.

"Yeah."

"And, of course, the man who murdered the pilots."

"Yeah. Chiun got him."

"I assume you interrogated this person?" Smith said.

"You assume wrong."

"How is that?"

"Because you're assuming a person, and not what tried to kill us," Remo said.

"What tried to kill you?" Smith parried.

Remo handed the receiver to Chiun, who was hovering nearby.

"It was a not-bee," Chiun explained.

"A bee brought down the plane!" Smith said, his lemony voice skittering high into the stratosphere of the musical register.

"No, a not-bee."

"Talk sense," snapped Smith.

"I am," said the Master of Sinanju in an injured voice. "It had the form of a bee, but it was not a bee."

"Put Remo back on," Smith directed.

"Why?"

"Because I need to speak with him," explained Smith tightly.

Face quirking up, Chiun surrendered the receiver to his pupil, sniffing, "The conversation has taken an unimportant turn, Remo. Emperor Smith wishes to speak with you."

"Not-bee theory didn't exactly go over well?"

"That man is old. No doubt his faculties are failing. It is the burden of the kingly. Nero was much like this in his snowy years."

Remo took the phone and said, "I can't tell what he's talking about, either."

"Remo, start at the beginning."

"Which beginning?"

"From the time you left the morgue."

Remo did. He told about the bumblebee that had followed him from the parking lot and all that had transpired at the airport.

"And he had the same death's-head markings as the morgue bee," Remo finished. "The outside morgue bee. Not the inside one."

"It could not be the same bee," Smith stated flatly.

"Why not?"

"Bees do not fly that fast."

"This one was pretty light on his wings. Speaking of which, we mailed you a wing from the first bee."

"I will be very interested to see that."

"That was the good news. The bad is that the second bee looked like it read your address when we mailed the package."

"Preposterous!"

"This bee was out to get us," Remo said heatedly. "I'm just letting you know what it knows."

"It knows nothing. It is dead. And I want the body."

"Well, that's going to be kinda hard," said Remo, looking out through a plate-glass window to where the 727 was awash in fire-retardant foam. "Chiun mashed it flat as a wafer, and the plane is crawling with airport personnel. The NTSB should be along at any moment."

"Then I will have the bee's remains requisitioned on my end," said Smith.

"Good luck," said Remo. "So what do we do now? Risk flying again or what?"

Smith was silent for a long space. "I want that bee's wing."

"It's on the way via Federal Express."

"Not soon enough. I want it today. Recover the package and bring it here. Wurmlinger can wait."

"If you say so."

"I say so," said Smith, terminating the connection.

Hanging up himself, Remo addressed the Master of Sinanju. "He sounds pretty P.O.'ed."

"I heard. We will bring him the wing of the not-bee."

They had their first stroke of luck that day when they went to the Federal Express pickup box. A driver showed up. He was in the act of unlocking the deposit box—which saved Remo the bother of ripping it apart with his bare hands in front of witnesses—when Remo tapped him on the shoulder.

"I need to get back a package I sent."

"Sorry. Once it's in the box, it's ours. Company rules."

Remo smiled pleasantly. "Sure. I understand."

And he and Chiun followed the man to his awaiting orange-and-purple-splashed white van. They were not at all secretive about it. In fact, they carried on a loud running conversation.

"Don't you hate it when big companies take your

money and blow you off when you have a problem?''
Remo told Chiun.

''Customer satisfaction is the soul of the professional assassin,'' Chiun replied. ''So said Wang the
Great, who understood such things.''

The driver, knowing he was being followed, cast
several nervous glances over his shoulder. He looked
more worried each time. Just as he inserted his key
into the door, he looked back again.

He saw no sign of the thick-wristed white guy or
the old Oriental who had been following him.

Still looking back over his shoulder, he rolled the
rear van door up.

Then he climbed aboard, threw his satchel in the
back and lowered the door. It locked with a resounding clunk of steel latching.

He drove out of LAX at a good clip, pausing only
at the main entrance.

That was when the rear door unexpectedly rattled
up, and he saw California sunlight beaming in from
the back.

Braking and swearing, he ran back.

The cargo door was fully up, but there was no sign
of whoever had opened it. He ran it down again and
decided not to report any of what had happened.

But as he eased onto the freeway, he had the uneasy feeling that at least one of those two had been
hiding in back of the van.

*How* was another matter. The only way into the
van was through a locked side or rear door. And the
rear door had been unlocked only long enough for

him to check to see that the coast was clear and climb aboard.

Surely that was too short a time for a grown person to slip on board. Surely.

BACK AT THE TERMINAL, Remo was saying to Chiun, "That guy was looking everywhere except where we were."

"No," corrected Chiun. "We were everywhere his gaze did not fall."

Remo shrugged. "Same difference. Okay, let's get this thing to Folcroft."

"What of the bug man, Earwig Wormfood?"

"Smitty said he can wait."

"Thus, he waits."

**19**

Harold Smith was deep in cyberspace when his secretary buzzed him that he had visitors.

"It's those two," she whispered.

"Send them in, Mrs. Mikulka," said Smith, looking up from his desktop screen. It was a relief, he thought, not to have to reach for the old concealed stud under the edge of his old desk to send the old-style monitor humming down into its concealed desktop well. That was in the days before he had the new system with its screen mounted flush under the black glass desktop. He still sometimes missed that system with its comforting green monochrome screen. It matched his Dartmouth tie.

When Mrs. Mikulka popped her blue-haired head in, Smith merely looked up and nodded his gray head. No one could see the buried screen except the man seated before it.

Mrs. Mikulka withdrew as Remo and Chiun entered.

Remo said, "Hiyah, Smitty," and tossed the FedEx envelope across the room.

It went sailing over Smith's head, out of reach. At the last moment, it abruptly boomeranged back to settle before him, square with the corners of the desk, unnoticed by Smith, who was still looking over his shoulder, expecting it to bounce off the office picture window.

Smith blinked, looked about and finally saw the package, resting on the desk as if it had been there all along. He cleared his throat, unimpressed with Remo's theatrics.

Stripping back the cardboard zipper, he emptied the contents on the smooth desktop.

A single wing fluttered to the black glass. It was backlit by the amber screen below. Touching a key, Smith reset the screen to a pure white. The light highlighted the outline and veins of the tiny wing.

Chiun was uncharacteristically silent as Smith studied the wing's delicate structure.

"You're being ignored," Remo whispered to him.

Chiun shook his head. "I ignored him first."

"Well, he's ignoring you back."

"He is too late. He is the ignoree, while I am the true ignorer."

"Well, you know the etiquette of ignoring," said Remo in an unconvinced tone of voice.

Smith's patrician nose was almost touching the desktop now. He made assorted faces he was entirely unaware of.

"What do you say, Smitty?" Remo prompted.

Smith looked up, squint eyed. "It appears to be a bee's wing. Unremarkable."

"Well," said Remo. "Is it a bumblebee or a drone?"

Smith sat back and began working his keyboard.

Remo came around the desk to watch.

Smith had brought up a color replica of a drone honey bee and was manipulating it. One wing broke off and enlarged itself. It matched in outline and vein patterns the detached wing resting on the desk.

"It is a drone's wing. An ordinary drone," he said.

"No, it was a not-bee," Chiun corrected.

"I am unfamiliar with that terminology," Smith admitted.

"Examine that wing more closely," Chiun suggested.

Smith did.

"What do you see?" asked Chiun.

"A common drone honey bee wing, according to my data base."

Chiun shook his head slowly. "The creature that possessed that wing owned intelligence and malevolence. It was not a bee, common or otherwise."

Smith brought up an image of a killer bee.

It was completely different and the wing structure was different, as well. The killer bee was no different than a typical honeybee—long of body but not as long or distinctively colored as a yellow jacket. The drone, on the other hand, was plump and fuzzy.

"This is not a killer bee's wing," Smith said flatly.

"True. It belongs to a killer not-bee."

Smith looked to Remo for help. Remo rolled his eyes and pretended to find the overhead fluorescent lights of interest.

"I fail to understand," Smith said helplessly.

"You are excused," Chiun said, and floated over to the picture window to contemplate Long Island Sound.

"I guess we came a long way for nothing," Remo told Smith.

"There is word out of the L.A. Coroner's Office."

"Yeah?"

"The new coroner has pronounced the deaths of Dr. Nozoki, Dr. Krombold and the others as the result of killer-bee stings."

"That can't be!" Remo exploded. "We saw how those people bought it. A garden-variety bumblebee got them."

"Drone honey bees," Smith said carefully, "cannot sting. And more importantly, the venom of the Africanized killer bee is a neurotoxin, which is to say it affects the nervous system, not merely the breathing passages, as does ordinary bee venom."

"That makes no sense."

"It does if someone has crossbred a new kind of bee."

"That's possible...."

"Since the advent of killer bees in this hemisphere, Remo, there have been many attempts to interdict the killer bee in its northern migration. All have failed. The defense of last resort has been to cross these feral bees with more-gentle domestic bees in order to obtain a less virulent and aggressive strain."

"How's it coming?"

"It has been an utter failure. But that is not to say that someone could not attempt to create a more virulent strain of bee, if they chose to reverse the breeding program.''

''What's the point of that?''

''It is obvious,'' said Chiun, turning from the window.

Remo and Harold Smith looked at him, unspoken questions in their eyes.

''To kill,'' said Chiun.

Remo and Smith looked at one another, their faces undergoing various changes of expression—Remo's dubious, Smith's lemony.

Clearing his throat, Smith swept the bee's wing into the FedEx container and attacked his keyboard. He brought up a list of the dead to date, including the two pilots.

''Doyal T. Rand was the first,'' he said.

''We don't know that,'' said Remo. ''He wasn't stung. His brains were eaten out.''

''Let us assume he was the first because the man who autopsied him subsequently died of anaphylactic shock.''

''Okay,'' allowed Remo.

''That was Dr. Lemuel Quirk. The New York coroner—''

''M.E.,'' Remo corrected.

''—also was killed by the sting of a bee, although no bee was found.''

''Why?''

''Simple. To cover up the first killing.''

''In Los Angeles, three people died at a new restaurant of bee venom, although none appeared stung and no bee parts were found in their stomachs, according to Dr. Wurmlinger.''

"How did you know that?" asked Remo.

"I talked to the assistant deputy coroner in Los Angeles."

"Oh."

"A Dr. Nozoki who autopsied them died of a bee sting. As did a Fox cameraman. As did Dr. Gideon Krombold. Again, let us assume a cover-up."

"By bees."

"Using bees," said Smith.

"Idiots," said Chiun.

"What was that?" Smith asked the Master of Sinanju.

"Nothing," said Chiun, resuming his enjoyment of Long Island Sound.

Smith returned to his glowing amber list. "The bee attempted to kill you and Chiun. It died. Yet another bee followed you from the coroner's office and apparently attempted to finish the job by bringing down your flight."

"It's a chain of BS, but it's solid," Remo admitted.

"That leaves but one question."

"Actually, it leaves a zillion. But what's the one on your mind?" Remo asked.

"If the intelligence behind this—and there can be no mistaking that one does exist—is intent on killing everyone involved with those two deaths, why are Tammy Terrill and Dr. Wurmlinger still alive?"

"Search me."

"Because they are useful," said Chiun.

"Useful to whom?" asked Smith. "Who could so perfectly control this new strain of feral bees that they function as assassins?"

Chiun made a face at the misuse of the honorable term *assassin*.

"And how are they controlled?" added Smith.

"Sounds like Bee-Master to me," muttered Remo.

"Who?"

"Bee-Master. It was a comic-book character I used to read about back at the orphanage."

Smith made the lemony face of a man who had bitten into a persimmon unsuspectingly.

"We are dealing with reality here," he said.

"Not if bees can think and attack people they don't like," Remo returned.

Smith made an uncomfortable noise in his throat.

"If this chain of deaths began with Rand and the owners of that restaurant, what do they have in common?" Remo queried.

Smith posed the question to his computer, and it came up with side-by-side profiles of Doyal T. Rand and the Notos.

"Rand is a genetic genius. It was he who perfected the current method of roach-population control by shutting off their pheromones."

"What about the others?" asked Remo.

"They had just opened a restaurant that served bugs."

"I sure hope the thunderbug isn't back," said Remo to Chiun. Chiun made a disgusted face.

"Ordinarily," Smith mused, "I would not connect

two such dissimilar deaths were it not for the fact that in both cases the medical examiner who autopsied the victims succumbed to bee stings. That is the only link. The cover-up of the attacks. It is wrong.''

''It's criminal,'' Remo admitted.

''No, it is wrong in this sense—if a serial killer is at work, his signature should be static. The cause of death—the *modus operandi*—may vary.''

''You think we're dealing with a serial killer?''

''I am nearly certain of it. And the only connection between the two victims involves insects.''

''The killer is a bug on bugs, you mean?''

''An insane person who must be identified and apprehended.''

''Well, what can we do?''

''At this stage, little. I believe it is time to bring in the FBI. They have psychological profilers who can glean remarkably accurate information on the subject from details surrounding the killings and crime scene.''

''What about us?'' wondered Remo.

''Go home. Stand by. I will call upon you when I need you.''

''What about Wurmlinger?''

''He is in police custody, according to my sources. He is going nowhere for now.''

Smith had already turned his attention to his computer system, so Remo motioned for Chiun to follow him out.

Chiun passed from the room, presenting his disdainful back to the emperor who had neither heeded his wisdom nor understood it.

Before closing the door, he allowed himself to peek back at Smith the Mad.

The Mad One was still intent upon his oracles, so Chiun closed the door with a nerve-jangling jar.

No one ignored the Master of Sinanju without penalty. Not even the emperor of the wealthiest empire of the modern world.

## 20

At FBI headquarters in Quantico, Virgina, Edward E. Eishied received a strange inter-Bureau e-mail message signed ASAC Smith.

He had heard of Assistant Special Agent in Charge Smith. He had never met him. But Smith was an FBI legend. It was said he was a retired agent given special investigative status by the director. It was also said the faceless Smith was really a cover for whoever sat in the director's chair, going back to the halcyon days of Hoover. J. Edgar, not Herbert.

No one knew for sure. But everyone knew that whether it was a cross e-mail message or the man's graham-cracker voice on the line, what Smith said went.

In this case, it was an e-mail. The text read, "Require psychological profiles on unknown subject. See attachment for details. Needed ASAP."

Eishied snapped to attention. This was his meat. He had worked every serial-killer case from Ted Bundy to the Unabomber and he had nailed the essentials of every psychological profile he ever undertook.

The weird part was Eishied knew of no case not already under active investigation.

He sat back, expecting to find details of some horrific new killer of the ritualistic type.

Instead, he read the incoming data and slowly slumped in his seat.

"This is a test," he muttered. "No, it's a joke."

But ASAC Smith had no reputation for humor. In fact, by reputation he was the most button-down SOB in the Bureau hierarchy.

Downloading the file, Eishied went at it. It was going to take some real brainpower to profile this guy. He picked up the telephone and speed-dialed the Chicago office.

"Ralph? Eishied here. I need your assist on something."

"I was just going to call you. I just received the weirdest request from no less than ASAC Smith himself."

"Does it involve killer bees?"

"Yeah. You on it?"

"Just downloaded the file into my machine. The question is, are we supposed to work together or independently?"

"My guess is that Smith's looking for every pristine angle."

"Okay, no communication until we turn in our reports."

"Good luck."

"Same to you," said Eishied, then hung up.

As he fired up his laser printer for generating a hard copy, Edward Eishied muttered, "I sure hope we come up with the same profile...."

**21**

Tammy Terrill had never seen anything like it.

"What is with you people?" she complained to the L.A. chief of detectives.

"We're not prepared to give a statement at this time," he returned.

"I gave my statement to *you!*"

"That's different. You're a witness. You're obligated to give your statement."

Tammy stared at the transcription of her statement, which lay on Chief of Detectives Thomas Gregg's desk, along with a pen so she could sign it. They were in a brightly lit interrogation room in the downtown L.A. police headquarters. It looked nothing like the interrogation rooms Tammy had seen on TV. It was too nice.

"If you don't give me an interview, I won't sign that," she warned.

Chief of Detectives Gregg eyed her with no flicker of emotion. He didn't look much like a cop, though he talked just like one. He was too tanned to be a cop, and his hair was too sun bleached. Even for a California cop.

"Gary, have Miss Terrill here held as a material witness."

"You can't do that!"

Gregg looked Tammy dead in the eye the way a bird looks at a worm. "We need a signed statement or we need you. What's it going to be, Miss Terrill?"

Tammy signed the statement. "This is under protest."

"Just spell your name right," Gregg said woodenly. They had all been like that, wooden and unemotional, when they had descended upon the L.A. County Morgue and sorted through the bodies.

Tammy had tried to get their theories on the case before they got too busy.

"We just got here," Gregg had said.

"I saw it all," Tammy told him. "It was killer bees. Ask him. He's big on bugs."

At that point, Dr. Wurmlinger introduced himself and threw cold water on Tammy's new lead. "I confess I have no explanation for what has happened here," he said in a helpless voice.

"Tell them it was killer bees. You know it was killer bees. I know it was killer bees. Just tell them."

Wurmlinger looked as lost as a termite on plastic. "The bee that stung them could not have killed them. Other than that, I am at a loss for an explanation," he said.

After that, Tammy and Wurmlinger were separated and taken downtown. There, Tammy told them everything she had seen to the point when Dr. Krombold had succumbed, finishing with, "It stung me, too, but I have the skull of a crockery pot, so I didn't die."

Chief of Detectives Gregg seemed unimpressed by any of it. He just asked methodical questions and expressed doubt only when Tammy failed to identify her cameraman by name.

"They're so...common," she explained. "Like they're pod people, or something."

Now, with her statement signed, Tammy was being released. Out in the corridor, she hunted up Wurmlinger. He was coming out of another interrogation room and looked as lost as a cockroach in an hourglass.

"Hi."

"Hello," he said dispiritedly.

"Time for our interview."

"The police asked me to make no public statement."

"I'm the media. We outrank the cops."

Wurmlinger shook his long head slowly. "I am sorry. I must return home. I have had a very trying day."

"It's about to become the greatest day of your life. Because you're about to become Fox News Network's resident bug expert."

"No."

"Just think of it!" Tammy said, throwing her arms wide. "Your face will be telecast from coast to coast. You'll be famous. You'll be asked to lecture. Hey, maybe you'll even get a date or two."

Wurmlinger winced. "Goodbye," he said, exiting the building.

Tammy watched him get into a cab and overheard him ask the driver to take him to the airport.

Tammy whistled up a cab and gave her driver the same instruction.

There was no way she was going to lose her story now.

WURMLINGER WAS so preoccupied that Tammy had no trouble trailing him to the American Airlines counter, where he offered his return ticket to a clerk.

After he left for his gate, she barged into line and accosted the same reservations clerk.

"I need to go where that tall drink of ugly is going."

"Brownsville, Texas."

"Right. Texas. I'm going there."

The reservations clerk cut her an open-ended return ticket to Brownsville, Texas, and Tammy loitered at an adjoining gate until the last boarding call came. She slipped aboard and took her seat without being noticed by Wurmlinger.

At Brownsville, she was one of the first off the plane, which put her in a position to grab a cab before Wurmlinger collected his luggage.

The cabbie wanted to know where she was going.

"Just get me out of the airport, and I'll get back to you," Tammy told him, snapping open her cell phone.

She dialed Clyde Smoot in New York.

"What is Dr. Wurmlinger's address again?"

"Didn't you find him?" Smoot asked.

"I'm on center stage in something bigger than 'X-Files.' Just give me the address, Clyde."

After it hit her ears, Tammy repeated it to the driver, and he gave the cab real gas.

"This," Tammy said, "is the way to cover breaking news."

# Deal Yourself In and Play
## GOLD EAGLE'S
# ACTION POKER

# PLAY "ACTION POKER" AND GET...

★ 4 Hard-hitting, action-packed Gold Eagle novels — FREE
★ PLUS a surprise mystery gift — FREE

Peel off the card on the front of this brochure and stick it in the hand opposite. Then check the claim chart to see what we have for you — FREE BOOKS and a gift — ALL YOURS! ALL FREE! They're yours to keep even if you never buy another Gold Eagle novel!

## THEN DEAL YOURSELF IN FOR MORE GUT-CHILLING ACTION AT DEEP SUBSCRIBER SAVINGS

1. Play Action Poker as instructed on the opposite page.
2. Send back the card and you'll get hot-off-the-press Gold Eagle books, never before published. These books have a total cover price of $18.50, but they are yours to keep absolutely free.
3. There's no catch. You're under no obligation to buy anything. We charge nothing — ZERO — for your first shipment. And you don't have to make any minimum number of purchases — not even one!
4. The fact is thousands of readers enjoy receiving books by mail from the Gold Eagle Reader Service. They like the convenience of home delivery…they like getting the best new novels before they're available in stores…and they think our discount prices are dynamite!
5. We hope that after receiving your free books you'll want to remain a subscriber. But the choice is yours — to continue or cancel, anytime at all! So why not take us up on our invitation, with no risk of any kind. You'll be glad you did!

## AND THERE'S MORE!!!

• With every shipment you'll receive *AUTOMAG*, our exciting newsletter — FREE.

**SO DON'T WAIT UNTIL YOUR FAVORITE TITLES HAVE BEEN SNAPPED UP! YOU GET CONVENIENT FREE DELIVERY RIGHT TO YOUR DOOR. AT DEEP DISCOUNTS. GIVE US A TRY!**

© 1993 GOLD EAGLE

## THE GOLD EAGLE READER SERVICE: HERE'S HOW IT WORKS

Accepting free books places you under no obligation to buy anything. You may keep the books and gift and return the shipping statement marked "cancel". If you do not cancel, about a month later we will send you four additional novels and bill you just $15.80—that's a savings of 15% off the cover price of all four books! And there's no extra charge for shipping! You may cancel at any time, but if you choose to continue, then every other month we'll send you four more books, which you may either purchase at the discount price...or return to us and cancel your subscription.

*Terms and prices subject to change without notice. Sales tax applicable in N.Y.

## BUSINESS REPLY MAIL
FIRST-CLASS MAIL    PERMIT NO. 717    BUFFALO, NY

POSTAGE WILL BE PAID BY ADDRESSEE

**GOLD EAGLE READER SERVICE**
3010 WALDEN AVE
PO BOX 1867
BUFFALO NY 14240-9952

NO POSTAGE
NECESSARY
IF MAILED
IN THE
UNITED STATES

## 22

Remo Williams was walking the halls of Castle Sinanju in North Quincy, Massachusetts.

He was bored. There was nothing to do. Chiun was
closeted in his private room doing God alone knew
what while Grandma Mulberry—or whatever her
name was—haunted various rooms like a cantanker-
ous Korean ghost.

Remo avoided her at all costs, but it was hard. She
roamed from room to room dusting and cleaning and
cackling to herself. Chiun claimed she was singing an
old Korean love song. To Remo, it sounded like a
hen cackling.

At six o'clock, he checked in with the local news.
Since Chiun was busy, that meant Remo could watch
the newscaster of his choice. That meant Channel 4.
The other two channels both boasted a reporter named
Bev Woo. They were not the same person. It was a
local oddity that created no end of problems for Remo
if they had to watch any Woo. Chiun insisted on
watching the dumpy, middle-aged Bev Woo, whom
he had dubbed the incomparable Woo. Remo preferred the lithe and chipper Bev Woo, whom Chiun
detested. But since he had a real choice, Remo went

with the third option, Channel 4, where a new Asian anchorette with the unlikely name of Dee-dee Yee held sway.

It turned out to be a slow news day. A drunken car crash led the top of the news. A record-sized blue shark had been captured in a Kingsport fisherman's net, and the weather for tomorrow was promised to be "springlike." Since this was New England, that probably meant rain. Maybe even hail. Brimstone was also possible.

At the end of the broadcast, the anchor said good-bye, and the station immediately cut into a bumper that rehashed the lead stories the station had recapped two seconds earlier, adding, "Tune in at eleven for details."

"Why do they always do that?" Remo muttered. Increasingly, it seemed that the news had more teasers for the next segment or the next newscast than hard news itself. He wondered if there was some kind of plot afoot by commercial advertisers to hook America into watching what was fast becoming a perpetual, round-the-clock newscast. On second thought, maybe they saved more money teasing than reporting.

Then he remembered he had a fourth option. The Fox News Network.

The Fox report started with an update on the is-there-life-on-Mars? controversy and segued into a story about an Iowa corn farmer who claimed a "windless wind had devoured his crop."

"Are space aliens responsible for these mysterious events?" the reporter intoned. "Stay with Fox News for the other side of the news. The news the other networks dare not tell. Fox is committed to tracking down the stories no others will report. For news, think Fox.''

There was nothing on the killer-bee story or the strange serial coroner deaths on both coasts. And no sign of Tammy Terrill. Remo wondered if maybe she had succumbed to delayed bee-sting shock after all.

Bored, Remo decided to rattle Chiun's cage.

''Hey, Chiun. You busy?'' asked Remo, knocking on the door.

Chiun's querulous voice came through the panel. ''Go away!''

''What do you mean, go away?''

''Go away. I am improving my mind.''

''You're what?''

''Reading a book,'' Chiun explained.

''All right. All right. Sheesh.''

After that, Remo decided to go for a walk.

He happened upon Grandma Mulberry, who stuck her tongue out at him and said, ''Good riddance.''

''Who said I was going out?'' growled Remo.

''You wearing kiss-me-pretty-boy face,'' she tittered.

''That's it! I'm getting a room.''

''Better than crouching in bush with other faggots,'' she taunted.

''Remind me to string you up in the nearest tree for a scarecrow,'' Remo snapped.

Grandma Mulberry then bestowed upon Remo a

very respectable Bronx cheer. She sounded like old buzzard with stuttering gas.

On the way out, Remo noticed a book lying on the kitchen table. It was entitled *The Joy of Astral Sex*. Curious, he opened it up.

A quick scan showed it was some kind of New Age self-help book. Most of it concerned instructions on how to achieve an out-of-body experience. The rest focused on finding the proper disembodied sex partner, and how to do it the ectoplasmic way.

"It's the only way the old bat's going to get any," grumbled Remo, who rolled the book into a tight cylinder and fed it into the garbage disposal with grim glee.

He found himself walking along Wollaston Beach a few minutes later. The wind was flattening the gentle ripples of Quincy Bay, and in the distance Logan Airport's squat concrete control tower showed clearly.

There was no getting around it. He would have to move. Strangling the old bat was out of the question. Chiun would make his life even more miserable than she did. There was no way he was going to win. And he still didn't understand why Chiun had hired a housekeeper in the first place. They had gotten along fine, just the two of them, for more years than Remo cared to count.

It would be hard to live apart from the old reprobate, but it was either that or put up with snide insults for the rest of his days.

Remo was so intent on his thoughts he didn't notice

the auburn-haired woman until she practically stood in his path.

He looked up. She had long shimmering hair and wore a look that would make a Boston cop flinch. She was pretty. No, wait. Make that gorgeous. Her eyes were warm and brown, and she was wearing a blue spring dress that hugged her body like fresh linen. She looked young yet mature. Fresh but seasoned. Her face was radiant, but without that dewy look very young girls possessed.

"Excuse me," Remo said. "I didn't see you." He started to walk around her.

Shifting, she got in his way again. "You look bored," she said.

"That's me," admitted Remo.

She looked him dead in the eye. "Fine. Marry me."

Remo said, "What?"

She waved a ticket. "Look, I just won the lottery. Mass Millions."

"Good for you."

"And I quit my job."

"Congratulations."

"But I'm bored."

"It's a long line," said Remo, "and I was ahead of you."

She got in his way and fixed him with her striking eyes, which were growing steely. "Did you hear anything I just said?" she demanded.

"I have stuff on my mind."

"I just won seven million dollars and I'm free as

a bird." She smiled. "And you look like my kind of bird."

"Sorry. I fly alone."

"Don't tell me I'm not your type. I know different."

Remo decided she was crazy and turned on his heel, walking the other way. She followed along, growing more insistent. She had the slightly husky voice of a former smoker. That was a strike against her in Remo's eyes. He didn't care for smokers.

"I don't have a type," said Remo, wondering if the shark effect was wearing off. He found if he ate shark every other day, it quenched his powerful pheromones.

"Look, I'm not kidding about winning the lottery. It happened last week. See, this is the winning ticket. I'm afraid to turn it in. So I come here and try to think. Aren't you even slightly impressed?"

"I have my own problems," said Remo.

"Look, if you won't marry me, how about a date?"

Remo blinked. He stopped in his tracks. A cunning gleam grew in his deep-set dark eyes.

"I gotta take you home to meet someone first," he said quickly.

Her voice took on an edge. "If it's your wife, I withdraw the offer."

"No. Come on."

They walked back to Castle Sinanju. She told Remo her name was Jean and she had six kids and one grandson. "No two alike," she added.

"You don't look that old," he said.

"I'm not. I was just testing your nerve. How is it?"

"Holding up."

"You're doing better than most guys I meet. For some reason, guys are intimidated by me. Puts a big damper on my love life." Her smile turned sly. "By the way, how's yours?"

"Ever hear of astral sex?"

Her eyes bloomed. "You can do astral sex? I thought I was the only one who knew that stuff."

"I just read about it," Remo lied. "What's it like?"

"You lie in separate beds, sometimes separate homes. You never touch in the physical sense. But your souls mate."

"Is it good?"

"It's transcendent. Did I ask you your name?"

"Remo."

"I'm half-Italian, so we should get along just fine. Assuming you believe in prenuptial agreements."

"I wouldn't ask the woman I was going to marry to sign one," said Remo.

"You got it backward. I'm the one who hit Mass Millions."

"Oh. Right."

"Anyone ever tell you that you're a little slow sometimes, Remo?"

Remo nodded. "You'll meet him."

Grandma Mulberry met them at the door, took one look at Jean and said, "Do not fall for his act. He is a faggot."

Jean burst out laughing. "She's cute."

"She's not the one I want you to meet," Remo growled.

"Oh, I think she was."

They found Chiun in the bell-tower meditation room. The Master of Sinanju looked rested and bright of eye on his reed mat. Without skipping a beat, he said to Jean, "You are very beautiful."

"Thank you."

Remo broke in. "That's Chiun. Chiun, this is Jean. We're talking about getting married."

"If you marry for money, love cannot fail to follow."

Remo blinked. "I know this is kinda sudden but—"

Chiun lifted a long-nailed hand. "You have my permission to wed. I bless this union."

Remo blinked more rapidly. Jean laughed out loud, a happy, infectious sound.

"May you bear my adopted son many squawling infants," Chiun said expansively.

"Don't you at least want to know her heritage?" Remo asked.

"A good thought," said Chiun. "Child, what is your father's last name?"

"Rice. My name is Jean Rice."

Chiun brought his deceptively delicate hands together, and his face assumed a rapturous expression. "You will be an excellent influence upon my wayward son, who has sowed his wild oats for too long now. It is time he settled down to a steady diet of rice. Even if it is white rice."

"We haven't set a date yet," Remo said quickly.

Chiun arose from his mat. "There is no need. I am prepared to marry you now."

Remo stepped back with nervous speed. "Wait a minute! What's the rush?"

"You have made the decision. It is done. As head of the House, it is my duty to join you in matrimony."

Remo started backing out of the room.

"But first you must know certain things about my adopted son, Remo," added Chiun.

"Shoot," said Jean, folding her arms.

"He is a fearsome killer."

Jean cocked an eyebrow. "Him?"

"Yes. Second only to myself. Many enemies of this country he has slain in cruel and merciless ways. For we secretly work for no less than the emperor of America."

Jean eyed Remo. "He's funny. I like him."

"He's a pain in the butt," returned Remo.

"He's using reverse psychology, you know."

"I am not," Chiun flared. "If no one objects to this union, I pronounce you assassin and consort."

"Wait a minute. *I* object," Remo said.

Jean wrapped one arm around Remo and said, "Too late. We're wed."

"I hardly know you. And this is just a date."

"Don't sweat it. I'm rich. I'll support you."

Chiun's eyes narrowed sharply to conceal their growing merriment.

"Look," Remo sputtered. "I just met her. I

thought I'd use her to get that old bat off my back. I can't walk by her and she makes a crack about my masculinity.''

Face reddening, Jean released Remo and stepped away.

''You were just using me!'' she said, her voice squeezing down in shock.

Remo caught himself. ''I didn't mean 'using' like that.''

She grabbed his arm again. ''So we can get married, after all.''

''You *are* married,'' said Chiun.

''No!'' said Remo.

''If you jilt this woman who loves you, Remo, it will bring shame to the House,'' Chiun scolded.

Remo grabbed Jean by the hand and dragged her down the stairs. Her laugh bounced off the walls. Remo, visibly annoyed, fumed until they were out of the building.

Once outside, Jean looked up at the fieldstone monstrosity and said, ''If we end up living here, I want some changes.''

''Don't get ahead of yourself,'' Remo growled.

She looked up at him, her eyes appealing. ''You weren't *really* using me?''

''I need to get that iron-haired scold off my back.''

''Uh-huh. Let's go back to the beach. You look like you could use a good smooch.''

''I'm a little rusty in the romance department,'' Remo admitted.

She took his hand. ''I have just the cure for that....''

23

The first psychological profile came by e-mail.

Smith's system beeped to alert him of the incoming transmission from the FBI Chicago office. Smith hadn't expected a report this soon, although he knew the Bureau profilers were very good at this sort of task.

The text report was succinct to the point of ridiculous:

> UNSUB is antisocial type. White male, age about thirty-five, intelligent, detail oriented and keeps bees. Probably had an ant farm as a child and fell into fantasy world inhabited by insects. Lives in isolation. Minimum to no social life. Drives Volkswagen Beetle. Follows the Charlotte Hornets.

Smith input the text into his own profile generator and commanded the program to generate a rough artist's representation of the UNSUB.

Moments later—the speed of modern computers still sometimes astonished Smith, who had cut his analytic teeth in the halcyon days of Univac—a color image appeared.

It showed a nearly featureless white man, bearded, but wearing dense wraparound sunglasses and a deer-stalker cap.

Smith blinked. The system had generated a face that was a cross between Sherlock Holmes and the Unabomber.

Obviously, he was working with insufficient data.

Saving the image as a file, Smith returned to the task at hand. Perhaps one of the other profilers would do better. After all, profiling was not an exact science....

## 24

Midway through dinner—Remo had ordered mako shark out of habit—he realized the merry look in Jean's eyes wasn't there because she had won seven million dollars courtesy of the state of Massachusetts, but because she was in love with him.

Not lust like most women, but love. It had been a gleam in her eye from the first, but now it was open and unconcealed.

"So," Remo said, putting down his fork, "what's the attraction? It can't be my pheromones. They've been pretty quiet lately."

She smiled. Her lips were very red. They went with her eyes somehow.

"Last summer, I had my Tarot cards read," she said, leaning forward. "Guess what the woman said."

"Search me."

"'You're coming into money.'"

"They all say that."

"It came true, didn't it? Now shut up and listen. Then she flipped a couple of cards over and said, 'I see you on a beach. There's a man walking the beach with his head down. Dark hair and dark eyes. He has unusual energy.'"

"That could be anyone."

"'And wrists like two-by-fours.'"

Remo's knife and fork froze in midair. "She said that?"

Jean nodded. "Her exact words. So when I saw you, I knew exactly who you were."

Her smile lit up her crinkling eyes.

"Who am I?"

"Let's just say this—there's still time to run."

"I don't run from anything," said Remo. But his dark eyes were worried.

They drove to the beach and walked its entire length and back again. A cold moon came up and washed them in its pristine light.

They were still there when the sun rose.

**25**

If Mearl Streep hadn't had the misfortune to be christened Mearl Streep, a lot of things might have been different.

For one thing, he wouldn't get all those annoying telephone calls at all hours asking for an autographed picture of himself in drag.

For another, he'd still be teaching the fifth grade.

Mearl Streep's rise to fame changed all that. Between the calls at night and the scrawls on the blackboard of James L. Reid Grammar School in the daytime, Mearl Streep had been practically drummed out of polite Iowa society.

In the beginning, it was only miserable. Then his brother passed on, and Mearl inherited the family farm. That made it bearable. Nobody cared what a simple corn farmer called himself.

But Mearl's heart wasn't in corn. It was in being somebody, and being Mearl Streep was a plain losing proposition.

"How the hell do I get me some respect?" he asked his dog, the only companion he had who didn't snicker behind his back.

Old Blue barked a time or two and lay down and began snoring.

"Life is against me. That's all there is to it," he muttered.

Old Blue rolled over and passed gas.

"And if it's against me, then by damn, I'm going to be against it," Mearl said firmly, fanning the air with his seed cap.

It was one thing to blow off steam on a farm in the middle of the Corn State where no one cared. It was another to keep doing it. Mearl got tired of listening to his own complaints and took to listening to the radio.

There were some pretty interesting new personalities on the radio during the good days before the Great Flood. First there was Thrush Limburger. He really got the blood coursing. But after a while, he started sounding more and more like an eastern windbag, shifting with the changing political winds.

Others came. They went, too. Louder, more feisty than the ones before. After a while, all the sound and fury died down and there was nothing good on. Nothing for a hardworking but bored corn farmer to listen to.

Then interesting things started happening. Ruby Ridge. Waco. Folks were talking about how Washington was going to be moving against the people pretty soon, and some of the loudest voices in radio started disappearing. Folks blamed bad ratings, but Mearl wondered. It sounded vaguely sinister. So Mearl bought himself a shortwave set and took up listening to Mark from Minnesota, a program devoted to warning folks about the coming insurrections with the black helicopters and the New World Order and suchlike.

Not four months after Waco, came the Great Flood of 1993. The hundred-year flood, they called it.

It wiped out Mearl Streep. He barely escaped the moving wall of black puddinglike mud that rolled over his farm after the Raccoon and Des Moines rivers overflowed in the wake of a four-hour goose-drowner of a rainstorm. Eight dirt-drumming inches fell. A crest of water twenty-seven feet high rolled off the Raccoon and ran smack into the swollen Des Moines.

From that tumultuous collision, it spread out in all directions like a cold wrath of the Almighty coming to clear off the earth.

That night, Mearl sat on high ground in his red Dodge pickup and listened to Mark from Minnesota proclaim God's honest truth.

"This so-called flood was no act of God. God don't flood the farms of God-fearing people. This was Washington. They are experimenting with their weather-control devices and figure the best people to try it on are farmers. What do farmers know? They get rained on, droughted on and hailed on all the time. They'll get over it. Well, listen my brothers out there in the heartland. Don't get over it. Get even. You who are organized into militia, get ready. Those who aren't, what are you waiting for?"

"By damn, what *am* I waiting for?" Mearl asked

himself over the relentless hammering of raindrops on his truck roof.

Thus was born the Iowa Disorganized Subterranean Militia, led by Commander Mearl Streep.

At first, no one wanted to join. There were no militia in Iowa. It was a peaceful state and folks were too busy cleaning up the black mud and trying to get back to normal to join anything but the unemployment line.

When the first unemployment checks ran out, Mearl started doing business. First, all he had was a squad but before long, he had himself an honest-to-God unit.

They trained in the deserted cornfields taken over by the banks. If they happened upon a banker, sometimes they used him for target practice. It was only fair. An eye for an eye. An ear for an ear. And Mearl wasn't talking about corn.

For three years, Mearl had drilled his men, and trained them to prepare for the black helicopters that were certain to fill the skies when zero hour came.

No one knew when zero hour was, but he was all but certain it would take place on April 19.

"Why April 19?" a new recruit asked, as they invariably did.

"That was the hallowed date of the shot heard round the world, in Lexington, Massachusetts, in 1775. That's when the First American Revolution started. In 1991, another shot was taken against tyranny at a place called Ruby Ridge on the same date. Two years later, also on April 19, the battleground was called Waco. These events turned the tide against the new tyrants so bad that on April 19, 1995, they created a diversionary tactic, blowing up that federal building in Oklahoma City.

That was the turning point. Everything after that is what we called AO—After Oklahoma. We are now at war with our own unlawful government. And we gotta drill for the next April 19 or bend our proud backs under the iron boot of Washington.''

Two entire April 19s passed without incident.

Then they came. Exactly on time.

First it was the Garret cornfields. Stripped by what was described as a wind that wasn't a wind.

"What was it?" Streep demanded after rushing to the scene in his camouflage uniform on the latest April 19.

"It sounded like a cross between a tiny twister and a locust swarm," Gordon Garret himself had told him.

"Sounds like Washington to me."

"I don't know what it was, but it bankrupted me," Garret said dejectedly.

"Then you might want to take a gander at this," said Mearl, pulling an IDSM membership form and introductory booklet from the cargo pocket of his cammies.

Garret read right along.

"That'll be thirty dollars, your first quarter's dues," Mearl added.

"I'm flat busted."

"No man is busted who marches with the Iowa

Disorganized Subterranean Militia,'' promised Mearl Streep.

The twister from hell had hit other farms, too. Not all of them in a straight line. A number were skipped.

"Collaborators," muttered Mearl. "That proves Washington's behind this. No storm or swarm picks its targets. Look at this."

They looked. Everyone saw it plain. It was as if some supernatural thing had taken random bites out of the waving green prairies and fields. But the bites weren't random. Any farm that was hit was completely destroyed. Those that were spared were absolutely untouched, not an ear as much as nibbled on. In his mind, Mearl saw them as collaborationist farms. And there were more of them than there were of the downtrodden. A whole lot more.

"We gotta take the fight to the enemy now," Mearl exhorted.

"To Washington?"

"We are gonna take Washington back for the God-fearing people," promised Mearl Streep. "First we gotta put the fear of God into Washington."

## 26

When Remo returned home with the dawn, Grandma Mulberry met him with a disapproving expression and a short, pungent oath.

"Slut."

"You're pushing it, you old bag of bones. Nothing happened."

"Not mean redhead, but you. Out all night. Shame on you. Tomcat slut."

Remo inched closer. "You know I can break your neck like a twig?" he said in a low growl.

The old woman sneered back. "Master Chiun bounce your butt over moon if you do."

Remo's teeth met with a click. His hands floated up as if they had lives of their own. They hovered at choking height.

Catching himself, Remo dropped them to his sides.

"Give me a second," he told Jean, who observed the entire exchange in silent bemusement.

The Master of Sinanju was already up. He was transcending with the sun in his white muslin morning kimono.

"Hey, Little Father. I need to know some Korean."

"'I love you' is *Song-kyo Hapshida*."

"Thanks. But I already know that. How do you say 'F you'?"

Horror froze Chiun's wrinkles. "You have broken up with the most wonderful woman you have ever met or will ever meet?"

"No, I want to tell that rusty battleax off once and for all in language she'll understand."

"I forbid you to do this."

Remo's face fell. "Thanks a lot, Little Father."

Remo ran down the stairs and found an old Korean-English dictionary. It didn't have the correct phrase. Not even a reasonable facsimile.

Remo decided he had only one person to turn to.

HAROLD SMITH ARRIVED for work with the rising sun. He greeted his secretary, nodded to her routine "No messages" and brought up the system linked to the Folcroft Four in the basement of the complex.

He was not long at this when he heard a click behind him. He ignored it. The click came again.

This time, he turned around in his swivel chair.

There, on the other side of the picture window, hovered a common bumblebee. It bumped into the window.

"Impossible," said Smith.

Then the blue contact phone rang.

Not taking his eye off the bee, Smith scooped up the phone.

"Smitty, I need your help" came Remo's voice.

"Not as much as I may need yours," Smith said, his voice drained of all emotion.

"How's that?"

"There is a bee on the other side of my office window. It is trying to get in."

"The two-way window? How can a bee see through it?"

"I suspect he cannot. But as you know, the window faces the Sound. It is not visible except to boaters. Yet this bee appears fascinated by it."

"Maybe it's trying to head-butt his reflection."

"Perhaps. But it seems very determined to enter my office."

"Got any bug killer?"

"I'll get back to you," said Smith.

"When you do, look up the Korean translation for 'F you.'"

"I am not going to ask why you need that information," Smith said thinly.

"Good. Because I'm not going to tell you."

Smith hung up and buzzed his secretary.

"Yes, Dr. Smith?"

"Have maintenance bring me an insecticide fatal to bees."

"Yes, Dr. Smith."

It wasn't long before the maintenance man set the can of Deet on Smith's desk, and Smith dismissed him.

Then Smith went up to the Folcroft roof and, getting down on his stomach after doffing his gray jacket and vest, looked down over the roof combing.

The bee was still hovering at the window not four feet below. Smith could see its back clearly. It was brownish black, except for the fuzzy yellow-and-black midbody, where the wings were rooted. The fuzzy thorax was marked with a distinct skull whose tiny black hollows stared sightlessly upward.

Smith aimed the can, steadying himself, and released a jet of noxious spray.

The stuff spurted down, enveloping the bee. It bobbed off to one side. Smith redirected the spray at it. It dropped, came level and continued to buzz the window.

The can ran empty before the bee got annoyed. Then, like a tiny helicopter, it abruptly shot up to Smith's eye level.

Smith gave it a last shot and the bee, its multifaceted eyes turning white, retreated a dozen feet, blinded.

Discarding the useless can, Smith dashed back to the roof trapdoor and dropped it after him on his way down the ladder.

When he returned to his office, he was shaking.

And the bee was still there. Its tiny face was dripping foamy insecticide now. Otherwise, it was unbothered. The eyes were clearing.

"No normal bee could survive what I just subjected you to," Smith said in a low voice.

He lifted the blue contact receiver and decided that this was a crisis that required the intervention of his enforcement arm....

Tammy Terrill expected a big rambling Victorian out of *The Addams Family.* Or a long white lab building. Maybe even a rustic ranch or adobe fort.

She didn't expect a mud hut.

Actually, it wasn't a hut. It was too big. It was more like a wasp's nest, but it was made from dried mud. Not piled mud, but sculpted and smoothed mud. Its flowing skin was blistered with strangely shaped windows like bug eyes made of glass. If not for the fact that it was the same color and texture as a Mississippi riverbank, it might have been beautiful in a weirdly futuristic way.

"Can you believe this place?" she whispered to her new cameraman, whose name was Bill. Or maybe Phil. He had come down from the Baltimore affiliate.

"Takes all kinds," said the cameraman.

"Okay. Let's see what we can see."

They circled the hive. It was dotted with glass blisters. There was a front door and a back. In back, there was some kind of shed made of steel. From the shed was coming a strange humming.

"Sounds like bees," whispered Tammy.

"Sounds like sick bees."

"Or killer bees who haven't been able to kill as much as they like," suggested Tammy.

"Better leave it alone, then."

"I'm more interested in what's inside this big hive thing."

"I want no part of any break-in."

"No law against shoving a camera up against somebody's window and taping away," Tammy argued.

Bill—or Phil—shrugged. "I'll go along with that."

They picked a window at random. Creeping up to it, they pressed their faces against the chicken-wire-reinforced pane.

What they saw inside made their eyes grow round as saucers and their jaws fall open.

"Damn! Frankenstein's lab wasn't this weird," the Fox cameraman mumbled.

"If this isn't the story of the century, I'll eat shit and like it. Now, get to taping before Wurmlinger shows up...."

**28**

The bumblebee had moved to the main entrance of Folcroft Sanitarium by the time Remo drove the rental car through the stone gates with their foreboding lion heads on either side.

Folcroft was in a state of lock-down. No one could get in or out. And through the car telephone, Harold Smith was sounding nervous.

"Find that thing and crush it!" Smith was saying. "We cannot afford to call attention to the organization."

"Relax, Smitty. You run a sanitarium and you have an extermination problem. The exterminators are here. We'll take care of it."

"Hurry," said Smith.

Remo drove up to the main door, and the hovering bee seemed to take almost instant notice of Remo and Chiun.

It was completely white now, carrying a coat of drying insecticide as if it had just emerged from a happy bubble bath.

It flitted before their windshield, regarding them with what looked like cataract-gazed eyes.

"Okay," said Remo, "let's take this guy."

Chiun lifted a calming hand. "Wait. Let us observe it for a time."

"What's to observe? It's another of those super-bees. Our job is to kill it and turn the body over to Smith."

"No, our task is to survive our encounter with this devil in the form of a bee."

"That, too," Remo agreed. Turning off the engine, he settled back in his seat.

They watched as the bee grew increasingly curious, zipping to Remo's side window, around the back, then to Chiun. It butted its head against the glass at several points.

"It wants in," Remo muttered.

"No, it desires us to step out."

"Just say when."

Chiun was stroking his wispy beard. "We must foil its evil intentions, Remo."

"Hard to believe a bee has *any* intentions, evil or whatever."

The Master of Sinanju said nothing. His eyes were intent upon the hovering bee. They studied one another for several moments, then gradually, imperceptibly, Chiun slipped his fingers up to the small wing window on his side of the car.

"Remo," he undertoned, not moving his lips.

"Yeah?" said Remo, equally stiff lipped.

Chiun wrapped ivory fingers around the window latch. "When I say jump, you will jump from the vehicle as quickly as you can, taking care to slam the door behind you, also as quickly as you can."

"And what are you going to do?"

Instead of answering, Chiun flipped open the wing window and squeaked, "Jump!"

Three things happened in very quick succession. Remo jumped from the car. The bee slipped through the open window, and the Master of Sinanju simultaneously shut the window behind it and exited the vehicle.

So perfect was their timing that both doors clunked shut with one dull sound, and the bumblebee found itself trapped in the vehicle with no escape. It went into a frenzy of aerial acrobatics and glass-butting.

Harold Smith came down to see it for himself.

"Behold the fruits of your power, O Emperor," proclaimed the Master of Sinanju in a lofty voice. "The assassin that sought your life awaits your tender mercies."

Smith frowned with all his lemony intensity. "It should be dead."

"This can be arranged," said Chiun.

"Yeah," added Remo. "We'll just push the car into the water and drown it."

Smith shook his head. "No. I need to examine it."

"That's going to be a trick," said Remo. "It was a trick getting it in there. Getting it out safely, I don't know about."

"There must be a way."

"There is," said Chiun.

Remo and Smith looked at the Master of Sinanju with studied interest.

"But I do not know what that way is—as yet," Chiun admitted thinly.

All three men gave it considerable thought.

Smith said, "Insects breathe by diffusion, which means air comes in through their bodies. It is not possible to suffocate it in the normal sense."

"Insecticide is out," added Remo. "You tried that."

"Ah," said Chiun.

"Ah?"

The old Korean flitted into the building and returned moments later carrying the separate parts of a Pyrex cake holder in his long-nailed hands, undoubtedly scavenged from the Folcroft cafeteria.

"I don't think that's going to work, Little Father," Remo cautioned.

"Ordinarily, what I have in mind would never work," Chiun allowed. "But you are not undertaking the task at hand, but me. I will make it work."

Addressing Smith, he said, "Emperor, seek a place of shelter from which you may enjoy this display of the power you control so artfully."

Smith retreated to a position behind the glass door and watched intently.

"Remo, when I say open the door, you will open the door," Chiun said, eyeing the agitated bee.

"What about shutting it again?" Remo asked.

"It will not be necessary."

And the Master of Sinanju stationed himself at the side door where the bee was most active. Remo grabbed the door handle and set himself.

Chiun lifted the cake holder and its Pyrex bell in either hand like a musician about to clash together a pair of cymbals.

"Now!"

Remo yanked open the door.

The bee obligingly bumbled out. And was captured.

It was a near thing. The cake-holder sections came together with an unmusical crack. But when Chiun uprighted the cake holder, the bee was buzzing around the interior in angry, frustrated orbits.

Smith came running back down, and Chiun presented the cake holder to him. Smith took it gingerly in both hands.

"Thank you, Master Chiun. Now come inside."

They took the elevator to the administration floor, and Smith informed his secretary to inform the guard staff that all was well.

"The killer bee has been captured," he said, rather unnecessarily inasmuch as Mrs. Mikulka's wide eyes followed the Pyrex-protected bee until the point it disappeared into Smith's office.

Inside, behind closed doors, Smith set the cake holder on his desk.

The still-dripping bee orbited a few more moments, then settled down to stand tensely on its multiple legs.

"It looks like an ordinary bumblebee," Smith was saying as he took a red plastic object from his desk. He flipped it, and a red-ringed magnifying glass slipped out. Holding it by the combination lens protector and handle, Smith trained it on the quiescent bee.

As if equally curious, the bee obligingly stepped closer— giving Smith a better view. Its foamy feelers quivered and dripped.

"This is a bumblebee," Smith said.

"Wurmlinger said it was a drone," said Remo.

The bee turned around once and mooned Smith. The gesture of disrespect was entirely lost on Smith.

"I see a stinger," he breathed. "Drone bees do not possess stingers."

"That one does," Remo declared.

"Clearly," said Smith, returning the magnifying glass to his desk drawer and shutting it.

Dropping into his ancient, cracked leather executive's chair, Harold Smith addressed Remo and Chiun while not taking his eye off the bee, which had turned around to regard him with tiny blind-looking orbs.

"This is not an African killer bee or any genetic mutation of one. It is a common honey bee drone equipped with a stinger."

"And a brain," added Chiun.

"Not to mention a death's-head on its back," Remo said.

Smith frowned deeply. "Somehow, this bee was sent here to spy on me. The only way this could have happened is if it were able to communicate with the bee you killed in California."

"Get that body yet?"

"No. It has not been recovered from the crashed 727."

"I don't see how bees can talk across three thousand miles of country," Remo said.

"Somehow, there is a way they do."

"Don't bees talk to one another by touching antennae?"

"You are thinking of ants," said Smith.

"I thought bees operated the same way."

"No, they communicate by giving off chemical scents, as well as via aerial acrobatics such as the honey dance."

"Where did I get the idea they touched feelers?" Remo wondered aloud.

"I do not know. Nor can I imagine how we will discover the truth."

"Why not ask the bee?" suggested the Master of Sinanju.

They looked at him, their faces growing flat as plaster.

"You speak bee?" countered Remo.

"No, but if the bee was able to read the address of Fortress Folcroft in California and impart this intelligence to the bee we have captured, they must speak American."

"That's crazy!" exploded Remo.

"If you do not care to try, I will," sniffed Chiun.

Remo backed away with an inviting bow and flourish of one arm. "Be my guest."

The Master of Sinanju hiked up his golden kimono skirts and addressed the bee in the bell jar.

"Hearken, O foiled one. For I am Chiun, Master of Sinanju, royal assassin to the court of Harold the

First, current Emperor of America, in whose merciless toils you have found yourself. Before you are consigned to the cruel fate you so richly deserve, I demand you divulge all you know of the plot against Smith the Wise. Failure to do so will result in a beheading by a dull, rusty headsman's ax. Cooperation will grant you the boon of a sharp blade and a swift, painless death."

Remo snorted. "You can't behead a bee."

"Shush," said Chiun with a double upward flourish of his expansive kimono sleeves. "Speak now, doomed insect, and spare yourself an ugly ending."

The bee hadn't moved through all of this. Not even its feelers.

Then, after twitching its wings once, it emitted a high, tiny sound.

It wasn't a buzz or a drone. Nor was it the sharp *ziii* of a bee in flight.

Remo and Chiun leaned in. The sound was too small for Smith's normal aging ears, but there was something about it that touched their senses.

"Speak louder, O bee," Chiun instructed.

The bee seemed to make another sound.

"I feel like an idiot," said Remo, backing away.

Chiun eyed Smith and asked, "Have you a device for capturing sounds?"

"Yes." Smith dug out a pocket tape recorder with a suction mike attachment made for recording telephone calls.

Chiun nodded. "Affix this device."

Smith attached the cup to the glass and pressed the Record button.

"What the hell are you doing, Smitty?" Remo asked in exasperation.

"Perhaps its sound can be identified by an entomologist," Smith said defensively.

Remo rolled his eyes.

Lifting his arms like a conjurer invoking a genie, Chiun exhorted, "Speak again, O bee."

The tiny sound was repeated, and when it stopped, Smith hit the Stop switch, rewound and then pressed Playback.

He fingered the volume control to the highest setting and waited.

The tape hissed loudly. Then came a tiny, metallic voice. "Release me now, or my brethren will swarm down in deadly numbers."

"What!" Remo exploded.

Gray face slack with shock, Smith replayed that part again.

"That was you throwing your voice, wasn't it?" Remo accused Chiun.

"I deny this accusation," Chiun sniffed.

Smith hit the Record button and asked Chiun, "Inquire who it is."

"To whom do I have the privilege of speaking?"

"I am but a drone in the service of the King of Bees," replayed the tape recorder after Smith rewound it.

"Who is this ruler?" demanded Chiun. "Speak the fiend's name."

"I serve the Lord of All Bees."

"Is that anything like the Lord of the Flies?" grunted Remo, who couldn't quite believe what he was hearing but went along anyway.

Smith stared at the bee, open-mouthed and bug-eyed.

"I have a question for it," said Remo.

Chiun gestured him to go ahead.

"Who told you to come here?" asked Remo.

"My master." This time, Remo heard the voice clearly. The tape playback verified what he had heard.

"How'd you find this address?" asked Remo.

The tape recorder replayed the tiny reply. "One of my brethren read the address off the package you mailed from Los Angeles."

Harold Smith groaned in a mixture of horror and disbelief. "Our cover is blown."

"To the freaking bee kingdom, Smith," Remo said in exasperation. "It's not like it's going to be spread over tomorrow's *New York Times!*"

Smith eyed the bee. "Your terms are rejected."

"Then my vengeance will be awesome to behold. Tremble, mankind. Tremble before the awesome might of the Bee-Master."

"Did he say Bee-Master?" asked Remo.

"He has been saying that all along," said Harold Smith.

Remo snapped his fingers. "That's where I read about bees talking by antennae. In old comic books."

"It served you right for believing it," said Smith.

"Give me a break. I was only a kid. What did I know?"

"Chiun, we must drown this vermin," Smith said grimly.

"The interrogation is over, O merciless one?"

"Find a way to drown it. I must have the remains for analysis."

Bowing, the Master of Sinanju lifted up the cake holder and bore it into Smith's private washroom.

The bee was racing around the inside of the Pyrex dome, with all the agitated impotence of a condemned prisoner when they last saw it.

As the sound of running water came, Remo looked at Harold Smith and Smith looked back. Smith's face was gray and haggard; Remo's was flat with a kind of shocked bewilderment.

"Bees don't talk," Remo said.

"That one did," Smith said tonelessly. He fumbled with his hunter green Dartmouth tie.

"Bees don't talk," Remo repeated.

"That one did," Smith insisted, his voice rising in anger.

When Chiun returned, he was holding an aquarium in the form of a cake holder. The bee floated in it, upside down like a defunct goldfish.

"It is done. The fiend will trouble you no more."

"Thank you, Master Chiun."

A worried silence hung around the room.

Remo broke it. "That bee said he served the Bee-Master."

Smith had his head in his hands as if he were experiencing a severe migraine headache.

"I only know of one Bee-Master," Remo added.

Smith looked up. The expression on Remo's face was approximately that of a man who had tried to scratch his nose only to find he'd grown a tentacle where his hand should be.

"Bee-Master was a comic-book superhero when I was a kid. He was a scientist who invented a radio that could translate the language bees spoke."

"Bees do not speak," Smith snapped. Then he caught himself.

Remo kept talking in a distant voice. "Bee-Master became a friend to the bee kingdom. When spies tried to steal his insecto-radio to sell to Russian agents, his bee friends stung them into submission. From that point, they were a team. Bee-Master became a crime fighter. He wore a black-and-yellow costume with a helmet that looked like a high-tech bee's head. Everywhere he went, bees flew with him. They communicated through their antennae. Funny how I remember that story. I haven't laid eyes on an issue of *The Bizarre Bee-Master* in a zillion years."

"It is not possible to communicate with bees in the manner you describe. The person who created that story knows nothing about bees," Smith said firmly.

"Hey, I'm only telling you what this crazy stuff reminds me of."

"Nonsense."

"Sure. But you could check it out."

Smith did. Grimly, he input "Bee-Master" into his system and executed the search command.

Up popped a heroic figure dressed somewhat along the lines of a yellow jacket, with an aluminum helmet concealing his head. The helmet sported antennae and great crimson compound eyes in place of human ones.

The figure was labeled The Bizarre Bee-Master.

"That's him!" said Remo. "Where'd you find it?"

"This is the official Bee-Master web page, sponsored by Cosmic Comics," Smith said dryly.

Remo's face lit with surprise. "I didn't know they were still making Bee-Master comics. Check it out. It has Bee-Master's complete history."

Remo read over Smith's gray shoulder. Chiun, after looking briefly, made a face and went back to examining the dead bee corpse floating in water.

"According to this," Remo said, "Bee-Master is really Peter Pym, biochemist. He controls his bee friends through electronic impulses from his cybernetic helmet." Remo grunted. "I always wondered what *cybernetic* meant. None of the nuns at the orphanage knew."

Smith tapped a key. The word *cybernetic* was highlighted. Another tap brought up a dictionary definition.

"*Cybernetic,*" Smith explained, "means the science of control. And the concept described here is ridiculous. Insects do not communicate through electrical impulses, but via chemical scents only other insects comprehend."

Remo grinned. "Maybe you should run a search on the name Peter Pym."

"Why? It is a fictitious name."

"Just a thought. It's the only lead we have."

"It is no lead at all," said Harold Smith, escaping from the official Bee-Master web page. His eyes went to the floating bumblebee under Chiun's silent scrutiny. The expression on his lemony face suggested he had already begun to doubt his memory of the bee communicating in tinny English sentences.

Briefly, he replayed the tape, and the bee's nervous little voice was so disturbing, he clicked it off again.

"Find that info I wanted, Smitty?" Remo asked after a moment.

Smith snapped out of his daze. Attacking his keyboard once more, he brought up a phrase in Hangul, the modern Korean alphabet.

Remo read it.

"*Dwe juhla,*" he said. Turning to Chiun, he asked, "Did I get the pronunciation right?"

Turning dull crimson, the Master of Sinanju lifted his kimono sleeve before his face out of shame over his pupil's severely coarse language.

Remo grinned. "I guess that's my answer."

**29**

Helwig X. Wurmlinger drove his grasshopper green Volkswagen Beetle from the airport to his private residence outside Baltimore, Maryland.

When the mud dome appeared, his twitchy face began to relax. He was home. It was good to be home. It was often useful and necessary to travel, but Helwig X. Wurmlinger wasn't a social insect, but a solitary one. His preference for solitude enabled him to toil long hours and perform experiments that would frighten those who didn't share his appreciation of the insect world in its multitudinous harmony with nature.

Friendless, wifeless, Wurmlinger saw nothing wrong with living in what was for all intents and purposes a mud nest. There were no dissenting opinions in Helwig X. Wurmlinger's life. No one to gently inform him that he had crossed the line from the merely eccentric into the truly weird.

When, turning up the path to his home, he saw the white satellite truck marked Fox News Network, Wurmlinger became agitated. His mouth twitched, and his face joined in.

He was shaking when he unfolded himself from the cramped confines of his Beetle. And when he saw the cameraman with his minicam jammed up against a side window, he ran so fast his arms flapped loose as sticks at his sides.

"What is the meaning of this!" he demanded. "What are you doing on my property?"

The cameraman flung himself around, and Wurmlinger found himself looking into the glassy eye of the camera.

A frosty female voice intruded. "Maybe you're the one who has some explaining to do...."

It was that Fox woman. Wurmlinger had already forgotten her name, but he recognized her voice and facial contortions.

"You are trespassing!" Wurmlinger told her with studied indignity.

Instead of answering the undeniable charge, the blond woman said into a microphone she lifted to her mouth, "I am here with insect geneticist and etymologist—"

"Entomologist," Wurmlinger corrected tersely.

"—Helwig X. Wurmlinger of the USDA Bee Research Lab. Is that correct, Dr. Wurmlinger?"

"Yes, yes."

"If you work for the federal government, why do you have your own private laboratory here in the outback?"

"This is the backwoods. The outback is in Australia!"

"Answer the question, Doctor."

"This, my private laboratory, is where I do my work for the USDA. Here, I also conduct other experiments. None of them the business of the general public or yourself.''

''I draw your attention to the strange buzzing coming from the boxes in back of your property, Dr. Wurmlinger.''

''That is my apiary. It is where I keep my bees.''

''Is that so? If ordinary bees are your business, why are they making such a strange sound?''

''What strange sound?''

''Are you denying your bees are abnormal?''

''These are perfectly normal Buckeye Superbees. I employ their products to sweeten my tea and maintain my health.''

''Step this way.''

Walking backward, Tammy and her cameraman worked their way to the rear of Wurmlinger's odd home. He walked after them, his thoughts confused. Why were these people here? What did they want? And why were they filming him walking around his hive?

When they reached the back, the cameraman swung around to capture the apiary on film.

From the bee boxes came a weird, doleful humming.

''My bees!'' Wurmlinger bleated. He rushed toward them.

The sound was sinister and eerie. It wasn't a drone, nor was it a buzz. It was something unhappy and anguished.

Dropping to one knee, Wurmlinger unlatched one of the steel frames that contained honeycombs. He lifted it up and scrutinized the bees crawling along it with naked concern on his long face.

"Mites!" he groaned. "Mites have gotten to my poor bees."

Dropping the comb frame back, Wurmlinger went to another bee box. Another batch of bees was brought to light. They moved sluggishly among their waxy honeycomb cells.

"More mites!" he groaned.

A third box came up with honey and a gooey mass but no bees.

"Foulbrood! These bees are dead."

"What happened to them?" Tammy demanded, sticking her microphone into his bitter face.

Woodenly, Helwig X. Wurmlinger came to his feet. He steadied himself. "My bees are ruined," he said helplessly.

"Are these killer bees?"

"No, I breed only European honeybees and a few exotics."

"Are you aware, Dr. Wurmlinger, of the rash of killer-bee-related deaths in New York and Los Angeles, information that the U.S. government is withholding from the public?"

"I know nothing of New York—and you know as much as I do about the inexplicable events in Los Angeles!" Wurmlinger said in exasperation. "You were there."

"Answer the question," Tammy undertoned.

"Yes, yes, a new species of venomous feral bee

has been introduced into the ecosystem of North America.''

"Do you deny knowing the true origin of these killer bees?''

"Please do not use that unscientific term. The correct term is 'Bravo bee.'''

"You sound like a man sympathetic to bees?'' Tammy prompted, all but scaling Wurmlinger's greenish teeth with her mike.

"Bees are the most beneficial insects known to man. They pollinate eighty percent of crops in the country. Without them, mankind would not eat.''

"I'm not talking about friendly bees, but the death's-head bee that the United States government has unleashed upon the world.''

"What are you talking about?''

"New, vicious kinds of bees created by the USDA for reasons still unknown. Bees that sting over and over again. Bees that inject a fatal poison to which modern medicine has no antidote. Bees that have so far inflicted horrible deaths on eight persons with no end in sight. Do you deny, Dr. Wurmlinger, that in Los Angeles three people alone have succumbed to the bite of the death's-head superbee?''

"Sting,'' Wurmlinger said testily. "Bees do not bite except for a few harmless species.''

The insistent reporter stepped in and demanded in a stern voice, "Only a trained insect geneticist could create a race of superbees. Only someone with the scientific knowledge, the funding and a secluded laboratory away from curious eyes.''

Tammy ducked behind the cameraman and pointed an accusing finger so that the camera captured it from its own point of view.

"Only you, Dr. Helwig X. Wurmlinger!"

"Nonsense."

"Nonsense? Do you deny conducting secret genetic experiments in this lab of yours? Do you deny unleashing unknown horrors on an unsuspecting world?"

"I do deny these insane allegations," Wurmlinger sputtered.

"Then how do you explain this!" Tammy crowed.

And turning to her cameraman, Tammy said, "Show America what Dr. Wurmlinger has been doing with their tax dollars."

The cameraman pivoted and trained his minicam at a handy window. He zoomed in.

And in the Baltimore Fox affiliate, a news director watched tensely as the feed came in. Clearly visible through the chicken-wire-reinforced window was a dragonfly whose body and legs were studded with dozens of unwinking compound ruby eyes.

It looked for a reassuring moment like a weird model of a dragonfly from another dimension.

That illusion was broken with startling suddenness when the dragonfly's wings came to life and it floated away, leaving the unnerving impression that it had been staring at them with its narrow rear end.

**30**

Mearl Streep watched the Fox broadcast from the comfort of his RV barreling along Interstate 80 to Washington, D.C.

He had purchased the RV with the monthly dues from his loyal Iowa Disorganized Subterranean Militia, christening it the IDSM Mobile Guerrilla Command HQ and Recreational Center, and installed a close aide to drive it.

He was leading a convoy of pickup trucks, sport utilities and off-road vehicles—all made in the USA—to Washington. They were taking the long way around, because Mearl understood that taking the capital of the greatest nation in the world required more manpower than his thirty or so militia members, none of whom had actually served in a peacetime army or national guard, much less fought in an actual war.

After all, they were corn farmers mostly.

Their war fever was pretty high by the time they rolled out of the Corn State with its mysteriously precise checkerboard of desolation.

"When we get back, we're taking over the surviving farms," Mearl boasted. "Taking 'em back from the collaborators."

"We'll run 'em off," his aide-de-camp, Gordon Garret, called from behind the wheel.

"Naw. You can't merely run collaborators off. That's why I'm calling it Rope Day."

"You're going to hang farmers, Mearl?" Gordon asked in horror.

"No. But I am bound and determined to hang any collaborators and traitors to the Constitution of the United States that I find, agricultural affiliations notwithstanding."

"Oh, that's different."

Along the way, they kept watch out for the much-dreaded black rotary-winged aircraft of the New World Order, but no mysterious helicopters came into view.

They checked for bar codes on the back of highway signs, and when found, spray-painted them black because these were the guide posts by which the combined forces of the Trilateral Commission, the UN peacekeepers and ethnic irregulars pulled from the nation's worst ghettos, would use to find their targets on zero hour of H Day. They also defaced various billboards advertising the latest Meryl Streep film.

Along the way, they took in some mighty fine countryside, and Mearl got to swig a refreshing assortment of locally brewed beers. It was the good life in its way, and sure beat shucking corn.

When the Fox special entitled "The Death's-Head Superbee Report" came on, he immediately took notice.

A blond reporter with the suspiciously foreign

name of Tamara Terrill started off the broadcast by asking some fascinating questions.

"Has a new species of killer bee been unleashed upon the United States of America? How many have died, and how has the United States Department of Agriculture covered up the growing threat?"

At the mention of the USDA, Mearl sat up straight. He never trusted the Agriculture Department, or any branch of the federal government except where it came to farm subsidies that he figured were his due. And the word *cover-up* was one of the most active in his vocabulary.

"More importantly," Tamara Terrill was saying, "has the federal government itself created this death bee in hidden USDA laboratories? And for what sinister purpose? Are these merely superbees or the vanguard of a new kind of bee destined to ravage the globe?

"For the answer to these questions, we begin with the strangely underreported death of insect geneticist Doyal T. Rand in Times Square several days ago."

At that, Mearl Streep hollered for his driver to pull over. Behind him, the Convoy to Freedom likewise pulled over.

"Hey, you men gather around. You gotta see this."

They clambered into the RV, hunkering down on the floor and open seats. Those who didn't fit, crowded around the outside, listening from the open windows.

There by the dusty dirt of the road in Pennsylvania, they watched in growing fascination as an unassailable chain of logic was woven from rumor, facts, innuendo and sloppy reportage. But to Mearl Streep and his Iowa Disorganized Subterranean Militia, it not only rang with truth, but it fit perfectly with everything they believed.

The clincher came when footage from Iowa was shown—footage of the bizarre hours-old ravaging of previously sacrosanct corn country.

"Is this, too, the work of the superbee of doom?" Tamara was asking.

Mearl brought a fist down on his padded armrest, crushing an empty can of Sam Adams. "As sure as the CIA has a surveillance microchip in my left butt cheek," he said, "it's gotta be. I can feel it in my bones."

The program grasshoppered from Iowa to Los Angeles and the successive deaths of two county coroners and "a brave but nameless Fox cameraman who dared to investigate the truth," according to Tamara Terrill.

Then came the portion of the program that made their blood run cold. The program had been hinting at USDA involvement and denials and was leading up to some incredible revelation. When it hit, it left Mearl Streep and his men sitting slack jawed in their seats.

The program cut to a weird mud hive of a building in God alone knew where. And it showed a long drink of weird with the alien name of Helwig X. Wurmlinger denying all manner of schemes and horrors.

The capper came when the TV screen filled with

the image of a big dragonfly with red eyes everywhere except on his head. When it took off, showing it was alive, the assembled militiamen jumped in place and began scratching themselves as if feeling vermin on their patriotic hides.

There were other things glimpsed through the window of the "laboratory from Hell," as Fox was calling it.

Roaches with prosthetic limbs. Two-headed spiders. And other things God never meant to be.

And over these accusations came the disembodied voice of Helwig X. Wurmlinger protesting his innocence over and over again, as the evidence of his ungodly tampering with nature filled TV screens all over America.

After the program ended with the promise of further reports from Fox, Mearl Streep sat in his cammies, oblivious to the spilled can of Sam Adams in his lap, and said, "You freedom fighters listen up now."

They perked up.

"Washington can wait. That tall glass of bug juice is responsible for the plague that descended upon God-fearing Iowa. And we as the lawful Iowa Disorganized Subterranean Militia are duty bound to find, interrogate and squash him and his traitorous works flat."

They locked and loaded, piled into their respective vehicles and right-turned toward Maryland and righteous revenge.

## 31

An Iowa National Guard helicopter ferried Remo and
Chiun from the Des Moines airport to the affected
area. They were not the only helicopter in the sky.
News choppers were everywhere, like noisy crows.

The Guard pilot was ordering them to keep the air-
space clear. He wasn't being ignored. Not at all. In
fact, a lot of the news teams flew in tandem pointing
their glassy-eyed cameras his way and tried to interview him by radio.

The pilot ignored all entreaties to offer a semiof-
ficial opinion of the blight that had descended upon
central Iowa.

In back, the Master of Sinanju looked down at the
wavy rows of growing corn and made a disgusted
face. "Corn. It is a pestilence."

"Get off it, Chiun," Remo said.

"You have tasted its forbidden grains. You are
prejudiced."

Remo tried changing the subject. "What do you
think caused this, Little Father?"

"A plague. Of course."

Remo looked interested. "Locusts?"

"A plague. More I cannot say until I have stood

amid the terrible yellow stalks that have conquered the white world.''

''Are we talking about corn?''

''*I* am talking about corn. You are only listening.''

The helicopter descended upon a ruined cornfield, and Chiun stepped out. Standing with legs apart, he girded his kimono skirts and surveyed the damage.

Remo got out on the other side, ducking under the still-turning main rotor. It made his short dark hair ripple anxiously.

Not a cornstalk was standing. The ground was littered with immature yellow kernels and shredded golden cornsilk. The air smelled of fresh-picked corn.

Remo inhaled it with pleasure. Chiun cast a disapproving eye in his direction. Remo had developed a taste for corn a year or so back, something Chiun violently disapproved of. No grain but pure white rice was permitted in the Sinanju diet. Remo had protested that there was nothing wrong with corn.

''I ate some and didn't get sick,'' he had said. ''American Indians eat it all the time.''

''I care not with what the red man filled his lazy belly,'' Chiun had replied. ''You are Sinanju. You are of the East now. Not of the West. You are forbidden corn.''

''According to the best experts, American Indians came from Asia. They're a mix of Mongols, Chinese and Koreans.''

''South Koreans, perhaps,'' sniffed Chiun, whose ancestors came from the cold, forbidding north. ''Our blood is northern. We do not pollute it with yellow grains.''

And that had been the end of the discussion.

As they stood on the black Iowa loam, Remo decided to pick up the argument. ''I don't see what's so terrible about corn,'' he muttered.

Chiun considered for a time. Whether he was considering Remo's question or the fragrant desolation about him wasn't clear at first. Finally, he spoke. ''It is too sweet.''

''It's a nice change of pace from rice,'' Remo said.

''Rice is sweeter than corn. Rice is sweet in a clean way. Corn is heavy and starchy and honey sweet.''

''Nothing wrong with honey,'' remarked Remo, kicking at a well-chewed ear of corn.

''Honey is permissible in tea. You would not honey your rice.''

''No,'' Remo admitted.

They walked. Remo picked up pieces of fallen cornstalks and examined them. Chiun's hazel eyes raked the surroundings, taking everything in. He seemed uninterested in the details.

''No twister did this,'' Remo remarked.

Chiun nodded sagely. ''A plague. It has all the earmarks of a plague.''

''Speaking of ears,'' said Remo, ''I still don't see what's so terrible about corn.''

''Your foolish question reminds me of Master Kokmul.''

Remo made a thinking face. ''Kokmul. I don't know him.''

"He lived long ago. But you and he would have enjoyed one another's company," said Chiun.

Remo brightened. "How's that?"

"He was very much like you—foolish."

Remo's shoulders fell.

They continued walking.

"Kokmul lived after the unthinking Columbus came to the so-called New World and brought back to Europe the pestilence called corn," Chiun said slowly, his eyes roving over the fields as if expecting the dead corn to rear up and jump them.

"Pestilence?"

"Corn grew in the Spain of the spendthrift Isabella, from there spreading east and west until it reached Cathay," said Chiun in a doleful tone.

"China, huh? Funny, I never saw corn in Korea."

"Corn *did* come to Korea, thanks to Kokmul the Foolish. But it was cast out by his successor."

"I guess I'm about to hear another legend of Sinanju," said Remo, his feet tramping corn leaves without making them rustle.

"Then listen well, for this is a lesson the House cannot afford to learn twice."

Chiun's voice became low and grim. "In the days of Kokmul, there was work in Cathay. The nature of this work was unimportant. It is only important to know that from time to time, Kokmul ventured north of Sinanju on foot to ford the river known today as the Yalu and performed certain services for a certain prince of Cathay.

"On one occasion, Kokmul came to a grove that

he first took for young sorghum. Except it was not the season for young sorghum, but tall sorghum. But these green plants, which grew in orderly rows, were neither.''

Remo looked around. The corn had been planted in orderly rows with the stalks well-spaced before they were cut down.

''Now, farmers tended these plants that were sown in rows, and it was harvest time,'' said Chiun. ''Weary from his journey, Kokmul stopped and asked a farmer about his unfamiliar crop.

''The farmer, honoring the Master of Sinanju, snapped off the top of one plant and stripped it of its green leaves, exposing a vile yellow thing like a demon's smile with numerous blunt teeth protecting it.''

''An ear of corn,'' said Remo.

''Yes.''

''Never heard it described in such appetizing terms,'' Remo grunted.

Chiun waved the remark away into the corn.

''The farmer showed Kokmul how to boil the yellow thing in water so that its hard teeth did not break human teeth when bitten, and how to eat it safely, as well as how to prepare it as bread or meal. And Kokmul, being an innocent in the ways of corn, became hooked by the wondrous ways in which corn could be eaten.''

Remo cocked a skeptical eyebrow. ''Hooked?''

''You would call it hooked. Kokmul became a slave to corn, is the way it is inscribed in the Book of Sinanju.''

"Okay…"

"So taken with his new addiction was Kokmul that instead of venturing on to the princely court that had summoned him, Kokmul gathered up ears of hard corn and bore them back to the unsuspecting village of Sinanju, then a paradise of rice and fish."

"And laziness," added Remo.

Chiun said nothing to that. He went on. "As you know, Remo, the ground around our ancestral village is not the best. Little grows, except rice in paddies, and often not even that. It was thought by Kokmul that this new thing called corn would grow where other plants did not. So, planting the corn as the Chinese farmer had instructed, Kokmul brought the demon corn to Korea."

They walked along, their feet seeming to float over the loose black loam. At least they left no footprints, though they walked with a firm tread.

"In time," Chiun resumed, "the green stalks rose up. Thick they became. Heavy they grew. The sinister gold threads that made more corn grow showed themselves like painted harlots peeping out from their hanging tresses. It was much work to raise corn. Not so much as to harvest rice, which is backbreaking work. But it was difficult nonetheless.

"And when the corn was sufficiently tall and ripe, Master Kokmul summoned the villagers and showed them how to strip and shuck the ears and how to store them for the long winter with the winter cabbage. That autumn and winter, the bellies of the villagers were heavy with corn, Remo. And they grew fat."

"Not to mention dumb and happy," said Remo.

A withering glance from Chiun's closest eye stilled Remo's grin. This was serious business to Chiun.

"The First Corn Year passed peacefully. There was no trouble. The second was not so bad, for the corn grew steadily, but not consumingly. Then came the Third Corn Year."

"Uh-oh. What happened? The crops failed?"

Chiun shook his aged head. "No, the pestilence began."

Chiun walked along, narrowed eyes taking in minute details of the ruined corn in his path. Where he could step on a loose kernel, he did. The old Korean seemed to take special delight in extinguishing the half-ripe grains.

"I have warned you, Remo, that corn is not as good or as pure as rice. I have told you it is to be avoided. I have never told you why it is a plague and a pestilence to be crushed wherever it rears its lurid, toothsome head."

Remo grinned. "As they say, I'm all ears."

"You will not laugh when my story is over." Chiun kicked a corncob out of his path. "Rice, when it is digested, nourishes. No grain of rice enters a man's stomach that is not consumed. Not so the sneaky and insidious corn grain."

They came upon a herd of spotted cows busily munching the fallen cobs. The cows hardly took notice of them.

"The corn kernel is hardy and stubborn," Chiun continued. "It cries out to be eaten, but once digested, it does not always surrender its nourishment to the consumer. Some kernels survive, to pass undigested from the body of man and beast alike.''

Chiun stopped and gazed down at his feet.

Remo looked down, too.

"What do you see, my son?" asked Chiun.

"Looks like a meadow muffin to me," Remo said.

"Look closer."

Remo knelt. It was cow dung, all right, already dried by the sun. Peeping from the dark mass were glints of smooth golden yellow.

"What do you find so interesting, Remo?" Chiun asked in a thin voice.

"I see the cows have been at the corn."

"Yet the wily corn has escaped the cow's diligence."

"Cows don't chew their food as thoroughly as they could, I guess," said Remo.

"Nor do people. Not even the villagers of Sinanju."

Remo got up. Chiun met his gaze with his thin hazel eyes.

"In the Third Corn Year, Remo, the yellow heads reared everywhere. Where it was planted. Where it was not planted. The villagers ate it in great abundance, with shameless relish, and whenever they squatted in their laxness, they released undigested corn kernels, which took root and grew.

Chiun closed his almond eyes and all but shuddered.

"Before long, the horrid eyesores were everywhere. Even in the rice paddies," he said.

Remo made a mock face of horror. "Not the rice paddies. No."

Chiun nodded grimly. "Yes. By the Third Corn Year, there was no rice. Only corn. This was all right for the villagers, but the Master of Sinanju, on whom the village feeds, required rice to sustain his skills. But there was no rice. Only corn. Kokmul began losing his skills and grew fat and sated on corn."

"What brought him out of it?"

"A simple thing. Death. He died, and his successor took his place. That was Pyo, who went out into the cornfields and with his flashing noble hands decapitated the archdemon's offspring, restoring the bounty of rice to the village of Sinanju and exiling the demon corn from Korea forever. To this day, in the north, it is a crime punishable by death to willfully and knowingly plant corn."

Remo grunted. Looking around, he said, "Well, it's a safe bet Pyo didn't come back from the Void to lay waste to Iowa."

"No, it was not Pyo. It was a plague of another kind."

"What kind?"

"That, we must determine," said Chiun, starting off to a farmhouse beyond the cows.

Shrugging, Remo followed. If Chiun could figure out what happened here, it would have been worth listening to that cockamamy story.

Remo still didn't see what was wrong with a Master of Sinanju eating corn. As long as he chewed his food thoroughly.

**32**

There were no satellite trucks or reporters, no sign of life surrounding the mud-dome laboratory of Helwig X. Wurmlinger as the Freedom Convoy wound its dusty way to the place Commander Mearl Streep of the Iowa Disorganized Subterranean Militia called "the center of the USDA plot against the heartland."

It didn't look like much when it came into view. A high dome of mud maybe two stories tall. The windows were cut in strange, flowing shapes like bulging insectoid eyes. The only sound that could be heard was the weird, doleful drone of afflicted bees.

"I don't like how that sounds," Gordon Garret said from behind the wheel of the lead RV, which for purely tactical purposes was now bringing up the rear.

"We can't afford to lose our communications nerve center in case point takes a direct hit" was the way Commander Streep put it when they made the switch.

"That sound," said Commander Streep, fingering his lawful AR-15 sport rifle with its sniper scope and full clip of Black Talon bullets, "is the feared anti-American and anti-Christian devil bee. Our sworn enemy."

Garret shivered, his nervous foot hovering over the brake.

"Column, halt!" Streep called over his PA system hookup. The Freedom Convoy came to a jouncing and dusty stop.

"Dismount!"

From the pickups and sport-utility vehicles, the shock troops of the Iowa Disorganized Subterranean Militia poured out, locking and loading and racking their Remington shotguns, those that had them.

In the relative security of his command RV, their leader dialed the PA system to its highest setting and lifted his mike to his lips.

"Attention! This is Commander Mearl Streep! I call upon Dr. Helwig Wurmlinger to exit his awful abode to answer for his crimes against American agriculture."

The bee buzzing abruptly dropped. Silence fell.

Then an oval door opened, and out into the moonlight stepped a tall, gangling figure whose eyes were wobbly discs of moonlight.

"Are you Wurmlinger?"

"I am. Did you say you were Meryl Streep?"

"Mearl, dammit! Mearl Streep of the Iowa Disorganized Subterranean Militia."

"Then I have never heard of you, and you are on my property."

"We have come to make you answer for crimes against America and Iowa."

"What rubbish are you speaking? Step into the light where I can see you."

"So you can assassinate me with your devil bee? No. We are not such fools, Wurmlinger." A pause, then he went on. "Boys, get ready to torch that Frankenstein mud-hut!"

The Iowa Disorganized Subterranean Militia looked around helplessly.

"With what?" one asked. "We ain't brought any torches."

"Well, go into that devil hut and find some flammables."

No one moved. They were too afraid, and the humming started anew. It was unhappy, like the drone of dying honeybees.

Then a bee did appear. It was big and fat and bobbed up and down in the moonlight, finally coming to a point at the window glass of the RV where Commander Streep was issuing his demands.

It went tick against the glass. This caught Streep's attention, and he turned around.

In the moonlight, the compound eyes regarded him with an alien malevolence. But that wasn't what made the hairs rise on the back of Streep's thick red neck.

It was the unmistakable death's-head on its fuzzy golden black back.

"Assassin bee! It's an assassin bee!" Streep screeched. "Turn smartly, men, and chop it down if you value your lives!"

As one, the Iowa Disorganized Subterranean Militia wheeled, weapons snapping up and ready to fire.

If they could only find a target.

Questing muzzles remained cold. No gun flashes

painted the surrounding woods with their red, puri-
fying flame, Streep saw.

"What are you waiting on, you idiots?" he roared.

"Where is it? Where is it?" his men were saying.
Their weapons were tracking the trees, the moon, the
RV and the ground. Everywhere but where the soli-
tary devil bee hovered, patient and sinister.

That was when Streep fumbled a flashlight out of
a cargo pocket of his cammies. He clicked it on. A
light popped. He trained it on the bee and called out,
"There is your target! Shoot to kill!"

The Iowa Disorganized Subterranean Militia did.

The night air was lit by zipping yellow tracer
flashes. The percussive stutter of autofire and the ac-
companying din of the war cries of men more afraid
than angry shook the tense air.

When the guns stopped, there was no sign of the
bee or Dr. Helwig X. Wurmlinger.

"Did we get him? Did we get him?" a shaking
voice asked.

Coming up from under a pile of cushions on the
RV floor, Commander Mearl Streep wondered the
very same thing.

He was fumbling for his flash when a new sound
cut the disturbed evening.

It was a drone. High, metallic, it was nothing like
the sad drone of the hived bees that had greeted them.
It was angry, insistent and it filled the night like viciously sharp blades of sound.

The Iowa Disorganized Subterranean Militia
stretched and craned their necks all around them. Fear

warped their moonlit faces, their eyes bugged out and sweat oozed from exposed pores.

"Shoot at the sky! Shoot the sky!" Commander Streep called out. "It's a swarm of devil bees. They come for us!"

The Iowa Disorganized Subterranean Militia obeyed their commander with an alacrity that would have made a four-star general proud.

Except for one problem: they had neglected to reload their weapons.

Click-click-click went their weapons like so many cap guns firing. Or in this case, not firing.

Because, while their helplessness was dawning on them, the insistent buzz reached a crescendo and they began grabbing themselves at every exposed orifice. A few sneezed violently. But whatever had gotten up their noses wouldn't come back out. Some covered their ears with their palms, but just as quickly uncovered them when they realized the high buzzing was inside their ears already.

One militiaman stood with his head cocked to one side, slapping his right ear in hopes of dislodging whatever had gotten into his left auditory canal. He cried out with each self-inflicted jar of his skull.

From the relative safety of his command RV, Commander Mearl Streep watched in mounting horror. The cream of his militia was falling all around him, conquered by something they could neither see nor shoot at. All it was was a high noise that might have been the sound of the glassy falling moonlight under severe stress, if light could emit sounds.

One by one, the Iowa Disorganized Subterranean Militia began dropping.

At his post at the RV's wheel, Gordon Garret enjoyed a commanding view of the slaughter. "What's killing them? I can't see anything!"

By way of answer, Commander Mearl Streep retched uncontrollably.

When a man rolling on the ground in his death throes happened to turn his way, Commander Streep saw the thing that made him sorry he had ever elected to take on the dark forces of the federal government.

As he watched, the man's open, terrified eyes were disintegrating. Actually melting from sight like so much candle wax consumed by fire.

But there was no fire. And no sign of bees.

Mearl Streep was no fool. He knew a losing battle when he witnessed one.

"Retreat! Retreat! We're pulling back!" Streep said. "Get us the holy heck out of here!"

Hands shaking, Gordon Garret keyed the engine to life.

It was too late. Though every window was sealed, the vengeful buzz got him, too. Taking hold of his skull, he jerked out of his seat and began throwing himself around the RV's plush jungle-camouflage-motif interior.

The most awful thing about it was that something seemed to have gotten into his skull. Streep figured that from the way he deliberately banged his head into bulkheads and windows—even the microwave, which popped open.

Fumbling with the door, Garret stuck his head into the microwave oven and stabbed every button he could.

Nothing happened. The safety mechanism defeated his desperate attempt to microwave himself to death.

By the time Garret slid out, loose as a sack of cold manure, Commander Mearl Streep was cowering in back at the rear-exit door latch.

The drone was still in the air. The howling and threshing had all stopped.

Carefully, Streep turned on his haunches and reached for the exit latch. He took hold of it. Only then did he face away from the RV's green, brown and black interior.

When he turned, his blood ran cold.

For on the other side of the glass, hovering on moon-blurred wings, was a death's-head bumblebee. Its compound eyes regarded him without understanding or mercy.

"Oh, God." Streep gulped, releasing the latch.

That's when the buzzing seemed to lift from Gordon Garret's dead body and work its way toward him.

Streep's widening eyes saw nothing. But he knew with a nerve-numbing certainty that something he couldn't see—only hear—was moving toward him, seeking his life.

In desperation, he yanked on the latch and tumbled out.

That was when the killer bumblebee jumped him. Something else attacked, too. Streep could feel things in his ears and his nose. They felt like living sounds crawling into his skull, seeking his brain to quench its dark, un-American appetites.

Commander Mearl Streep died screaming as his tongue and eyeballs melted in his very head with the speed of candle wax vaporizing. The sound of his screaming grew so loud it almost rivaled that of the thing hungrily devouring the contents of his head. But not quite.

When he collapsed into a sunken heap of camouflage green, the sound ascended to the cold moon and faded in the night.

After a while, the death's-head bumblebee sought the hollow of a nearby elm tree to pass the night.

It was dawn before Dr. Helwig X. Wurmlinger dared to step out of his eccentric home. He took one look at all the eyeless, immobile corpses and said, "Goodness gracious me."

Then he went out back to check on his sick bees.

**33**

Remo and Chiun found the owner of the farm in his farmhouse.

It was a pretty good-size farmhouse. At least twelve rooms. The house was rambling, its clapboard skin painted white. The barn and grain silo behind it were as red as a hot brick, however.

Remo knocked on the door and received no reply. So he knocked again.

"I hear someone inside," he told Chiun.

"Do as you will. I will not cross the threshold of the house of corn." And Chiun walked off to survey the desolation that lay seemingly in all directions.

Remo tried the door. It wasn't locked and he stepped in.

Beyond the foyer, with its lace curtains and polished staircase leading upstairs, was a spacious living-room area.

The owner of the house was seated in a big recliner with his eyes fixed on a working television. It was a big-screen TV, tuned to the Fox twenty-four-hour news channel.

The man had the weathered look of someone who toiled in the sun. His eyes were squinted up, and the backs of his hands were red and raw as a blister. He wore bib-style coveralls over a red plaid flannel shirt, and on an end table sat a baseball cap that said Seedtec.

Remo said, "Howdy," figuring that was probably how farmers talked.

The man continued to stare.

"I'm from the USDA," he said. "The name is Remo Croy."

The man in the chair hadn't blinked from the time Remo had entered. He was going on sixty seconds of staring at the TV screen without blinking. His face had a loose, slack quality.

"Hey, did you hear me? I said I'm from the USDA. We're looking into the situation here."

The man blinked once, slowly. His mouth barely moved, but a low, toneless question issued from him.

"What's that you say?"

"I'm from the USDA. I need to ask you some questions about what happened here."

The man had his arms flopped over the sides of his recliner. The arm opposite Remo's position came up casually with a repeating shotgun. It smacked solidly into his free hand, and the farmer began twisting out of his seat in a preattack posture.

"USDA bastards! You broke my back!"

Remo moved in. It was no contest. While the farmer was still twisting around to draw a bead, Remo yanked the double-barreled shotgun out of his grasp. It came easily.

Stepping back, Remo broke the action, ejected the

fat red shells and, as the farmer came out of his seat bellowing, Remo casually made the twin barrels bend in opposite directions like a candelabra.

The farmer took in this example of raw power, blinked again and sat back in mute, sagging defeat.

"Do with me what you will," he said woodenly. "You already broke my heart."

"Hey, fella," Remo said gently, "I'm not here to hurt you. We're just looking into what happened out here."

"Don't fool with me. I know you Agriculture Department people are behind it. You and your genetic experiments, tampering with Mother Nature. Don't think because we're simple people out here wc can be fooled. Not for a minutc. We know it was your infernal bees that ran the corn down."

"Bees?"

"United States Department of Agriculture bees," the farmer snapped. "Bred to wreak havoc and make foul mischief. Which is what they done here."

"That's crazy! Who in their right mind would breed bees to ruin a corn crop?"

"The same ones who spent billions of dollars flying a man to the moon, where the soil won't yield and there's no air to breathe."

"That's a big leap in logic," Remo argued.

"I seen it all on the TV."

Remo looked at the screen. The station was coming up to its top-of-the-hour news segment. A purple-haired girl of about seventeen with jet black lipstick began reciting the headlines, pausing only to crack lime green bubblegum between items.

"New strain of voracious insects strikes at the heartland. Entire farms in Iowa have been leveled. Is there a connection to the mysterious assassin-bee deaths on both coasts that have authorities baffled? With us now is Fox star-reporter Tamara Terrill. Tammy, what's the latest?"

The familiar figure of Tammy Terrill appeared, clutching a microphone in her white-knuckled hands.

"Heather, official Washington is being stonily silent on this latest event in the looming insect crisis, but officials with the U.S. Department of Agriculture are issuing heated denials that they are behind the outbreak of vicious insects."

"How are these denials being met, Tammy?" the news reader asked.

"With skepticism. I myself have been investigating this threat for, oh, almost thirty-six hours now, and I don't believe a word of it. They're hiding something. Just like on 'X-Files.'"

The anchor nodded in agreement, adding, "'X-Files' rules. And it's on Saturdays now."

"Cool," chirped Tammy.

In his recliner, the farmer was also nodding. "See? Proof positive."

"That's no proof!" exploded Remo. "It's just two media dips throwing wild speculation into the air to see where it will land."

"It landed," the farmer said miserably, "in my corn."

"Look, I'm serious about looking into this. Can you tell me why some farms were stripped clean and others untouched?"

"Any fool can plainly see the why in that!" the farmer exploded.

"Well, I'm a fool from New Jersey. Humor me."

The farmer got up. He was taller than Remo expected. He walked with a stoop to his porch. There didn't seem much fight left in him, so Remo followed him out.

Standing out in the fading sunlight, he waved a plaid arm as if to encompass all of Iowa.

"What you're looking at is the first crop of the new Super Yellow Dent corn. Fool geneticists said it would resist corn borers, worms, cockleburs, you name it. Nothing could touch it. Nothing could lay it low. I paid a third more for that seed as any corn I ever bought. The slickers who sold it to me said the only thing that could kill it was drought. Now look at it. Bugs buzz sawed through it like no one's business."

The man whipped a red handkerchief out of the back pocket of his overalls and wiped his eyes on both sides. There was no moisture there. Remo figured the farmer had already cried himself out.

"I'm sorry this happened to you," Remo said simply.

"I got took. That's all there is to it. I got took for all I had. Super Yellow Dent is supposed to give off an odor that was poison to any pest known to prey on corn. Instead, it seemed to have drawn a worse pest than anyone ever heard of.''

''Maybe it wasn't the corn.''

The farmer expectorated noisily. ''Oh, it was the corn, all right. And I can prove it. You can, too.''

''How's that?''

''Take a survey of all the cornfields out this way. The ones that got hit grew Super Yellow. The ones that got off scot-free was ordinary corn. Golden Dent. Boone Country White. Champion White Pearl. Silver Mine. Early Huron. You name it. Everything except Super Yellow Dent, the savior of the corn farmer.'' The farmer spit a second time angrily.

The Master of Sinanju appeared at that point. He was carrying an ear of corn before him, carrying it by the corn silk, as if it were a distasteful yellow dropping.

The farmer straightened with a start of surprise. ''Who in hell is that?''

''My colleague,'' said Remo.

''Looks more like a refugee from Chautauqua Week, you ask me my opinion.''

''Behold, Remo,'' exclaimed Chiun, lifting his prize high.

''It's an ear of corn. So what?''

''See how it has been chewed on one side and not the other?''

Remo took the ear. It was chewed on one side. The other side showed rows of tiny kernels, each one indented as if nicked by a cold chisel.

"Looks like the stuff that survived had the moisture sucked out of it," Remo remarked.

"You idjit!" the farmer bellowed. "Don't you know corn? That's Dent corn. Them indentations are perfectly natural."

"I never saw corn like that," Remo said defensively.

"That's because Dent corn is purely cattle feed. You boil and bite that stuff, and it'll crack your teeth apart worse than Indian corn."

"Oh. What do you make of the fact the bugs ate only one side?"

"A freak of nature. That's what I make of it."

Chiun shook his head firmly. "Many ears show such signs."

The farmer took the ear from Remo, examined it with methodical interest, then stepped off his porch into the field.

He foraged about until he had picked up a double handful of corncobs. Every example had been stripped on one side and one alone.

"This is powerful fascinating," he muttered.

"Mean anything to you?" asked Remo.

"I could be wrong," he said, looking at the corn and not them, "but I would swear these ears were all chewed at from an easterly direction. The western sides are just fine."

"So what does that mean?" asked Remo.

"It means the pestiferous critters or whatever they were that ripped through my corn were headed away from the hellish place that spawned them, namely Washington."

"There is something else," said Chiun.

"What's that?" asked Remo.

"The corn has been chewed but not consumed."

"Can't be," the farmer snorted.

"Why not?"

"Insects don't chew through corn for purely mischief's sake. They need to eat. I don't know what new species of bug committed this travesty, but I do know it needs to eat. And if it ripped up my corn without eating any, that means but one thing I can think of...."

"What's that?" asked Remo.

"It ain't no insect made by God, but something else entirely."

Remo looked to the Master of Sinanju. Chiun beamed back at him. "Perhaps it was a not-pest," he said to the farmer but really for Remo's benefit.

Neither the farmer nor Remo knew what to make of the Master of Sinanju's comment, so they said nothing.

From the farmer's house, Remo called Harold Smith.

"Smitty, we don't have much, but here it is. Looks like every farmer that was hit grew a new kind of pest-proof corn, called Super Dent."

"Super Yellow Dent. Get it correct," the farmer's voice called from outside.

"Super Yellow Dent. According to a farmer who was hit—"

"And don't call us farmers. My pappy was a farmer. His pappy was a farmer. I'm an agribusinessman. I can not only say it, I can spell it, too."

"—this stuff was the only corn that got hit. Everything else survived. You should check it out," finished Remo.

"That is very odd, Remo."

"Also, I think we need to drop our USDA covers," Remo added in a lowered tone of voice.

"Why is that?"

"Tammy Terrill and Fox are painting the USDA as the fountain of all evil. I had to take a double-barreled scattergun away from the farmer I just questioned before he could perforate me with it."

"I will look into the supercorn theory, Remo."

"Add this to the mix," Remo said. "According to Chiun, the things that leveled the cornfields out here chewed but didn't swallow. And they traveled from east to west. Only the eastern sides of the cobs are stripped clean."

"What kind of insect is attracted to a plant and does not eat it?" Smith asked.

"Search me. Maybe one that's bred to wreck crops."

"Pesticide-resistant crops, in this case," Smith mused.

Dead air filled the line for too long, so Remo asked, "Anything on the dead talking bee?"

"The USDA laboratory is working on the corpse right now. I hope to have something soon."

"Okay, where next?"

"The FBI has generated another profile. It paints a portrait that fits only one individual my computers can find—Helwig X. Wurmlinger. It is time you paid that visit to his laboratory."

"There goes my date...."

"You are dating again?"

"Yeah," said Remo defensively. "Why are you surprised?"

"Because you did not request a background or marital-status check from me this time."

"That's right. I didn't. I guess I have a good feeling about this one."

"You said that about the last three."

"This is an extragood feeling. Even Chiun likes her."

"That is surprising."

"Yeah. I think he has a good feeling, too. Or maybe he's just taken by her last name."

"Which is?"

"Subject to change," said Remo, who then hung up, knowing that when the implications sank in, Harold Smith would start reaching for the Axid AR or Pepcid AC or Tagamet HB—or whatever he was using to ease his chronic heartburn these days.

**34**

The package was marked Rush.

No surprise there, thought USDA entomologist B. Eugene Roache of the USDA Honey Bee Breeding Center and Physiology Research Laboratory in Baton Rouge, Louisiana.

By now, everybody was reading or hearing about the new strain of killer bee that had struck on both coasts. They were calling it the death's-head bee, and the word was it was a new kind of Africanized Bravo bee.

It struck Roache as pretty strange from when first he heard about it. A new kind of bee appearing on opposite coasts in the same week. Normally, any new bee population entered through a single ecological gateway—and they wouldn't be bicoastal. Up from Mexico like the *scutellata*, sure. Down from Canada, maybe. But bees were not fond of the cold. The idea of bees coming down from Canada seemed farfetched.

A bicoastal entry suggested the cargo-ship theory. If it were just a Pacific deal, some kind of Asian superbee would be a possibility. With Atlantic attacks, the Asian theory looked thinner.

Those were the thoughts that ran through Roache's head as he waited for the rush package to be couriered from what he thought was another USDA laboratory in New York State. He had been alerted to the incoming package by a lemony telephone voice that said, "Identify this bee as quickly as possible."

That meant FABIS—the Fast Africanized Bee Identification System. They were better, surer methods of identifying a suspect bee to see if it were Africanized, or even a hybrid strain of Africanized European bee.

If it were a live bee, a stingometer would do the trick. It was an electrical box that recorded the number of bee stings—or attempted bee stings, since the suspect bee couldn't penetrate its hard shell. Four hits per second meant a Eurobee. Fifty-two hits, and it was a Bravo bee. That was how vicious the latter could be. It was the gang-banger among bees.

But this bee was coming in dead, and, after setting aside the foam and bubble wrap, Roache lifted the dead bee and set it on his workbench under a strong light.

He was surprised to see confirmation of the reports that it was a male honey bee drone. Or at least morphologically similar to one.

Under a magnifying glass, he examined the tip of the fat black abdomen. He gasped when he saw the stinger that shouldn't be there. It wasn't barbed, like a worker bee's or a yellow jacket's. This was the smooth hypodermic lance of a wasp.

"This bee can sting at will without penalty to itself," Roache muttered.

Excitement growing in his chest, he examined the death's-head markings at the back of the bee's fuzzy yellow thorax. It was distinctly a skull outline. It was almost perfect in its contours, like a tiny cameo.

"I have never seen anything like this. I can't believe anything like this exists," he muttered. "This is an entirely new species of bee."

Normally, the first step of the FABIS process was to dissect the bee in order to measure its significant components—the thorax, legs and wings. But this bee specimen came with an extra unattached wing, and Roache was loath to dissect the intact specimen just yet.

Taking up tweezers, he lifted the bee from the tabletop. He brought it closer to the light preparatory to setting it on an overhead projector for enlargement. He was curious to see the texture of the wing unassisted.

As the wing came closer to the desk light, he saw that the vein pattern was quite regular. In one corner, there was a tiny dot. A blemish of some kind.

Before Roache could take the wing away, a strange thing happened. Emitting a thin thread of smoke, the wing curled up and shriveled.

"Damn!"

The wing fell to the desktop. Roache blew on it. It continued to smoke. The stink was terrible. In the end, he was forced to press down on it to stop it from disintegrating completely.

The bee's wing, now curled into a blackened crisp of material, was pretty far gone, but the tip had survived. Roache placed it on the glass of the overhead projector anyway.

Clicking on the light, he projected the transparent image onto a clean white wall where preprinted outlines of Africanized and non-Africanized bee parts had been hung for comparative purposes.

The crisped wing was useless for comparison purposes.

But in the unburned corner, Roache saw the small dark blemish. He saw it clearly. And when he recognized it, his eyes all but bugged out of his head and he swore for ten minutes straight without repeating himself or running out of things to say.

Then he took his dissecting kit and attacked the complete specimen, his eyes bright and feverish.

**35**

They could smell death from a mile away.

The air was thick with the rotten, sickly sweet odor of bodies in the early stages of decomposition.

"Uh-oh," said Remo at the wheel, and slowed the rented Jeep Grand Cherokee.

"Death hangs over these woods," intoned Chiun, drawing a silken sleeve to his nose and lips to ward off the offending stench.

"A lot of death," said Remo.

They came upon the string of parked vehicles just short of the end of the dirt road that led to their destination. The vehicles blocked the road completely, forcing Remo to brake.

Getting out, they moved off the road and saw the top of the mud hive as the morning began painting its flowing contours in smoldering colors.

"What the hell is that?" Remo wondered aloud.

"The den of iniquity and bees."

"Looks like a beehive."

"A fitting abode for the self-styled Lord of All Bees."

As they moved in a circular-approach pattern

around the weird place, the low sound of bees awakening with the sun began to fill the morning air.

Remo paused in midstep. "Hear that, Little Father?"

"Bees. Bees that are not happy."

"That's exactly what I thought."

They moved closer. That's when they found the first body. He was dressed in military-style camouflage fatigues. An AR-15 rifle lay next to him. His eyes were open and they were empty. Literally empty.

"Check it out," said Remo.

Chiun knelt. He saw the empty red caverns already crawling with ordinary flies. The mouth lay parted. Chiun forced it open. The dead jaw popped in protest, but the sun sliding into the open mouth revealed no tongue, only a raw root and the dry enamel of teeth. The smell from the mouth was rank.

Chiun arose. Moving closer, they found more bodies, all without eyes or tongue. Some had fallen in such a way that their brain matter leaked from an ear or nostril—even from the mouth, as if they had died vomiting out their own brains.

"Just like that guy in Times Square," Remo said grimly.

Chiun nodded.

Checking a corpse wearing more stars and braid than a six-star general deserved, Remo discovered a black Velcro patch on the dead man's shoulders in place of insignia. He stripped it.

Under the black patch was an embroidered one showing an ear of corn over crossed muskets. It said

Iowa Disorganized Subterranean Militia—*E Pluribus Unum.*

"Hey! These guys are from Iowa. And they're militia."

Chiun made a shriveled-yellow-raisin face. "Here, Remo, is proof that the fiend who breeds talking not-bees will be found lurking here."

Remo stood up. "Maybe. But if militia are involved, I wouldn't bet on their being right about anything. Most of these guys are weekend warriors with delusions of civil war."

Chiun's eyes grew intrigued. "A civil war might be advantageous. Prince against prince. There would be much work for the House. And opportunity for raises."

"Can it. Let's pay a call on Wurmlinger."

Chiun got in Remo's way. "Have you forgotten the first rule of survival?"

"Yeah. Don't walk into anything blind."

"The scourge that felled these soldiers is unknown to us. Perhaps it is the very plague that brought sweet peace to the land of garish corn."

Remo considered that a moment and went to a handy body. It turned out to be Commander Mearl Streep's, but he didn't know that.

Kneeling, Remo took the dead man's head in both hands and turned it to one side so the left ear was suspended over the dirt. Shaking vigorously, Remo got a sound like scrambled eggs being agitated.

Gray brain matter began dropping from the left ear.

It was already congealing. Remo hurried it along with a few more encouraging shakes.

When he got the head emptied, Remo set it off to one side and stood up to regard the malodorous custardlike pile with the Master of Sinanju.

"What do you think? Is that all his brain matter?" he asked.

Chiun regarded the dead man's head a moment. "Yes. It is more than enough to fill his narrow skull. No doubt his eyes and tongue lie in that puddle, as well."

"Brains chewed but not eaten. Just like the corn in Iowa."

"It is the curse of corn descending upon the sons of corn, Remo," Chiun warned. "Take heed. Stick with rice for the rest of your days."

"I plan to. But not the rice you're thinking of."

"What other rice is there?"

Remo grinned. "Jean Rice."

Chiun turned to face the mud nest. "Now we must confront the author of the not-bees."

"I only see one door."

"We are Sinanju. We make our own doors."

"Lead the way," said Remo.

The Master of Sinanju approached by the back way. Coming to the boxes where bees made unhappy sounds, he skirted them carefully. Remo did likewise.

Going to a window, Chiun peered in.

Remo took up a position beside him. When Chiun withdrew one eye from the porthole, he motioned Remo to take his place.

Peering in, Remo saw that he was looking at a bedroom. It was an ordinary-looking room except for one thing. The wallpaper was done in a distinctive spiderweb pattern.

Eyeing Chiun, Remo shrugged, as if to say, So what?

Chiun drew near and hissed, "This is the lair of the fiend."

"We don't know that yet. So let's not jump to conclusions until we talk to Wurmlinger."

"Look again," said Chiun.

When Remo did, he frowned.

"Look at the wall above the head of the bed, and tell me that I am not correct, as always."

Angling around, Remo's eyes fell on the spiderweb-pattern wall above the bed. What he saw made his mouth hang open in surprise.

Before he could say what was on his mind, Chiun had turned, emitting a warning hiss more venomous than that of a cornered cobra.

Remo spun, too.

The Master of Sinanju had dropped into a defensive crouch, long nails floating before his face, ready to snap out and fend off the threat that had slipped up behind them.

Hovering in the air only three feet before them was an unmistakable death's-head bee. Its tiny legs were gathered up under its body, and it made no move to attack.

"Remo," Chiun urged, "prepare to execute the Silken Noose with me."

Remo frowned. Out of the side of his mouth, he asked, "Is that the maneuver where one of us gets behind an opponent while the other distracts him from the front?"

"No, you are thinking of the Meeting Palms," hissed Chiun. "The Silken Noose requires—"

The hanging bee interrupted his next words. In a voice tiny but loud enough to be heard clearly, it said, "Fools! How dare you molest the one who is protected by Bee-Master."

"Bug off," said Remo, whose own hands were crossed at the wrist before his chest in case the bee made a lunge at him.

"This dwelling, and all who dwell within, are under the all-encompassing protection of the Bizarre Bee-Master."

"Bizarre is right," grunted Remo. "You zap those nuts in the camouflage outfits?"

"They dared to thwart the Bee-Master's supreme will."

"Looks like they tried to hit Wurmlinger the Weird."

"And they paid the ultimate price, as do all who challenge the true protector of the insect kingdom."

"I don't know what makes me feel stupider," muttered Remo to Chiun, "having a conversation with a bee or having the bee parrot dialogue out of an old comic book."

"His stinger is not made of paper," warned Chiun.

"Gotcha. Okay, bee. Let's lay our cards on the

table. We're here to talk to Wurmlinger. You planning on getting in our way?"

"No," said the bee. "I am but a guard bee. The wrath of the Bee-Master will soon be upon you, would-be thwarter."

"In that case, you're so much beeswax."

Without warning, Remo turned in a flashing sidekick. His foot snapped out with such blurred speed that it had returned to the ground before the bee could react.

The bee, however, continued to float in place, unfazed.

"You missed," it taunted.

"Yes, you missed, Remo. How could you miss?" Chiun demanded.

"Look at my foot," Remo undertoned.

Chiun did. Remo's right foot rested on the ground. It was barefoot. His Italian loafer was missing.

A moment later, it dropped from the sky to catch the waiting bee unawares.

The open mouth of the shoe enveloped the bee. Bee and shoe hit the ground. Reacting with perfect timing, Remo's fist jammed the shoe into the ground. There came a satisfying crunch.

"Got the little bugger!" he crowed.

Recovering his shoe, Remo shook it out. A thoroughly mashed bumblebee fell out. After it hit the dirt, it didn't twitch. Not once. Its wings relaxed open in death.

Grinning, Remo restored his shoe to his foot. Facing the Master of Sinanju, he said, "I'm learning."

"Have you forgotten the wrath of the Bee-Master?"

"I'm more interested in talking to the Bee-Master himself."

With that, Remo went around to the front door and lifted his fist as if to knock. His knuckles traveled a short way. When they struck the door, it traveled a longer way.

Right off its hinges and across the living room.

Remo went in after it, calling out, "The jig's up, Wurmlinger."

A toilet flushed. And a cracked voice asked, "Who is there?"

"You remember us."

A door fell open with a creak, and around the corner of the door, Helwig X. Wurmlinger peered. He blinked his magnified tea-colored eyes slowly. He was very pale.

"What are you two doing here?" he demanded.

"We just snuffed your superbee. He gave you up first. You might as well come clean."

Chiun had slipped into the room, too, to take a position beside his pupil. "Yes. Your perfidy is known."

"Perfidy? I have committed no perfidy," Wurmlinger said.

"The bee told us everything," Remo bluffed.

"Bee. What bee? How could a bee tell you anything?"

"It talked." Remo folded his arms before him as

if to signal that he would listen to no BS to the contrary.

Helwig X. Wurmlinger looked back at Remo as if Remo were mad. "You are mad," he said.

"P.O.'ed is closer to the truth," said Remo, who shot across the room and dragged Wurmlinger into the living room by the collar of his white smock.

"Unhand me!" he complained.

Remo frisked him by patting his pockets. He frisked pretty hard. Wurmlinger went, "Ouch... yeow," and made other noises of pain.

When Remo was finished, he marched Wurmlinger into the spiderweb-motif bedroom.

"The bee that talked said he worked for the Bee-Master," Remo was saying. "Name ring a bell with you?"

"Yes."

Remo shoved Wurmlinger's face to the wall where a yellowed poster hung over the bed, featuring a grim face enveloped in an electronic helmet. It looked like the head of a chromium bee with crimson compound eyes.

"Explain this."

"That is my poster of Bee-Master," Helwig Wurmlinger said.

"It's a poster of yourself. I don't know how or why you did it, but you've bred a bee you can control with an electronic helmet."

"Are you insane? The Bee-Master is only a comic-book character. He doesn't exist."

"Then why do you have his poster over your bed?"

"Er, I—"

"Your hesitation betrays you," Chiun intoned, bringing his long, deadly nails up before Wurmlinger's long, nervous face.

"Go ahead," said Remo.

"This is very embarrassing."

"Not as embarrassing as having your head squeezed off your neck..."

Just then, the air filled with the growing metallic sound of a million angry insects.

"There is that sound again," Wurmlinger gasped.

"What sound?"

"The sound that killed all those men."

"Oh-oh," said Remo, looking to the window.

**36**

"Here. Hold this guy," Remo said as the high, angry sound grew louder, and Chiun accepted Helwig Wurmlinger's neck from Remo's grasp.

Moving to the detached front door, Remo lifted it and rushed it back to the doorway. The hinges were ripped loose, so he couldn't rehang it. Instead, he set it tightly in the door frame and leaned against it with his shoulder.

"I think we're okay," he called out.

The sound grew in volume and insistence.

Chiun went to a side window, taking Wurmlinger with him. The entomologist had to walk stooped over because of the difference in height between him and the Master of Sinanju.

From the bedroom window, Chiun asked, "What do you see, Remo?"

"Nothing," said Remo. "It's just a sound."

Chiun's facial wrinkles gathered up tightly. "I, too, see nothing."

Helwig Wurmlinger said, "I saw nothing when those men were killed. But it was dark."

"The not-bee informed us that the wrath of the Bee-Master was about to descend upon our heads.

What is the wrath of the Bee-Master?'' demanded Chiun.

"I have no idea," Wurmlinger said uncomfortably. "But it does sound rather beelike."

From the other room, Remo called out, "Chiun, I think I have a little problem here."

The Master of Sinanju flashed into the other room. He took one look at his pupil holding the door in place and squeaked, "What is wrong?"

"I don't know. The door is vibrating. But I can't see anything."

Then the door started falling apart.

"Remo! Retreat! Retreat from what you do not understand!" Chiun cried.

"I gotta hold the door shut, or that sound will get in."

Then Remo's choices all fled. The door simply came apart. It disintegrated into showering sawdust.

Backing off, Remo cleared the entire room and crowded Chiun into the bedroom. He slammed the door after him.

His back supporting the door, Remo said, "I didn't see a thing. But the door acted like termites were eating it."

"Termites chew. They do not eat," Helwig Wurmlinger said.

"Well, whatever they were, they made short work of that door. Chiun, how do we fight those things?"

"I do not know. But this one should."

Helwig Wurmlinger looked guilty as sin. He was sweating. He trembled.

`Then the door at Remo's back began to buzz.

"Here they come!" Remo said. "Look, I can hold the door. Get out the back way."

"No, I will not leave you!"

"Listen to him," Wurmlinger said. "Whatever that sound represents, it will eat your brains in your head. There is no defense."

"Listen to him, Little Father," urged Remo, his voice buzzing in sympathy with the agitated door.

His face a tight web of spidery wrinkles, the Master of Sinanju narrowed his eyes in thought. Then, flinging Wurmlinger onto the bed, he bounded to Remo's side. His hands flashed out and caught Remo by the front of his T-shirt. He pivoted. Remo went flying.

Retreating to the bed, Chiun took Helwig Wurmlinger by the throat and made his voice loud enough to be heard over the weird sound that was infiltrating the room.

"Halt in your flight, creatures unknown!" he called.

The sound filled the room. There was nothing visible, just a weird humming as if the air had been electrified.

In a corner, Remo crouched, his eyes going everywhere. His senses were telling him he was surrounded. But he could see no threat, only hear it. Cold sweat broke out all over his body.

Then a sharp sting made a red bump on one thick wrist. Remo slapped at it.

"Chiun..."

"Cover your ears," Wurmlinger screamed. "They get in through the ears."

Remo slapped his hands over his ears. He felt something tickle his left nostril. Expelling air from his lungs, he blew the unseen irritant out. Then, drawing in a deep breath with mouth closed, he sealed his nostrils shut against invasion and waited.

Through his pressing hands, he heard the Master of Sinanju.

"If my son is harmed, I will break this one's neck! Do you hear, Master of Bees? If you do not retreat, this man who you claim to protect will die at the hands of the Master of Sinanju."

The sound continued permeating the room.

Chiun's tight face was resolute. Helwig Wurmlinger was oozing perspiration from his face and neck. His hands covered his own ears, and his eyes were pinched shut against the eye-consuming phenomenon.

"I warn you," Chiun said.

The sound seemed to pause. For a moment, it changed pitch as it gathered itself into a tight ball in the center of the room.

Chiun's eyes went to the compressed source of that sound. Still, he saw nothing, but every sense screamed the threat had contracted to a space that was no greater than that of an egg.

For almost two minutes, there was a standoff. Chiun squeezed Wurmlinger's bony throat with sufficient skill that the scientist could just only breathe, although his face was turning redder by the moment.

In a corner, Remo crouched in a defensive posture

entirely unbecoming a Master of Sinanju. But he was facing a threat no Master had ever before encountered and against which he had no defense.

While Chiun held the balance of power in his bony hands.

At the end of two minutes, the humming, much subdued, even dejected, retreated from the room. Their eyes followed it even though it was really their ears that tracked its evacuation.

The unseen creatures poured from the mud nest of Helwig Wurmlinger and disappeared into the early-morning light.

When it seemed safe to do so, Chiun released Wurmlinger's throat. Remo came out of his crouch, his hands dropping to his side.

For a moment, he stood there rotating his thick wrists absently. His T-shirt was drenched in his own perspiration.

"What happened?" asked Remo.

"I saved you," said Chiun.

"I know that. But what—?"

Chiun eyed Wurmlinger. "The brain devourers valued the life of this man. It is time he explained why."

Helwig Wurmlinger looked back at the accusing gazes and flapped his hands helplessly. "I—I cannot," he managed to say.

And as they eyed the man, his head next to the fading poster of the Bizarre Bee-Master, Remo thought that there was a pretty strong resemblance between them. Especially around the chin.

**37**

Remo fixed Dr. Helwig X. Wurmlinger with his deep-set eyes and said, "You have a lot of explaining to do."

A giant cockroach walked into the room, twitching its feelers, and stopped and hissed at them loudly.

"Do not be alarmed," Wurmlinger told them. "That is a Madagascar cockroach. Perfectly harmless."

"What's it doing out of its box?" asked Remo.

"It is a pet. I keep it as a pet."

"Nobody keeps cockroaches as pets," said Remo.

Chiun floated over to the roach, which was as horny as an armadillo, and told it, "Do not hiss at me, vermin."

The cockroach hissed anyway.

And the Master of Sinanju brought a black sandal down on its back with a satisfying crunch.

Wurmlinger groaned and wrung his bony hands. "You had no right to hurt Agnes," he moaned.

"Worry about yourself," said Remo. "First, explain this poster here."

"That is the Bizarre Bee-Master."

"We know that."

"He was my hero as a child. My idol. I worshiped him."

"You're not a kid anymore. What are you doing with a comic-book hero on your bedroom wall?"

"I—I still retain a fondness for him. He was the lord and friend of the insect world. In many ways, I have patterned my life after his creed."

Remo frowned. "I don't remember any creed...."

Behind his Coke-bottle gaze, Wurmlinger's tea-colored eyes brightened. "You, too, were a Bee-Master fan?" he chirped.

"I wouldn't say fan. But I read a few issues here and there," Remo admitted.

"What was your favorite issue? Do you remember?"

"Get off it. Are you trying to tell us you've had that poster on your wall ever since you were a kid?"

"Yes. Since November, 1965. I never threw it away. I saved all my comic books, too."

"Why would you do that?"

"They are worth a lot of money. It is better than investing in gold. If you do not believe me, look under my bed."

Remo did. There were three long white cardboard boxes there. Remo pulled one out by the cutout handle, shooing away a scuttling spider.

"Mind you don't hurt my friends," Wurmlinger admonished.

"All I see are spiders."

"Wolf spiders. They eat paper-eating mites."

The box was filled with old comic books, each one

bagged in clear Mylar and backed by a cardboard stiffener.

The first one was titled *Tales to Amaze You* and showed the Bee-Master wrestling with a glowing green dung beetle against the backdrop of the Egyptian pyramids.

"Hey, I remember this one!" Remo said.

"Which one?"

Remo turned the comic book around so the cover showed. Wurmlinger's eyes lit up with undisguised joy.

"Beware the Dung Beetle of Doom! Yes, that was one of my favorites, too. Bee-Master discovered a mummified dung beetle in a museum and accidentally reanimated it. They fought seventeen cataclysmic battles until finally Bee-Master found a way to restore it to an Egyptian tomb in Karnak. They actually parted friends. It was very touching. You see, the dung beetle meant no harm. Bee-Master hadn't perfected his cybernetic helmet yet, so he couldn't communicate with the beetle family. When he finally did, he understood that all the carnage and death the dung beetle had inflicted on mankind was because he was misunderstood. Did you know that one day beetles will take over the world from Man?"

"I thought that was cockroaches," said Remo.

Wurmlinger winced at the thought of dead Agnes. "Before cockroaches inherit the earth, beetles will reign supreme. They are a very hardy race."

Remo dropped the comic book back into its box. "Look, your story doesn't wash."

"I don't have a story," Wurmlinger said in an offended voice.

Remo began ticking off items on his finger. "Number one, the mastermind killing people calls himself the Bee-Master."

"With or without the hyphen?"

"We don't know. So far, we're only hearing this stuff from—" Remo hesitated.

"Unimpeachable sources," inserted Chiun.

Wurmlinger cocked a skeptical eyebrow, but held his tongue.

"Number two," Remo went on, while surreptitiously stepping on a scuttling silverfish that had scooted out from under the bed, "whoever did this has attacked only people or things involved with pesticides or antibug inventions like worm-proof corn, or to cover up his killings. That means he's a bug lover. You are a bug lover."

"I am no insectophobe," Wurmlinger admitted. "But being an insectophile is not indicative of guilt."

"Hah!" squeaked Chiun. "He even speaks like Bee-Master."

Wurmlinger flinched.

"He's big on bees, too," Remo added.

"Everyone should be concerned about *Apis*," Wurmlinger exploded. "Bees are our friends. They pollinate crops as diverse as citrus and cranberry. Without bees, we would starve within a matter of a year or two. And the United States is currently in the throes of a severe bee crisis."

"Yes," Chiun said in a low, menacing tone of voice. "One that you have authored, bee lover."

"No. Not that bee crisis. But a much more serious crisis than a few insectoid casualties."

"Explain," said Remo.

"We are in the fifth year of what I predict will go down in history as the Great American Bee Crash. We are losing our wild bees. Some are the victims of man's thoughtless savaging of their habitats. But the recent droughts have reduced plant forage, and severe winter snow has aggravated bee fragility to elevated levels. All over this continent, *Apis* is succumbing to bee mites, which make them more vulnerable to bee diseases."

"Bees have mites and diseases?" Remo asked doubtfully.

Wurmlinger cupped one thin ear in the direction of the bedroom window. "Listen."

Remo and Chiun focused their hearing on the glass.

Outside, the doleful buzz of honeybees went up and down the sad end of the musical scale.

"Those are ordinary bees. They were healthy when I left for Los Angeles. I have returned to discover them infected with tracheal and *Varroa jacobsoni* mites. Some are already so weakened that they have succumbed to foulbrood, a disease that reduces the poor bee to a jellylike state. If my bees have come to harm, no bees are safe. Not feral bees. Nor domestic bees."

Remo looked at Chiun. The Master of Sinanju maintained his stiff, unsympathetic countenance.

"Okay, let's say that's all true."

"It *is* true," Wurmlinger insisted.

"There is an FBI profile of the Bee-Master out there, and it fits you to a T."

"And a *B*," added Chiun tightly.

"The Bee-Master has to be an insect geneticist. And everyone's seen your Frankenstein bugs on TV."

"My genetic creatures are mere experiments."

"A dragonfly with eyes all over its body?" Remo demanded. "Where is that thing, anyway?" he asked, looking around the room.

"In my lab. I have many unusual specimens in my lab. As for the dragonfly, it is merely an adaptation of a gene-transplanting technique previously accomplished using fruit flies. You see, the gene that creates eyes has been discovered. Simply by transplanting this gene to other spots on the insect's body, eyes sprout. They are unseeing, because they do not connect to the visual receptors of the brain, but they are perfect in all other ways."

Remo frowned. "What about the other stuff?"

"I have experimented with titanium prosthetics, yes. I admit this freely."

"Prosthetic limbs for bugs?" Remo said sharply.

"There is a need. And my discoveries may have human applications."

"Yeah. Like breeding killer bumblebees."

"Such a thing seems impossible," Wurmlinger said.

"If you can transplant an eye gene, why not a stinger gene?" Remo said pointedly.

"It is feasible," Wurmlinger said thoughtfully, "but it would be harmless unless a neurotoxin gland were also created. Bumbles are equipped with ordinary venom sacs." He shook his long, twitchy head. "No, I cannot envision this."

Remo took him by the arm. "Let's have a look at your lab."

The lab was in the rear of the mud hive. A semicircular room with brown curving walls and a window resembling a blister, it smelled like a festering boil when Remo pushed the door in.

The dragonfly zipped past them. Chiun decapitated it with a flick of his extralong index fingernail. The dragonfly fell in two dry parts to twitch on the floor only long enough for a speedy spider to dart out from beneath a test-tube stand and claim it for his lunch.

Wurmlinger closed his eyes in pain.

Around the room, there were ant farms, cricket terrariums and a goodly number of bugs roaming around loose amid the forest of test tubes and experimental equipment.

Remo found no bees. There was a praying mantis with a steely mechanical forearm and a jointed toothpick for a rear leg in a glass box, but that was as weird as it got.

Chiun frowned at all that he saw, but he said nothing.

"Okay, let's see your sick bees," said Remo.

"Allegedly sick bees," added Chiun.

They went out the back door to the bee boxes.

Wurmlinger lifted out of the hive boxes a sample honeycomb on a frame. The bees on it were absent of motion and humming.

None resembled the death's-head killer bee. Wurmlinger exposed a dozen honeycombs, including ones clogged with tiny winged blobs that had once been living bees.

"This is what foulbrood does," Wurmlinger said morosely.

"Tough."

"Insectophobe!" Wurmlinger hissed, dropping the frame back into its box.

A few bees clung to his body, and the Master of Sinanju asked, "Why do they cleave to you, if you are not the Bee-Master?"

"I wear an after-shave whose chief ingredient is bee pheromone. These bees think I am their queen."

Remo rolled his eyes. They went back into the house. Chiun drifted into the bedroom and studied the Bee-Master poster once more.

Remo looked Wurmlinger dead in the eye. "I need to ask you a question. I need you to answer it truthfully," he said.

"Yes. Of course," Wurmlinger said earnestly.

"Are you the Bee-Master?"

"No. Of course not. Everyone knows that the Bizarre Bee-Master is really Peter Pym."

Remo looked at Chiun and Chiun at Remo.

"He is telling the truth. His heart rate is normal," said Remo.

"Yes," said Chiun, nodding sagely. "Now tell us where we can find this Peter Pym."

"You cannot."

"Why not?"

"Because he doesn't exist. He's purely a figment of the imaginations of the greatest comic-book geniuses of their time, Irv Ray and Steve Starko."

"What he means," Remo explained to Chiun, "is that Bee-Master is a myth. Kinda like Mickey Mouse."

"I have met Mickey in the fur. He lives."

"Well, Bee-Master doesn't hang around amusement parks. He's strictly a paper tiger."

Removing one of the comic books from its plastic, the Master of Sinanju examined the story within.

"The artwork is terrible."

"How can you say that about Steve Starko?" Wurmlinger said.

"Everyone looks Slavic," said Chiun, dropping the comic book with undisguised disdain.

Wurmlinger lunged, catching it before it hit the floor. "Are you mad? That issue is worth over four thousand dollars in mint condition."

"People pay that much?" Remo asked.

"More for key issues. The origin of Bee-Master is worth ten. In mint, of course."

Remo muttered, "Guess I shouldn't have let Sister Mary Margaret throw mine out."

"You should sue her. It's been done."

"Forget it. She's long gone. Listen, you're the etymologist."

"Entomologist. Not to mention apiculturist," Wurmlinger said proudly.

"There's some nut out there who can communicate with bees. Just like Bee-Master. How could someone do it in real life?"

Wurmlinger's face twitched in thought. "It cannot be done. Not the way Bee-Master did it. That part of the Bee-Master legend was sheer fantasy. And I cannot see anyone possessing that remarkable ability to turn his talents to anything other than the good of mankind and the insect kingdom."

"Take it from us, these death's-head bees are under the control of a guy calling himself Bee-Master," Remo said hotly.

"Has he made public announcements?"

"No." Remo hesitated. "We know this because two of the bees talked to us."

Wurmlinger's upper lip curled. "Bees cannot speak."

"The death's-head bee does and did."

"Yes," chimed in Chiun. "We heard it plainly."

Helwig Wurmlinger looked at them both. "A bee spoke to you?" he asked.

"Yes," said Chiun.

"In English?"

"Yeah," said Remo.

"And understood you in return?"

"That's right," Remo said.

"Bees," said Helwig Wurmlinger in his most authoritative voice, "cannot speak—or understand English if they could. They do not possess a vocal apparatus. Nor are they equipped by nature with language-processing centers in their brains. Queen bees do pipe, it is true. Unfertilized females quack in responses, yes. But it is not language. There is no grammar.''

"Yeah, well, bumblebees aren't aggressive, either," Remo countered, "and look how many people are dead."

Helwig X. Wurmlinger had no answer to that.

**38**

Harold W. Smith was waiting for word from Remo in the field.

Waiting was often the hardest part of the dour Smith's job. He had the ability, through his computer links and telephone eavesdropping techniques, of keeping track of everyone from the President of the United States down to his own wife, Maude. With no more instruction than a flurry of keystrokes, he could tell if a telephone was in use, a specific computer was on-line or, increasingly in these days of global positioning satellites, the location of almost any car in the U.S., given sufficient search time.

But Remo and Chiun continued to vex him. They refused to carry cell phones. Remo because he kept losing them, and Chiun because the old Korean had heard on TV an erroneous report that frequent cell-phone use could lead to brain cancer. Smith doubted Chiun really believed this. It was just a useful excuse to avoid dealing with what he considered annoying technology.

While he waited, Smith sifted through strange reports coming off the wires.

In the Deep South, cotton fields had been decimated. As with the ravaged cornfields in Iowa, many fields were spared. Knowing what to look for, Smith got in touch with a USDA field agent and instructed him to look for problems with genetically engineered cotton.

A preliminary report confirmed his suspicions.

"The fields are a mess down here," the USDA field agent reported, after having dialed a Washington, D.C., number that was rerouted to Folcroft Sanitarium. "The young bolls are all over the ground, like madmen have been playing toss-ball with them. Losses will be in the millions."

"Get to the point," Smith instructed.

"They have a new crop of cotton growing down here. Supposed to be genetically engineered to resist weevils and cotton bollworms by emitting a natural pesticide. That's the crop that got it. The traditional crops are just fine. It's spooky. As if the pests that did this knew exactly what they wanted to hit."

"Verify and report back to me," Smith instructed.

Next, it was Texas wheat.

"Stubble fields down here look like they have been scythed," another unwitting USDA field agent reported.

"Are the fields pest-resistant?"

"That will take a lot of proving, but that's my guess."

"Verify this theory and report back."

Smith hung up and made a grim face.

The pattern was holding. From the killing of geneticist Doyal T. Rand to this. The mastermind was attempting to wage war on that segment of humanity that had waged war against the insects of the world. But why? What was his objective? Why were there no demands or statements of intent?

He checked his wrist Timex. Remo and Chiun had to have reached Wurmlinger's home. If, as the FBI had assured him, Wurmlinger was their man, the pair would make short work of him.

When a telephone rang, Smith knew from its muffled bell that it wasn't Remo. He had dreaded this call, but knew it was coming.

Extracting the fire-engine red telephone from his desk drawer, Smith set it on his glassy desktop and lifted the handset to his ear.

"I am aware of the situation, Mr. President."

"Our breadbasket is under attack," the President said hoarsely.

"Under selective attack," Smith replied calmly.

"How can you be so calm? This is a national emergency," the President sputtered.

Smith tightened the already too-tight knot of his tie. "The farms and crops have been targeted in such a way as to achieve a specific result."

"Result! What result?"

"That is becoming clearer by the moment, but I can tell you that it is tied in with the so-called death's-head-bee attacks on both coasts."

"It is?" the President stammered.

"It is," Smith said with unflappable earnestness.

The Chief Executive lowered his voice to a dull

hum. "Am I better off knowing about this, or not knowing about it? Politically speaking, that is."

"You are better off awaiting the results of my investigation, Mr. President."

"Those two. The one with the wrists and the old guy with the wrinkles. You have them on the case?"

"They are closing in on a suspect."

The presidential voice grew audibly relieved. "Then I'm going to sit tight. Do you think this will be over by the six-o'clock news?"

"I hope so. But the resolution may be one to which you are better off not being privy."

"It's that grisly, huh?"

"It is," Harold Smith said truthfully, "unbelievable."

"Okay. I'll just sit back and watch CNN and those Fox people. They seem to be right on top of this thing."

Smith hung up, visibly relieved. He had not wished to take the President into his confidence. Not if it risked exposing to psychological scrutiny the head of the supersecret government agency whose existence, if it were revealed, would surely topple his administration.

There was no telling how the Commander in Chief would react to descriptions of talking killer bees. It was more than possible that he would conclude that Harold Smith had slipped into senility and give the one lawful order a U.S. President was chartered to give CURE.

Disband.

Smith had been concerned that the talking bee's discovery of Folcroft might precipitate such a drastic step, but in truth, it had been such an unbelievable thing that he had all but put it out of his mind. For to disband CURE would be to bury it forever, along with its obscure director.

Smith patted the poison pill he kept in the watch pocket of his gray vest against that dark day and returned to monitoring his system. He wondered how the USDA Honey Bee Research Center was doing with the death's-head-bee specimen.

**39**

The wires were buzzing with report after report.

"Down south, the cotton's been cut down," an intern said breathlessly. "Isn't that great?"

"Fantastic!" Tammy agreed. "I've always wanted to tour the Deep South."

She was packing her overnight bag and calling down to the cameraman pool when the intern poked her green-streaked blond head into Tammy's New York office and relayed another bulletin.

"Texas wheat's come a cropper!"

"I love it!" Tammy screeched. "I can just see me now, doing a dramatic stand-up against waving fields of amber grain."

"Breakfast-cereal prices will go back through the roof again."

"Who cares? I'm a certified media star now. I can afford any size Wheaties they make."

And she could. Her bee report had electrified the nation.

Then her news director showed up and closed the door behind him, leaning his body against it and grinning from ear to ear.

"Guess what?" he asked.

"Don't tell me—California oranges are so much juicy pulp?"

"Not yet. But we think it's coming. We're retitling the 'Fox Death's-Head Superbee Report.'"

Tammy's eyes flared like blue brakelights. "You can't do that! It's the main hook."

"It's going to be called 'The Tamara Terrill Report.' Congratulations, kid. You've made the big time."

Tammy shot a fist into the air. "I have my own show!"

"That's right. And we're going live this afternoon, so get that saucy little butt of yours ready."

"But I'm going to Texas."

"Make it Alabama. Cotton is white. It'll show up better on the screen. You'll premiere in a field of smashed cotton."

"Just like Dorothy in *The Wizard of Oz!*"

"I think that was poppies. Just get ready, Tam."

"I've been ready ever since I graduated from broadcast school," Tammy exulted.

After Smoot had left, she finished packing and stopped to close her office window against the April chill.

A fuzzy bee zipped in before she could complete the task. She caught a glimpse of it out of the corner of her eye. It seemed to look back with its skull emblem. Her blood ran cold as fifth-place ratings. By then, it was too late. The window had thunked into place.

Tammy stood rigid for a moment, thinking.

"I'm going to pretend I didn't see it," she said to herself as a cold trickle of perspiration ran down the gully of her back.

Swallowing hard, she went to her desk, grabbed her bag and steeled herself to make a dash for the door. If she had to, she'd brain the bee with the bag.

Tammy took three steps. And froze.

The killer bee floated between her and the shut door. It hung on its blurry wings, tiny legs suspended like the landing gear of a miniature helicopter.

Then a tiny voice said, "Tamara Terrill!"

"Who's there?" Tammy called to the door in a dry, nervous squeak.

"Tamara Terrill," the voice repeated. "You have been chosen."

"Me?"

"Chosen for an important destiny."

The sound seemed to be coming from the door. Tammy was virtually certain of that. But it wasn't muffled as it should be. It was just small, almost tinny.

"Whoever you are, I need a quick favor," Tammy whispered urgently.

"What is that?" the tiny tinny voice asked.

"First, I need you to open that door. Then I need you to be very, very brave and jump on something for me."

"What is that?"

"I've got a killer bee in here with me and I need you to sacrifice your life for me."

"There is no need for that," said the voice that had

to be coming from the other side of the door, despite its unmuffled sound.

"Oh, there is. I have my own show now. I need to survive. It's for the good of the network. You *do* have insurance, don't you?"

"You are in no danger," the tinny voice assured her.

"I'm staring down a death's-head super-duper killer bee, buster. I most definitely am in danger."

"I am the bee."

"Huh?"

"You are speaking with one of the drone bees of the Bizarre Bee-Master."

Tammy blinked. "I am?" She gulped.

The bee floated closer.

"There is no one on the other side of the door. I am speaking to you," said the voice, which to the dazed Tammy started to sound as if it *might* be coming from the bee.

"This is a joke, right? Somebody in the writing staff is playing ventriloquist."

"This is no joke. Upon your shoulders rests the awesome responsibility for dissemination of the Bee-Master's demands to a trembling, unsuspecting world."

The voice sure sounded as if it was coming from the bee.

"I like how you talk," Tammy said. "But I don't understand a thing you're saying."

"I wish you to interview me."

"A bee?"

"Yes."

"You want me to interview a bumblebee on live TV?" Tammy repeated.

"It will be a television first," assured the bee.

"And if I don't, what? You're going to sting me or something?"

"Yes."

"Why?"

"Because you have failed your insect brethren."

"My insect what?"

"Obey the commands of the Bee-Master, and you will go down in history, Tamara Terrill," the bee insisted.

Tammy frowned. "Television history or history history?"

"Both," said the voice that was definitely coming from the bee. "For the Bizarre Bee-Master is about to reveal himself to the world."

"Now wait a minute. You've been assassinating people, right?"

"I have been exacting revenge," the bee countered.

"And covering it up by siccing your killer bees on assorted medical examiners."

"I was not yet ready to reveal myself to the world at large," the bee said flatly. "Now that my Revenge program has been implemented, that time has come."

"Gotcha. But now you do?"

"That is correct. The Bee-Master is weary of all pretense, all secrecy. It is time mankind knows the incredible truth."

"Okay, I got it. So answer one last question—why me?"

"Because my chosen publicity organ, the *Sacramento Bee,* has been ignoring my faxes."

Tammy's blue eyes narrowed. "Didn't one of their editors just die?"

"No," said the bee calmly. "He did not *just* die."

"Oh," said Tammy, understanding perfectly. She reached for her desk telephone. "Well, I guess you and me are about to share the most famous two-shot in broadcast history."

The bee showed that it was more than just a talking bee when it jumped on the switch hook, cutting off the line.

"No tricks," it warned.

"Honey, I wouldn't double-cross you for Ricki Lake's ratings."

"Don't call me honey," buzzed the bee.

"Oh, right. It's sexist."

"No, it is offensive to bees."

"Good point," said Tammy as the bee jumped off the switch hook so she could complete her call. "I'll try to remember that."

**40**

"Okay," Remo was saying, "you're not the Bee-Master."

"I used to wish I was," Dr. Helwig X. Wurmlinger muttered wistfully.

"But someone is."

"Someone does seem to have bred genetically superpowered bees," Wurmlinger admitted.

"And something else," Chiun inserted. "A swarm of things that drone and are invisible to the eye."

"There are some species of bees that are quite small," Wurmlinger said, "but they are not invisible. I have never heard of an invisible insect."

Chiun began to pace the room. "If these creatures are truly invisible, how do we know that one does not lurk here in our midst, observing all?" he asked suspiciously.

"It's possible," Remo said worriedly.

"It is *not* possible," Wurmlinger snapped. "Bees cannot be invisible."

"Name one reason why," challenged Remo.

"No such bee has ever been discovered."

"If you weren't looking for invisible bees, you wouldn't find them."

Wurmlinger blinked. He had no ready answer to that.

"Perhaps they are not invisible, but exceedingly tiny," he said after some time. "*Trigona minima,* for example, is the size of a mosquito."

"It's a thought," Remo acknowledged.

"It is a good thought," said Chiun.

They went to the door, which had been gnawed to sawdust by the invisible swarm of insects.

Wurmlinger scooped up sawdust samples into a dustpan with a whisk. He brought this into his insect lab and started preparing glass slides of sawdust samples.

While he was doing that, Remo and Chiun examined the loose dust in the pan. They were very intent in this work. Their eyes didn't blink at all.

Wurmlinger noticed this and asked, "What are you doing?"

"Looking for tiny bugs," said Remo, not looking up.

"Insects so small would be microscopic—or nearly so."

"That's what we're looking for," Remo said, nodding absently.

"You would need Bee-Master's superacuity compound goggles to see such a thing," he said tartly.

"We work with what God gave us," Remo replied distantly.

Shrugging, Wurmlinger clipped the first prepared slide into his microscope. Several minutes of careful observation revealed only sawdust. The grains were

marvelously fine, as if run through an infinitely re-
fined disintegrating process.

The next slide was the same. The third also showed
no evidence of insect parts.

Wurmlinger was selecting yet another slide when
Remo asked rather casually, "What kind of bug is all
mouth and has only one eye on the center of its forehead?"

"Why, no insect known to man," Wurmlinger told
him.

"Check this out," said Remo, handing over a pinch
of sawdust he had lifted from the dustpan.

He did not look to be joking, so Wurmlinger caught
the pinch in a glass slide, covered it and clipped it in
place under the microscope tube.

When he got the correct resolution, he saw it, lying
on its side. It had eight barbed legs, classifying it as
a member of the arachnid family, which included spiders and scorpions. Except it possessed wings, which
was impossible. Arachnids do not fly.

Lifting a probe, he moved the specimen around in
its sawdust bed, excitement mounting in his pigeon
chest. He got it turned around so that it faced the lens
tube.

"My God!" he gasped when its burning red cy-
clops eye glared back at him.

"You found it, huh?" Remo asked.

Wurmlinger swallowed his shock. His knobby
Adam's apple bobbed spasmodically. Still, he
couldn't get any words out. He nodded vigorously,
then shook his head from side to side as his educated

brain began denying the evidence before his very eyes.

But it was there. A long silvery green body, more like a scorpion than anything else in the arachnid family, boasting eight barbed and pincer-tipped legs and a pair of dragonflylike wings. And instead of a multieyed spider face, or the compound eyes of a fly or a bee, there was only a single smooth round orb mounted above an oval mouth with tiny serrated teeth all around the edges. The mouth made Wurmlinger think of a shark, not an insect.

"This is new!" he gasped. "This is incredibly new. This is a new class of insects. And I will go down in history as its discoverer."

"I found it first," Chiun squeaked.

"Are you accredited in any university?" Wurmlinger asked, regarding the old Korean with disapproval.

"No."

"Then your discovery does not count. I am one of the leading experts in the field of insects. This is my laboratory. Therefore, I am the discoverer of—" He paused, regarded his shoes a long moment while his long face worked. *"Luscus wurmlingi!"* he announced. "Yes, that will be its scientific name."

"You named that ugly thing after yourself?" Remo blurted.

"It is not ugly. It is unique. The name means One-eyed Wurmlinger."

"Is that anything like one-eyed wonder worm?" Remo asked dryly.

Wurmlinger ignored that. Reaching for a wall telephone, he said, "I must inform my colleagues before one of them happens to stumble upon a *wurmlingi* specimen in the field."

Remo beat him to the phone, pulled it bodily from the wall and handed it to Wurmlinger. Wurmlinger took it, saw the trailing wires and said, "Um..."

"Let's consider this classified for now, okay?" said Remo.

"You have no authority over me."

At that, Remo placed one hand on Wurmlinger's bony shoulder and said, "Pretend my hand is a tarantula."

Wurmlinger's eyes went to the hand, which started creeping up his neck on plodding fingers.

"Here comes the stealthy tarantula," Remo warned.

Wurmlinger flinched. "Stop it."

"The tarantula is on your neck. Feel its padded feet? Feel how soft they are?"

"I don't—"

"The tarantula is unhappy with you. It wants to bite. But you don't want it to bite, do you?" said Remo.

"No," Wurmlinger admitted, shrinking from the soft pads of Remo's fingers. He had tarantulas for pets. It was amazing how Remo's naked fingers felt like plodding tarantula feet on his neck.

"Too late," said Remo, his deliberately creepy voice speeding up. "The tarantula strikes!"

Wurmlinger felt a pinch. The hand withdrew, and Remo stepped away.

Wurmlinger had been bitten by tarantulas before. It was an occupational hazard. Their mandibles are poisonous, but not fatally so. Still, there is pain and numbness.

Wurmlinger felt no pain. But the numbness came on him very suddenly.

In a matter of seconds, he stood paralyzed on his feet. He swayed. Like a tree in the wind, he teetered from one side to the other. The horrible thing was that he couldn't move, couldn't stop himself from swaying.

Chiun padded up on one side and, when Wurmlinger swayed toward him, he blew out a strong breath.

The force of the breath pushed his swaying body the other way, and Helwig X. Wurmlinger felt himself tipping precariously even as his mind assured him screamingly that this couldn't be happening.

Fortunately, Remo caught him and carried him stiff as a stick to the bed and left him there, immobile. Time passed. Considerable time. During which the pair left without a word of farewell.

Having no better option, Helwig X. Wurmlinger drifted off to a mindless sleep.

When he awoke hours later, the slide containing the only known specimen of *Luscus wurmlingi* in the world was gone.

But at least they had left his Bee-Master collection intact.

And when he went out into the yard, the dead soldiers had begun fruiting, their mouths and empty eye sockets squirming with the most lovely maggots imaginable.

AT A PAY PHONE, Remo called Harold Smith.

"You want the bad news first or the good?" asked Remo.

"Why do you always have good news and bad news to report?" Smith asked glumly.

Remo looked to Chiun helplessly. Chiun got up on tiptoe, cupped the mouthpiece with one hand and whispered briefly into his pupil's ear.

"Because we're thorough," said Remo, into the phone. "Isn't that right, Little Father?"

"If we bear only bad tidings and not good, or good tidings, but no bad," Chiun said in a too-loud voice, "we would be accused of doing our duty without sufficient diligence. If in the future, Emperor Smith prefers not to know certain things, let him tell us of these things in advance and we will scrupulously avoid them in our travels."

Smith sighed.

"Give it to me as you wish," he said glumly.

"Okay," said Remo. "Wurmlinger isn't our man."

"How do you know this?"

"We know when a guy is lying to us. He wasn't. He's just a bug nut, pure and simple. And the only bees we found were sick ones."

"That proves nothing."

"But we found a whole bunch of dead guys scattered around. Ever hear of the Iowa Disorganized Subterranean Militia?"

Smith was silent, so Remo assumed he was working his silent keyboard. A sudden beep confirmed this. Then Smith said, "I have almost nothing on them other than they are commanded by a former corn farmer named Mearl Streep."

"Well, that gives us one solid motive. He jumped to the same conclusion Tammy Terrill did and tore off to avenge the cornfields."

"Odd," said Smith.

"What?" asked Remo.

"I have input his name, but the system keeps spell-correcting it and giving me information on a Hollywood actress."

"Forget it. Those guys are out of the picture," said Remo. "Oh, there was one of those talking guard bees here. It tried to warn us away from Wurmlinger."

"Is that not proof of his complicity?" asked Smith.

"Nope. Not to us."

"Then we are at a dead end," Smith said morosely.

"Not exactly. The Bee-Master tried to sting us again. This time, he sent one of those swarms after us. You know, the things that got that guy in Times Square."

"What did they look like?"

"They looked like the way bees sound, only louder and meaner."

"Excuse me?"

"They're too small for the naked eye to see. We beat them off, but captured one. I guess it died in all the excitement."

"You have another bee specimen?"

"Sort of. It's no bee. It looks like something out of a monster movie except it's smaller than a nit."

"Remo, an insect that small would be microscopic."

"This one practically is. And it's the ugliest thing you ever saw. What do you want us to do with it?"

"Bring it here."

"We're on our way."

Hanging up, Remo turned to Chiun. "I guess it's back to Folcroft for us."

Chiun held the glass slide up to the afternoon sun. "I pronounce you...*Philogranus remi.*"

"What does that mean?" asked Remo.

"Seed-lover Remo."

"Why are you naming it after me?" Remo flared.

"Are you not both brainlessly drawn to corn seed?" huffed the Master of Sinanju.

## 41

Edward E. Eishied couldn't be wrong. He wasn't wrong about Wayne Williams. He hadn't been wrong about the Green River Killer.

How could he be wrong about this?

All events leave a mark. All minds create emotional or circumstantial footprints. That was the key. Figuring out the whys and the wherefores of criminal acts.

A serial killer had been assassinating people who had only one thing in common: insects. They either killed them, or ate them and killed them. Therefore the unknown subject felt a kinship with insects.

That much seemed reasonable.

Eishied had generated a profile. Certain elements were basic. Well educated. A WASP. Drove a Volkswagen Beetle. It was amazing how many serial killers were WASPS who drove VW Bugs. The irony of that linkage had never occurred to Edward Eishied until these insect-related serial killings. He wondered if this might open up an entirely new psychological aspect to serial killers, but he had no time for that now.

He was the FBI's chief profiler, and the word coming back from ASAC Smith was that his profile was in error. An UNSUB fitting the profile perfectly had been investigated and it wasn't him.

When he received the e-mail message from ASAC Smith to that effect, Eishied had e-mailed back, "Then look for another UNSUB fitting that profile. I have never been wrong."

ASAC Smith had replied almost before the message was sent:

"Your profile is in error."

To which Eishied rebutted, "Your data may be in error."

Smith said nothing to that. Maybe he was steamed, but Eishied took the silence as a signal to keep working.

So he did.

There were certain unavoidables. The UNSUB had to be highly educated. An idiot doesn't breed new kinds of insects. That was a given.

The UNSUB was a Charlotte Hornets fan, but maybe that wasn't an indicator of geographic locality as much as a need to announce his kink to the world.

The longer Eishied pondered the facts in the case, the more maddening it became.

For some reason, his mind kept drifting back to his childhood. There used to be a cartoon character on TV. Bee-Man. No, Bee-Master. Yeah, that was the name. Guy could fly like a bee, sting like a bee and control bees like a queen bee, even though there was nothing fey about him. Other than his leotards, that is.

Maybe it was the long hours. More than likely, it was the growing indignation Edward Eishied felt that his ability as a profiler had been called into question. But he decided to have some fun with ASAC Smith. He began typing.

UNSUB was traumatized by multiple bee stings as a child. As time went on, he learned to master his fear of the insect kingdom. A more serious tragedy in his young adult life—possibly the murder of parents or spouse—had caused him to dedicate his life to causes he believes to be worthwhile. However, owing to trauma, even this positive expression takes a dark turn.

It was as near as he could dredge up the thirty-year-old memory of the origin of the Bizarre Bee-Master.

"UNSUB's initials will be 'P.P.,'" he added, grinning in the privacy of his office.

"Let that Smith bastard figure this one out," he chortled, and he pressed the Send key.

## 42

Harold Smith was looking at the insect through a microscope borrowed from the serum lab of Folcroft's medical wing.

Remo and Chiun were hovering beside his desk like expectant parents.

"Brace yourself," said Remo as Smith brought the slide into focus. "It's uglier than sin."

"I have named it *Philogranus remi*," sniffed Chiun, "in honor of its corn lusts, but its hideousness of countenance also played a role in my decision."

Remo glared at Chiun.

"A minor one," Chiun amended.

Smith brought the slide into focus. His rimless glasses lay on the desk. One eye was pressed to the microscope eyepiece.

He said nothing. There was no gasp of surprise, no outburst or expression of shock.

But when he looked up from the lens, his grayish face was drained bleached-bone white.

"The mind that created this hellish thing," he said thickly, "is that of a twisted genius who must be stopped. This infernal insect has been bred to be a combination flying shark and multilimbed buzz saw capable of ripping through flesh, grain and wood in an instant. There is no defense against it. All it has to do is enter the human ear and attack the brain. Death is almost instantaneous. No wonder the various medical examiners found nothing.'' Smith actually shuddered.

"What's the latest on the farm crisis?" asked Remo.

"The swarm—and it appears to be a swarm—has reached California. There is considerable crop damage. But again, it is fiendishly selective. In this case, citrus growers experimenting with a new pesticide have been hit."

"Don't all farmers use pesticides?" asked Remo.

"Yes, of course," said Smith, uncapping a bottle of Zantac 75 and swallowing two dry. "But these— these vermin seem to be targeting only the latest or most advanced insect-resistant crops."

"Why not get them all?"

Smith considered. "To make a statement. Perhaps this is just the first wave."

"If this guy is so big on bees, he's not going to kill every crop. Bees pollinate crops. Take crops out, and bees are out of work."

Smith considered. "Very good, Remo. That is an excellent observation."

"But it still doesn't get us anywhere," Remo muttered.

Smith was about to acknowledge that unfortunate state of affairs when his computer beeped a warning of an incoming message. He called it up, read it and his jaw sagged.

"What is it?" asked Remo.

"It is the latest psychological profile from FBI Behavioral Science."

"I thought they gave up on that stuff after they fingered Wurmlinger."

"This particular profiler is the Bureau's top man. He has never been wrong. Until now."

"He still flogging the Wurmlinger theory?"

"No, he has revised his profile. It is radically different." Smith's voice grew marginally excited. "We may have something here."

Remo looked over Smith's gray-flannel shoulder at the buried desktop screen and frowned the longer he read.

"Smitty, that's Bee-Master he's talking about."

"Yes, of course."

"No. That's the story of how Peter Pym became Bee-Master, right down to being stung by a swarm of radioactive bees."

"I don't see the word *radioactive*."

"He left that out," said Remo. "Look, he's even claiming the guy has the initials 'P.P.' How can he know that from the facts of the case?"

Smith frowned. "He is the best. These profilers can perform miracles of induction."

"He's pulling your leg. You're just too stiff to see it."

Smith frowned. Remo looked out the window, and

the Master of Sinanju paced the room. Back and forth, back and forth, in incredible concentration.

"What are you doing?" asked Remo.

"I am attempting to conjure up a vision of the wretch."

"Oh, yeah?"

"Yes. This thing you call profiling is known to Sinanju, only it is called Illuminating the Shadow."

"Illuminating the Shadow?"

"Yes, from time to time, Masters of Sinanju were called upon to divine the identities of shadowy persons who plotted against thrones or had struck in vain against those thrones only to escape into the shadows. I am attempting to divine the identity of this man by piercing the shadows that surround him."

"Feel free," said Remo. "But if it turns out to be Lamont Cranston, we're no better off than we were before."

But Smith looked interested.

"I envision," Chiun said at last, "a Byzantine prince."

"Byzantium no longer exists," Smith argued.

"Told you it was a crock," muttered Remo under his breath.

"A prince of Byzantium who conceals his face from view with a crown of great complexity," added Chiun.

"Sounds like the Man in the Iron Mask," said Remo.

Smith hushed him. Remo subsided.

"This prince rules over a kingdom of subjects who are not of his flesh."

"Bee-Master rules over the insect kingdom," Smith said.

"But these subjects that are not of his flesh are not of any flesh," continued Chiun.

"Insects are not made of flesh, but of a material like horn," said Smith. "Very good, Master Chiun."

"I don't believe you two are doing this...." Remo moaned.

"Can you envision where this person can be found?" asked Smith.

Chiun continued pacing. His face was twisted up in concentration, his eyes squeezed to the narrowness of walnut seams. "I know that this prince is drawn back to the scene of his depredations."

"Sure," said Remo. "The criminal always returns to the scene of the crime."

"No, that is not it," said Smith. "That is an old adage, but it is not exactly true. Criminals are not drawn to the scene of their crimes so much as they feel compelled to insinuate themselves into official investigations. It is very common that the chief murder suspect is the first person to offer eyewitness testimony or suggestions on how to solve the murder. It is a control issue with them."

"That's Wurmlinger again," said Remo.

"No, it is not Wurmlinger," said Chiun. "But another prince."

Smith was at his computer again.

"What are you doing, Smitty?" asked Remo.

"Calling up the facts in the Rand killing, the one that started this chain of fantastic events."

Smith skimmed the report carefully. "Here is something."

"What?" asked Remo.

"I hadn't noticed this before, but the killing of Doyal T. Rand occurred in Times Square at the intersection of Broadway and Seventh Avenue."

"So? We knew that."

"There is an old saying that Times Square is the crossroads of the world. If one were to seek a specific person, you have only to stand on that corner long enough and that person will almost certainly appear there. Because sooner or later everyone passes through Times Square."

Remo grinned. "Somebody should set a trap for Saddam Hussein, then."

Smith shook his humorless gray head. "Our man first showed up in Times Square. Perhaps he might return."

"Yes, he will return to the scene of his depredations, for he must," said Chiun firmly.

"You don't expect us to stand on a freaking street corner for the rest of our lives until he turns up again," said Remo.

"No, I will put the FBI on it."

"Good," said Remo.

"Not good," said Chiun. "For we must be the ones to vanquish this prince of Byzantium."

"You go, then. I have a date with a rich girl," Remo said.

Chiun started. "Jean is rich?"

"Won the lottery. Seven million bucks."

"Rich?" squeaked Chiun. "And you have not yet married her?"

"I don't marry for money."

"Then you are a dunderhead," spit Chiun. "She comes from the illustrious Rice family and swims in wealth, yet you stand there in your ignorant bachelorhood. For shame."

"I'll get around to her. Business comes first."

"See that you do," said Chiun.

**43**

In a hotel room overlooking Times Square, a man calmly unpacked his suitcase.

It was a very large suitcase. It had to be to accommodate its contents.

Folded neatly inside was a black-and-yellow spandex uniform. The upper portion was jet black, while the legs were banded in alternating yellow-jacket bands.

Standing in his boxers, he drew this on, carefully Velcro-ing and zippering the striking uniform that was his badge of identity.

The gauntlets of rubberized fabric fitted over his long, strong fingers. He stepped into the gleaming black boots, which squished when he walked, thanks to the honeycomb of suction cups on the bottoms of the thick soles.

Finally, he drew over his head the cybernetic helmet with its compound locust green orbs and retractable antennae. The helmet gleamed like a bee's skull forged of polished copper.

"I," he said in a deep, commanding voice, "the avenger of insects, am now ready to go forth and face my destiny."

Squishing with each step, he took the elevator to the lobby floor and, oblivious to the gawking and staring of common mortals, stepped out into the bustle of the crossroads of the world for his rendezvous with destiny.

OFFICER ANDY FUNKHAUSER had thought he had seen everything.

He was directing traffic when he happened to look at the corner of Seventh Avenue and East Forty-fifth Street.

There, standing calm as could be, was a man tricked up like a human yellow jacket, for Christ's sake.

The man crossed the street and came striding down as big as life and twice as stupid looking. Some pedestrians stared at him, while others just ignored him. This was New York. It took a lot to get a rise out of New Yorkers.

The man seemed not to be bothered by the attention. If anything, he walked with his shoulders squared and his stride more jaunty. He looked like the jackass to beat all jackasses, but he was the last to know it.

"Probably some kind of goofy Fox stunt," Funkhauser muttered, returning to his duties. Ever since that Rand guy died, people kept expecting killer bees to descend on Times Square.

It had only been a few days since the eyeless stiff had been carted off. And yesterday a beekeeper had come to lure away the swarm of bees that had congregated around the streetlight when it had all happened. Funkhauser had watched. It was amazing. The guy had put on protective gloves and net veil pith helmet and shinnied up the pole.

Once he'd gotten close, the bees just took to him like honey. They clung to his well-protected body like glued-on popcorn.

He'd come down, got into the back of his van that said Bee Busters on the side, and when he'd come out again, there hadn't been a bee in his bonnet. Or anywhere else on him, for that matter.

Times Square had quieted down since then, if Times Square could ever be said to quiet down, and Officer Funkhauser went about his duties when he heard the high, shrill humming.

His eyes went to the light pole, thinking the swarm had returned. But there was no swarm. What there was was an earsplitting buzz that swelled and swelled, sounding as if it was all around him.

Then a man screamed.

Funkhauser tried to fix the sound. It seemed to be all around him. A *zit-zit-zit*, like tiny air pellets zipping by.

A black-and-yellow figure jumped into traffic, clutching his coppery green-eyed head and twisting as if stung by a million bees.

No bees were visible, Funkhauser saw. There was just the guy, and he was screaming to beat the band.

He ran across Broadway, reversed himself and pitched to his left. That didn't shake whatever was eating him. So he dropped to the ground and rolled up into a tight ball.

There, he curled up like a bug set on fire, as the life quickly went out of him.

Funkhauser was at his side by that time. The droning had fallen quiet. It seemed to pour up into the sky. It was only a distant, fading *ziii* now.

If it hadn't, there was no way Funkhauser was going to get near the dead guy.

There was no question the yellow-jacket man was dead. Nobody screamed like that just from pain. This guy made as if to scream the lining out of his throat.

One look, and Funkhauser decided against mouth-to-mouth and CPR.

The guy's mouth hung open, and there was no tongue.

"Oh, Jesus, not again."

He got the weird helmet off, and it was no surprise that the eyes were hollow caverns. Funkhauser replaced the helmet. That spared the gathering crowd the horrible sight of the dead man's eyes. Or lack thereof.

Jumping to his feet, Funkhauser blew a shrill blast on his police whistle. Impatient traffic was inching closer to him like a line of hungry tigers.

"Can't turn your back for a minute in this crazy town," he growled.

**44**

Harold Smith took the call from B. Eugene Roache of the USDA Honey Bee Breeding Center in Baton Rouge.

"I have the results you requested," he said breathlessly.

"Have you been running?" asked Smith.

"No, I've been working."

"Then why are you so out of breath?"

"Because," puffed Roache, "I have just gotten off the wildest roller coaster of my professional life."

"Explain," prompted Smith.

"First, I attempted to examine the detached wing. Inadvertently, I held it too close to a high-intensity desk lamp. The wing shriveled up from the heat."

"That was inexcusably careless."

"Not all of it was burned," Roache went on urgently. "I saved a corner of it. When I projected it onto the wall, I saw something that almost gave me a heart attack."

"Yes?"

"This bee has a death's-head on its thorax. It's almost perfect. You couldn't get a more perfect skull if an artist painted it."

"I understand that," said Smith, voice growing impatient.

"I should have suspected it from that evidence alone. But I had no idea. Who would have thought it?"

"Thought what?" Smith snapped, wondering why the man hadn't gotten to the point.

Roache's voice sank to an awed whisper. "In the corner of the wing was a machine-perfect black *T* in a circle."

"A marking you recognize?"

"A marking a five-year-old would recognize. It's a trademark symbol!"

Smith's unimaginative brain caught on. "Trademark?"

"Yes, a trademark. I examined the whole bee, and its right wing also showed the same marking. This bee is trademarked!"

"Then there is no question that the death's-head bee was created by some genetic program," said Harold Smith. "Just as certain enzymes and bacteria can be trademarked for commercial use."

"That was my thinking, too. Until I dissected the bee."

Smith's ears registered the low, amazed tone of the entomologist's voice, and he felt the first tingle of anticipation.

## 45

By the time Remo and Chiun reached the street, it was over.

They had stationed themselves atop the Disney Store overlooking Times Square, watching the surging crowds below. The sun was going down. Lights were coming on all around Times Square. They had been at their post a little more than two hours when Remo spotted the man with the yellow-jacket legs and green-eyed helmet.

"I don't believe this," Remo exploded.

On the opposite corner of the roof, the Master of Sinanju was watching a different quadrant of the square. His tiny ears were protected by padded earmuffs to ward against the brain-attacking insects.

"What do you not believe?" Chiun said thinly.

Remo pointed to the street below.

"Bug-eyed man at six o'clock low."

"The hour is not yet five. Why do you say six?"

Looking over, Chiun saw Remo's arm leveled at a comical figure striding down Broadway. He was dressed like a black-and-yellow insect. His step as he walked was springy. The antennae on his shiny forehead bounced happily.

"There's our Bee-Master!" Remo shouted. "Come on."

Remo raced to the door to the roof. Sensing the Master of Sinanju was not behind him, he paused. "Shake a leg, Little Father."

Chiun shook his head in the negative. "No. That is not him."

"What do you mean, it's not him?"

"Look at his legs. He is dressed as a wasp."

"Yeah. So?"

"A yellow jacket is a wasp, not a bee."

"That makes him a not-bee, right?"

"No," Chiun said stubbornly. "A not-bee is a thing entirely different. Go without me. For you go on a fool's errand."

Remo hit the stairs, flashing to street level faster than an elevator could carry him. By the time he got out into the rushing river of New Yorkers, there was no sign of his quarry.

Remo looked up Broadway. Then down. Then he heard the high, anxious droning filtering down from the sky.

Above him, Chiun gave a warning hiss. Remo knew that sound. He ducked back into the building and held the glass-and-brass door shut with both hands, and started wishing he had accepted that extra pair of earmuffs from Chiun.

The weird sound came and went quickly. When it was gone, Remo stepped out cautiously.

Moving with every sense alert because he had no defense against the voracious insects that were too

small to see, Remo worked toward a gathering knot
of people.

They were crowding around a dead man lying in
the middle of stopped traffic. The dead man was
dressed like a yellow-jacket wasp. A cop was kneeling over the body. When he got the man's golden
helmet off, the eyes behind the green compound
lenses looked as if they had been gouged out.

Remo looked away from the dead man toward
Chiun, still stationed several floors above, and
shrugged his shoulders elaborately.

Chiun ignored him. Remo waved him down. Finally, the old Korean disappeared from the parapet
edge.

When Chiun joined Remo a few minutes later,
Remo was saying, "This doesn't make any sense.
Look at him. Bee-Master's own bugs killed him."

Before Chiun could speak, a small voice at their
side said, "That isn't Bee-Master."

Remo looked down. A boy of about thirteen with
blond hair cut in a mushroom fade stood there.

"Who asked you?" said Remo.

"Nobody. But you called him Bee-Master. Everybody knows Bee-Master wears a silver cybernetic helmet with infrared goggles. That's Death Yellow-
jacket."

"Death Yellowjacket?"

"Yeah. He's much cooler."

"Not anymore," said Remo. "He's dead."

"That's not the real Death Yellowjacket, just some

guy dressed like him for the convention,'' the boy said.

"What convention?'' asked Remo.

The boy puffed out his chest. On his T-shirt's front was a legend of Day-Glo green and red: New York Comic Collectors' Spectacular.

"The comic convention,'' the boy said. "At the Marriott. I just came from there.'' He held up a fat sheaf of comic books sealed in clear Mylar envelopes.

Noticing this, Chiun asked, "Do you have any Donald Duck?''

"Naw. Nobody reads about ducks anymore. It's all superheroes.''

By now, an ambulance was pulling up, and the police were pushing the crowd back.

"Did you see this guy at the convention?'' Remo asked the kid.

"No. But there's a costume contest at six. He was probably dressed for that. Too bad he died. Bet he'd cop first prize.''

Remo and Chiun swapped looks. Remo's was puzzled, and Chiun's was bland.

"Tell me, kid,'' said Remo. "Why would Bee-Master want to kill Death Yellowjacket?''

"He wouldn't. Bee-Master wouldn't kill anyone. He's old-fashioned that way. On the other hand, Death Yellowjacket kicks butt and takes no names.''

"Humor me. If Bee-Master wanted to kill Death Yellowjacket, what's his motive?''

"That's simple. Death Yellowjacket outsells Bee-

Master two to one. And bees and wasps hate each other anyway.''

''Told you so,'' said the Master of Sinanju in a serenely smug tone of voice.

At the Marriott Marquis, they were told that the man in the yellow-jacket costume was registered under the name of Morris Baggot.

They were about to leave when Chiun happened to look up and noticed a man in black spandex descending in one of the capsulelike glass elevators. His head was encased in a stainless-steel helmet mask with glowing red eyes.

''Observe,'' Chiun hissed.

Remo looked up. ''Uh-oh.'' He called the desk clerk's attention to the descending elevator. ''You wouldn't happen to know who that is, would you?''

The desk clerk did. ''That's Mr. Pym,'' he said.

''Pym? Not Peter Pym?''

''That's right. Do you know him?''

''Only by reputation,'' growled Remo. ''What's his room number?''

The clerk looked it up on his reservation terminal. ''Room 33-4.''

''Where's the comic-book thing being held?'' Remo pressed.

''Ballroom.''

''Thanks,'' said Remo, pocketing his FBI ID.

Taking Chiun aside, he said, ''That's gotta be our guy. He's operating under Bee-Master's alias. Looks like he's headed to the comic-book show, no doubt to capture first prize in the costume contest now that Death Yellowjacket is out of the picture.''

"We will vanquish him and avenge the stalwart wasp," vowed Chiun.

"First, let's check out his room."

They grabbed an elevator.

THE DOOR to room 33-4 opened easily after Remo stunned the electronic lock with the heel of his hand.

Inside, they found stacks of sealed comic books, with the price tags still on the Mylar envelopes. Remo whistled at some of the prices.

Under the bed, Remo found a carrying case with an ID tag in the name of Peter Pym, along with an address in Johnstown, Pennsylvania.

"This guy takes his Bee-Master pretty seriously," said Remo. Setting the box on the bed, he forced it open. Inside was a purple plush shelf like a jeweler's display case except that in each depression sat a fat death's-head bumblebee instead of a precious stone.

Remo blinked. In that blink, his hands became pale blurs. When they stopped moving, the bees were so much mangled mush scattered at his feet.

"Whew! That was close," he said.

"You were in no danger," Chiun said dismissively.

"Only because I stung them first."

Chiun shook his head. "They slept the sleep of things that do not live—except at the will of their master."

And stooping, the Master of Sinanju plucked one

of the mashed bees from the rug and raised it to the
level of his pupil's eyes.

"Look more closely, blind one. And behold the
true nature of the not-bee...."

**46**

"What did you discover when you dissected the bee?" Harold Smith asked.

"At first," said B. Eugene Roache, "I was interested in taking measurements of the thorax, wings and legs. It never occurred to me to enter the body cavities and explore."

"Go on," said Smith, his voice growing tense. This entomologist's nervous urgency was infectious.

"The body parts of course did not correspond to the Bravo bee. I ascertained that from a casual examination. There is no such species as an Africanized bumblebee. But I wanted to record the measurements for future reference. As I was doing that, I felt the detached wing between my fingers. It felt wrong to the touch."

"Wrong?"

"I've handled many bee wings in my career. I know how they feel against naked skin. These were too slick, too smooth. A bee's wing feels something like old cellophane, if you know that texture. This was entirely different. So I did an analysis of it."

"What did you find, Dr. Roache?"

"I found," Roache said in a disturbed voice, "that the bee's wing was composed of Mylar."

"Mylar!"

"Yes. A man-made substance. At that point I attacked the bee's interior structure. What I found gives me the shivers. This bee is not a bee. It's man-made."

"Man-made!"

"Yes. Isn't that fantastic? Someone has engineered a replica bee. That means he's discovered the secret of how bees fly. We've been trying to crack that one for decades! Isn't that incredible?"

"Dr. Roache," Harold Smith said tightly. "Whoever created that bee has devised one of the most deadly killing tools ever unleashed on this nation. Against that threat, the secret of bee aerodynamics is unimportant."

"There's more. Its stinger is a tiny hypodermic needle. The entire abdomen is a reservoir for Africanized bee neurotoxin. It's not an Africanized killer bee, but it carried the same toxin. Isn't that ingenious?"

"Insidious," Smith said.

"And I'm not sure about this part, but the head seems to contain a scanning mechanism. I would have to examine it under an electron microscope, but I have the feeling there's a miniature television camera in there."

"In other words," said Smith, "the bee is a combination of flying spy and assassin in a single package?"

"This bee can do anything an ordinary bee can do

except pollinate flowers. And I wouldn't doubt for a minute it could perform that function, as well."

"Dr. Roache, what you have told me must remain classified until you have been cleared to release it to the public."

"I assume I will be allowed to author a paper on my discovery," Roache said huffily.

"You will. Assuming you find a safe and secure place to hide. Several people have already died so that the secret you have uncovered does not leak out to the world."

"Who would want to kill me?" Roache asked indignantly.

"The genius who devised that insidious little creature."

"It's a machine, actually. Not a creature."

"It has killed and will kill again," Smith warned.

"Oh," said Dr. B. Eugene Roache. "I think I'd better be going now."

"You do that," said Harold Smith. No sooner had he hung up than the phone rang again. He brought it back to his face.

"Yes, Remo?"

"We hit the jackpot. Our man's here. He's in town attending a comic-book convention."

"Ridiculous!" snapped Smith.

"No argument there," agreed Remo. "But listen before you jump to the wrong conclusion."

Smith waited. Remo explained everything that happened from the daylight murder of Death Yellowjacket to their breaking into the hotel room rented to a Peter Pym.

Then Remo said, "We found a case filled with those death's-head bumblebees, and guess what?"

"They are mechanical," said Smith.

Remo's voice lost its note of satisfied triumph. "Yeah. How'd you guess?"

"I didn't. I have just heard from the USDA Honey Bee Center. The dissection showed the sample bee to be a nanobee."

"A what?"

"A nanobee."

Chiun's voice floated over the wire. "Emperor Smith is trying to tell you it is a not-bee, as I have said all along."

"What's a nanobee?"

"An ingenious form of nanomachine."

"Okay," said Remo. "I'll bite. What's a nanomachine?"

"A miniature device engineered on the microscopic level. It is a new branch of engineering. Already, there are microscopic machines capable of performing simple tasks. As the state of the art advances, more-complex devices are expected to come into existence that will allow doctors to perform microsurgery by introducing miniature robots into a patient's body. Or, like an enzyme attacking a biological structure, nanomachines like those that are tearing through America's standing crops might safely demolish obsolete skyscrapers without high explosives."

"The little one-eyed bugs are machines, too?" Remo blurted.

"Obviously. The bees are a cruder form of nano-machine, not as miniaturized but certainly as lethal, not to mention useful for spying."

Remo's voice grew thoughtful. "I guess that explains how all those bees were able to follow us and talk, too. They're robots."

"No doubt controlled by this Bee-Master through radio signals," added Smith. "One assumes the country has been seeded with them."

"Well, I guess that explains that. Now we just have to mop this guy up without getting ourselves chewed alive."

"That will not be easy, Remo," Smith warned.

"You're telling me. Know anything that can jam his frequency?"

"Not without knowing much more about his equipment."

"I was afraid you were going to say that." Remo's voice was distant as he asked, "Any ideas, Little Father?"

"Ask Emperor Smith what an EpiPen is," came Chiun's squeaky voice.

"Chiun wants to know what an EpiPen is. He just found a big clear plastic pen in a drawer and it says EpiPen on the side."

Smith input the question into his ever-ready system. The answer came up instantly.

"An EpiPen is a syringe, not a pen," Smith said. "It is used to deliver epinephrine, an adrenaline."

Smith paused. When he spoke again, his voice was low and urgent.

"Remo, listen, EpiPens are carried by people who are highly allergic to bee stings. In the event of a stinging, they inject themselves in order to counteract the systemic symptoms of anaphylactic shock."

"Are you thinking what I'm thinking?" Remo said.

"That our Bee-Master is allergic to bee stings. Yes."

"Nice going, Little Father," Remo called to Chiun.

"It is nothing," returned the Master of Sinanju. "Any genius would have accomplished the same brilliant result."

"Remo, I think this affair can be resolved safely with no danger to Master Chiun or yourself."

"I'm thinking that, too," said Remo.

"Here is what I suggest you do...."

**47**

It was his hour of triumph.

It had been a long time coming, but at last it was here.

Peter Pym basked in the applause of the ballroom full of people as he accepted the pewter trophy giving him first prize in the twelfth-anniversary New York Comic Book Spectacular costume parade. And he deserved it. For his Bee-Master regalia wasn't only a faithful reproduction to the most minute detail, but it was fully functional, as well, from the suction-cup vacuum boots to the cybernetic helmet.

It was true that as Bee-Master he couldn't commune with actual living bees. But he had improved on the genius of the original Bee-Master concept. He created his own bees, more powerful, more formidable than any strain known to man or nature.

Now, walking offstage, clutching his trophy, he moved confidently through the crowd of his fellow comic-book fans to the glass elevator and his room.

It was nearly time to do the remote interview with Tamara Terrill of Fox Network News and announce to the world his demands. Demands that had been rudely ignored by the late publisher of the *Sacramento Bee.*

But Bee-Master would be ignored no more.

Pym ignored the rude stares of the common herd as he roved the hotel corridors. Let lesser mortals gawk as they would. In time, they would be forced to relinquish their dominance over the planet that rightfully belonged to its ultimate inheritors, the insect kingdom. A planet whose dominion would be returned to its proper lords, the crickets and the grasshoppers. The bees and the hornets.

And allied with them until the end of time, their true lord, Bee-Master.

It was a dream come true. A lifelong fantasy made flesh. And it had taken thirty grueling years to bring to fruit ever since that glorious spring day in 1962 when he had picked up his first issue of *Tales to Amaze You* and was enthralled by the cataclysmic exploits of the one and only Bee-Master.

Coming to his door, he inserted the plastic magnetic pass card, extracted it and twisted the knob when the red light turned green.

He closed the door after him.

Immediately, he sensed something was amiss.

His every insectoid sense went to red alert. His antennae quivered atop his helmet.

His new comic books were out of order. Perhaps it had been the hotel housekeeper.

Then Pym saw his box of death's-head bees lying open and strewed about the floor.

"Someone will pay for this," he said, dropping to one knee on the rug.

Every bee was destroyed. Each exquisite gem of miniaturized technology, pulped as if they were nothing more than winged raisins.

Slowly, fists clenched, he climbed to his feet, standing tall and proud in his Bee-Master uniform.

"I swear," he said, lifting a shaking black fist before his helmeted face, "to wreak my awesome vengeance on all who oppose me."

Then he smiled under his cybernetic helmet. He had always wanted to give that speech in real life. It was from *Bizarre Bee-Master #3*. The Crimson Cockroach issue.

From the closet, he detected a buzz. Low, curious, it sounded like one of his bumblebees had survived the heartless massacre.

Striding to the door, he laid one black-gloved hand on the doorknob. As he pulled the door open, he narrowed his eyes behind his scarlet eye lenses. If one of his bees was still alive, he should be able to receive its visual-telemetry signal and see exactly what the bee saw.

But there was no transmitted image on the inner side of his flat eye lenses.

Too late, he realized the sound he was hearing wasn't that of one of his death's-head bees, but the annoyed buzz of feral honeybees. Too late, he slammed the door shut.

Too late! For they were out and buzzing around the room.

"No! Stay back. You are not of my brood," he cried. "You are not in league with the Bizarre Bee-Master!"

The bees ignored him. They circled and dive-bombed him, whether out of anger or as an attack response triggered by his dark uniform, he didn't know.

A sharp prick between his shoulder blades told him he had been stung in the back.

"Nooooo!" he cried. "I am your friend! I am a friend to all bees. All insects."

His right shoulder twitched in sudden pain.

Another sting pierced the back of his right glove.

The bee, withdrawing its barbed sting, fell to the rug squirming in its twisty death throes.

His throat immediately constricted. His breath came in ragged gasps.

"No! Not this way! The Bizarre Bee-Master cannot meet his end this way. Not when I am poised on the threshold of my greatest triumph."

Then he remembered he had prepared for this dire contingency, and stumbled to the hotel-room bureau, where he began clawing through the drawer contents.

"My EpiPen! It will save me. My EpiPen. Where—where is it? Where is my EpiPen?"

But there was no sign of it amid his Bee-Master Underoos and T-shirts.

Meanwhile, the angry bees continued to attack. Their relentless *zit-zit-zit-zit* signaled each sharp sting that brought coldness to his body.

They were ferocious. Insistent. Indomitable.

He knew from the countless pinpricks erupting all over his body that these were no less than Africanized honeybees.

"How ironic," he moaned, "to die at the stings of those whose habitats I am sworn to protect…"

Falling to the floor, he made a last, desperate attempt to contact his nanomites in the vicinity. They would protect him. They would come to his aid….

But try as he might, he couldn't focus his thoughts. Couldn't broadcast the electronic signal that would bring the deadly creatures of his own devising to combat these bees who, in their blind fury, their unthinking ignorance, were slowly killing their only champion among a vicious humanity.

Then, like a miracle, an image swam before his eyes.

He was looking into the perfect features of Tamara Terrill. Of course. The interview. His bumblebee emissary was signaling that the interview had begun. It was time to speak. To tell America of his demands if they wanted the scourge he had inflicted upon their farms and cruel scientists to be lifted.

"I bring mankind greetings from the Bizarre Bee-Master, King of all Insects," he heard his drone announce. That was his cue.

He opened his mouth.

A feathery sensation alighted on his tongue. A sharp pain replaced it, and almost at once, his tongue swelled up, reacting to the potent venom of the bee that in its death spasms rolled down his open throat.

He could not speak. Thwarted. In the last ditch, he was thwarted! It was unbearable.

As he clutched up in a ball, like a dying insect himself, the Bizarre Bee-Master heard an insistent glassy tapping. Shutting off his helmet telemetry, he turned his flat scarlet eyes to the balcony window in response to the sound.

It was they! The nanomites had come to succor him. Somehow, some way, they knew! They were trying to penetrate the glass.

His leaping hope turned to crushing defeat when he saw, for the first time, that there were only two ordinary bipeds there. He recognized them. The tall man with the thick wrists and an old Asian who had challenged him before. He didn't know who they really were. Agents of the forces of darkness, without question.

The old Asian was waving goodbye. The other one was holding up the missing EpiPen, the one thing that could preserve his life and all his grandiose plans for the future of insectdom.

Slowly, painfully, as Bravo bees punished him mercilessly, he crawled toward them.

The bees continued to attack. But he would not fail. He refused to fail. He was the Bizarre Bee-Master and he was real. He was alive. He was indomitable.

"I," he moaned through his rapidly constricting throat, "am indomitable. I cannot be defeated. I refuse to be defeated. I refuse…"

And through the glass balcony door came a mocking rebuttal. "That s the biz, sweetheart.…

They were the last words the Bizarre Bee-Master heard before he ascended to the great beehive in the sky.

WHEN THE BEE-MASTER had finished convulsing, Remo opened the sliding glass door and stepped in, Chiun right behind him.

The bees in the room came at them with the same single-minded anger they had displayed all along. Casually, Remo and Chiun thwarted their every attempt to strike, urging them out through the open door and into the dusk of late afternoon.

Remo stripped the body of its helmet, lifted it to head height and collapsed it like a shell of tin. The helmet went *crunck*, and its red goggles shattered like bicycle reflectors.

Remo threw the remains into the wastepaper basket.

They looked down at the bloated, cyanosed face of the Bizarre Bee-Master and said, "I wonder who he was?"

"He is dead," intoned the Master of Sinanju. "Nothing else about him matters."

ACROSS TOWN, in the Manhattan studios of Fox TV, Tammy Terrill was getting ready for the interview of her career. It would be live. It would be real. And it would be a TV first.

She could hardly sit still through makeup. But she had to look her best. Fox was almost behind her now.

The majors would be after her by this time tomorrow, and may the highest bid win.

Rushing to the studio, she bumped into Clyde Smoot, who said, "Tam, this had better be good. I wanted you in tall cotton not under hot lights."

"Don't sweat it. It's going to be better than good. It's going to be spectacular."

Taking her seat at the Fox anchor desk, Tammy checked her lavaliere mike and waited for the red tally light that would tell her she was live.

The bumblebee was hiding under the desk. On cue, it would emerge and alight on the desk. Then the interview would begin. And so would Tammy Terrill's national career as a media superstar.

The spooky theme music trailed off into an appropriately long, sinister organ sting.

When the tally light came on, Tammy looked back at the camera with her cool blue gaze and said in her most self-important voice, "This is Tamara Terrill. And this is 'The Tamara Terrill Report.'" She took a breath. "Tonight, with America's heartland under siege and pocked with devastated crop circles, and with killer bees swarming in our major cities, Fox News Network brings you an exclusive that will rock the news world, and the world that watches the news."

The camera zoomed in for a close-up. Tammy lifted the bee onto the desk. It sat there.

"A being known only as Bee-Master has thrown down the gauntlet and is demanding to be heard. And Fox, the news network of the coming millennium, is the only network brave enough to give this mystery man a hearing."

Tammy flashed the quiet bee the okay sign. The bee stirred on its tiny feet.

"With me now is what might appear to be a common, ordinary bumblebee. But is it?"

The bumblebee jumped up into the lights and circled Tammy's head once.

"No. This is no ordinary bee. But a death's-head super-killer bee. But even that is not the entire incredible story."

The bee dropped back onto the desk and faced Tammy. The camera dollied in on the skull imprinted on its back.

"This bee," continued Tammy, "is an emissary of the Bee-Master, and through its own tiny bee voice we will hear what the Bee-Master has to say and how this will affect the future of civilization." Under her breath, Tammy added, "Not to mention my career..."

Tammy picked a microphone off the desk and pointed it at the bee. "Mr. Bee, speak your piece. America is listening."

The bee started to speak.

Later, there were those who denied the bee ever spoke. Or who swore that Tammy Terrill was practicing a cheap form of ventriloquism.

But at that moment, all over America, millions of viewers heard a tinny amplified voice that said clearly, "I bring mankind greetings from the Bizarre Bee-Master, King of all Insects."

"Is that anything like the King of all Media?" Tammy quipped.

The bee didn't reply. For a moment, Tammy thought she had offended the bee. So she asked, "Tell us about the Bee-Master."

The bumblebee just sat there.

Tammy said, "Go ahead. We're listening. We're live."

The bee just sat there.

Face frowning, Tammy nudged it with the mike.

The bee fell over. Its tiny legs stuck up stiff and lifeless in the air.

And seeing her great moment dispersing like pixels in a blown TV tube, Tammy attempted another broadcast first. She tried to give the bee mouth-to-mouth resuscitation.

All she succeeded in accomplishing was to accidentally swallow her guest interviewee.

In the control booth, there was a collective groan.

Coughing violently, Tammy gasped, "We—we seem to be having...technical...difficulties."

The set went black. So did the career of Tammy Terrill, AKA Tamara.

**48**

A week later, Remo was waiting for the doorbell to ring when the telephone rang instead.

"I have determined the identity of the Bee-Master," said the lemony voice of Harold W. Smith.

"Okay. But hurry up. I have a hot date."

"His real name was Palmer Pym," said Smith.

"Wait a minute. That's the real Bee-Master's real name. I mean, the fictitious one's real name."

"Peter Pym is a nanoscientist attached to UCLA. His diaries have been found. Evidently, as a young boy he discovered a Bee-Master comic book and, struck by the coincidence of their shared name, he resolved to become Bee-Master in real life when he grew up. He studied biology and biochemistry, but his plans were frustrated when he discovered it was impossible to commune with insects through electronic means. And further, that he was highly allergic to bee stings. So Pym pursued other avenues. In time, he was attracted to the field of nanotechnology, and there realized that his dream was not impossible after all. He needn't communicate with actual bees if he could instead create obedient artificial bees of his own."

"That is the nuttiest thing I ever heard," Remo exploded, looking at a wall clock. Jean was due at any moment.

"Nevertheless, it is true. Pym set out on a campaign to wage war on those who had waged war on the insect world, starting with Doyal T. Rand. His nanomites, as he called them, were created to demonstrate his power. But he was unable to make his demands public because his chosen vehicle refused to cooperate."

"Who was that?" asked Remo, not really caring and instead wondering what was keeping his date.

"The publisher of the *Sacramento Bee*."

"Well, that makes sense in a moronic kind of way," said Remo.

"Instead, he chose Tammy Terrill."

"Yeah. And we know what happened there."

"Your timing was fortunate. She has been so professionally embarrassed she is unlikely to resurface again. More importantly, the Bee-Master menace is over. There has been not a single attack since you vanquished Pym. All his equipment and insects we have found have been destroyed. I have so informed the President."

"Well, all's well that ends," grunted Remo, looking out the window for the zillionth time.

He saw a long white stretch limousine pull up. "And here's my date. Catch you later, Smitty."

Hanging up, Remo started down the stairs as the doorbell chimed. He heard the door open and Jean's smoky voice clash briefly with Grandmother Mulberry's witch's croak.

A moment later, the old bat herself came rushing up, her yellowed prune face crimson as an apple.

"How's it going, Granny?" he asked jauntily.

She glared at him and said, "Hope you and foulmouth white girl marry soon. You deserve each other. Good riddance."

"Have a nice evening yourself," returned Remo.

Jean was waiting at the door, dressed in a shimmering blue nightgown.

She took one look at Remo's casual attire and asked, "You're not going out looking like that, are you?"

Remo stopped in his tracks. "Oops."

Jean's frown turned into a grin as she reached behind her and hoisted into view a neatly pressed suit on a hanger.

"I cashed in my lottery ticket. So tonight we ride in style and you dress so I'm not embarrassed to be seen in public with you. Not that I would be anyway."

Remo took the suit. "What'd you tell Grandma Mulberry?" he asked. "She looked like someone spanked her good."

"She tried to give me a hard time, so I used the line you taught me to."

"*Dwe juhla?*"

"Yep."

"That got her, huh?"

Jean smiled mischievously.

"Well, I added 'you old bone bag,' too."

Remo grinned. "Okay, I just gotta let Chiun know not to wait up."

But they couldn't find Chiun anywhere. He wasn't in the bell-tower meditation room. Nor in the kitchen. The fish cellar was empty, too.

Finally, Remo knocked on the door of Chiun's private room. It fell open.

Inside, there was no sign of the Master of Sinanju.

But on a low taboret, Remo found a book. Recognizing the cover, he picked it up.

The title was *The Joy of Astral Sex.*

"Hey, this is the same book I caught Grandma Mulberry with!" Remo blurted.

"So? They're reading the same book. What's wrong with sharing?"

"Except I jammed her copy down the garbage disposal."

Remo's face turned shock white. "You don't suppose... Not Chiun. Not with her..."

"Hey," said Jean, beckoning Remo to follow her out the door, "he's old. He's not dead. Neither are you. And the night is young. Come on. You can change clothes in the car. I'll try not to peek."

Shrugging, Remo dropped the book and followed her out, muttering, "Now I'll never get rid of that old fishwife...."

# Take
# 4 explosive books
# plus a
# mystery bonus
# FREE

Mail to: Gold Eagle Reader Service
3010 Walden Ave.
P.O. Box 1394
Buffalo, NY 14240-1394

YEAH! Rush me 4 FREE Gold Eagle novels and my FREE mystery gift.
Then send me 4 brand-new novels every other month as they come off
the presses. Bill me at the low price of just $15.80* for each shipment—
a saving of 15% off the cover prices for all four books! There is NO extra
charge for postage and handling! There is no minimum number of books I
must buy. I can always cancel at any time simply by returning a shipment
at your cost or by returning any shipping statement marked "cancel." Even
if I never buy another book from Gold Eagle, the 4 free books and surprise
gift are mine to keep forever.

164 BPM A3U3

| | | |
|---|---|---|
| Name | (PLEASE PRINT) | |
| Address | | Apt. No. |
| City | State | Zip |

Signature (if under 18, parent or guardian must sign)

* Terms and prices subject to change without notice. Sales tax applicable in
NY. This offer is limited to one order per household and not valid to
present subscribers. Offer not available in Canada.

AC-96

When terrorism strikes too close
to home...

# DON PENDLETON'S
# THE EXECUTIONER®

## THE ★ AMERICAN TRILOGY

An ultraright-wing militia force is using acts of
terrorism to splinter American society. But a greater
conspiracy is at the heart of the violence on U.S. soil
as a foreign enemy seizes the chance for revenge
against a nation in turmoil. It's up to Mack Bolan to
infiltrate the group and bring it to its knees—before
it's too late.

Available this June, July and August
wherever Gold Eagle books are sold.

GOLD
EAGLE®

AT-G